My Australian Adventure

Book 1 in the Clarence Duval Series

Also by Rob Bauer

Fiction

The Nightmare Kingdom

The World Traveler

The Buffalo Soldier

Darkness in Dixie

The Long Way Home

Nonfiction

Outside the Lines of Gilded Age Baseball: Alcohol, Fitness, and Cheating in 1880s Baseball

Outside the Lines of Gilded Age Baseball: Gambling, Umpires, and Racism in 1880s Baseball

Outside the Lines of Gilded Age Baseball: The Origins of the 1890 Players League

Outside the Lines of Gilded Age Baseball: The Finances of 1880s Baseball

My Australian Adventure

Book 1 in the Clarence Duval Series

Rob Bauer

Although the people who participated in the Spalding Tour of 1888 and 1889 described in this book were real people, this is a work of fiction. My portrayal of each character is fictional, and so are many of the events of the tour I've written about. This story should not be interpreted as an accurate description of the Spalding Tour or its participants.

This is a work of historical fiction. Names, characters, places, and incidents are the product of the author's imagination or are used fictitiously. Use of actual historical events, authentic texts, and names is of public access and public domain.

For any inquiries regarding this book, please contact Rob at robbauerbooks@gmail.com.

No part of this book may be reproduced in any form or by any electronic or mechanical means, including information storage and retrieval systems, without written permission from the author, except for the use of brief quotations in a book review.

For my dad, Bob.

Even though you didn't live to see this book yourself, I want
the world to know how much you meant to me.

Author's Note on Language

One of the difficult things about writing historical fiction featuring African Americans is the use of racist language. Words that are painfully demeaning today were, sadly, commonplace usage in the era when this story is set. I've chosen to keep these words for the sake of historical accuracy. I mean no offense to any of my readers.

Contents

Chapter 1

October 25, 1888
Omaha, Nebraska, United States

"How old are you, boy?" the man passing on the street asks me.

"I'm twelve, sir," I respond as I wipe my eyes on the ragged sleeve of what's left of my linen shirt. It was white when I got it, but now most of it is a dirty brown.

"Why are you crying?" Then, the man frowns down on me with an angry look and adds, "And where are your parents?"

I look up at him from the sidewalk, then stand up and face him. In addition to his expensive-looking leather shoes and steel-tipped cane, the stranger wears a black vest over a freshly pressed white shirt. A gold watch chain dangles from one vest pocket. He adjusts his black, stovepipe top hat while he questions me.

"I'm crying because I've just lost my job for the second time in three months. And because I don't have parents," I reply with a sniffle. "Well, I suppose I have parents somewhere, but wherever they are, they aren't here in Omaha."

"Just what I suspected. A no-account nigger begging on the streets. Your kind doesn't belong here. Why don't you go someplace where you're wanted?"

Before I can respond, smack! He whacks me on the shoulder with his walking cane. That hurts! Then the man shuffles away, muttering to himself.

I rub my bruised shoulder and sit back down on the wooden sidewalk. That man was the second person to hit me so far today. But I've had worse days at home in Chicago.

Chicago. How am I ever going to get back there? The thought makes me start crying again. I sit back down, and another tear plops into the dust between my legs. The dust swirls around my feet in wispy eddies when I shuffle my feet. What's left of my old shoes aren't much help keeping the dust off my cracked, calloused toes.

My stomach growls in hunger. Again. Where can I get some grub? Maybe some man will let me sweep the floor of his shop for a little money. I could probably do that. The problem is, I don't know any shopkeepers here in Omaha. If I ask the wrong one, he'll hit me again, like as not.

I look up and down the street, which happens to be California Street. Earlier in the day, I wandered past Creighton College, which is now down the street on my left. On the right, the railroad tracks are just a couple blocks away. I decide to walk north, toward the train depot. Nothing better to do, I guess, especially when I can smell the odor of rotting meat and decaying animal carcasses from the slaughterhouses wafting up from the south.

I wipe my eyes and get up, my knees sticking out of the hole in each leg of my trousers. It's warm enough today that I can get by without a coat, and from what I've overhead people say, that's a lucky thing for late October in Nebraska. Since I don't have a coat anyway, I suppose I should enjoy my good luck now because it will probably be gone tomorrow.

The streets in downtown Omaha are wide enough for carriage traffic going both ways, and a few leafy trees stand on either side of

2

the street. Most of the buildings in this part of downtown are brick or wooden frame buildings with two stories. Many have broad plate-glass windows looking out on the street. I pass both a dry goods store and a store selling leather goods on my way to the train depot.

There it is, just up ahead on my right. It's one of the largest buildings in town, with a long wooden platform surrounding it where people can get on and off the train. The platform has iron hand rails around the outside, all painted black. The station building is three stories, and as it comes into view, I see that it's a long, skinny building.

As I get to the depot, another stagecoach rolls past. The billowing dust makes me cough. The dust blankets everything. It's all over my clothes. What's left of them. Coughing again, I brush some dust off out of habit, but it's pointless. I wish Omaha had more paved streets, like in Chicago where I'm from. The city does have some paved streets, some with asphalt, even, but most of them are south of the depot. I close my eyes to keep out the dust from the next passing carriage, so I don't see it stop, or see the head that pokes itself out of the carriage's open window, until someone in the carriage speaks. Then, to my surprise, I hear a familiar voice I never expected to hear again.

"Stop the carriage! There's the little coon. Come on, Clarence, hurry up!"

I blink my eyes open. Is that Tom Burns with his head sticking out of the carriage window?

"Who are you talking to, Tommy?"

Glancing behind Burns and into the carriage, I see a man with short brown hair and a thick mustache slightly turned up at the ends. He's wearing a black suit jacket over his beige vest. "Who could a guy from Pennsylvania like you possibly know in Omaha?"

"That's Clarence Duval, the mascot we had with us in the East. I wonder what in the world he's doing here?" Burns says to the man in the carriage. To me, he says, "Clarence, get in the carriage. Hurry now!"

3

Because I have nothing better to do, I dart between two carriages going the other direction and clamber in to get a better look at the other man with the mustache. I recognize him. It's Harry Palmer. He writes for the newspapers in Chicago. Palmer is a man of good size, not fat, but he sure must eat better than I do. Beneath his jacket and vest, he wears a white shirt with a black tie. Tom Burns, the man who noticed me first, has a full mustache just like Palmer's, except not turned up at the corners. He is of medium height and somewhat stocky, and he has his baseball uniform on.

Two other baseball players are in the carriage as well. I recognize Jimmy Ryan; he's an outfielder who plays with Burns on the Chicago White Stockings. The other man is John Tener, a pitcher who just joined the team this past season. Tener's one of the tallest men I've ever met. Burns and Ryan are about average height, but Tener must be at least half a foot taller than they are. Burns, Ryan, and Tener are all in their baseball uniforms. The uniforms are white cotton cloth, but have the word "Chicago" arcing across the chest in black block letters. Above the lettering, the uniform shirts are open, but the players can lace them up, too. Each uniform shirt has a collar, and everyone but Palmer has on a black baseball cap as well. Ryan adjusts his as I climb in.

"Bless me, it *is* Clarence Duval," Palmer says. "Wherever have you been these months, Clarence? I haven't seen you since, what, our last eastern trip in Philadelphia. Isn't that right, Tom?"

"Yeah, that's it, Harry," Burns says. "Come, Clarence, tell us your story. You traveled with us for our series against the Quakers in early August, and then we bought that new suit of clothes for you to fix you up right, and then you disappeared. We had bad luck without you, too. We had a three-game series with the Quakers, but rain canceled one, and we lost one of the others. We lost badly. Then we lost two more games right after that. Against Washington! No one should lose two of three against Washington. Where did you go?"

"Well, you see, Mr. Burns, Miss Jarbeau wanted me for her company. She said they couldn't have their show just right without me, and so I've been on the road with her these past months since August, trying to get a little money for the winter. I've still got my baton, see?"

"And little else, it would appear," Palmer says. "Although I'll admit I always liked your brass baton. Is that a croquet ball covered in gold paint at the end?"

"Yes, Mr. Palmer, it's just so. I can still toss and catch it, too. I'll show you when we get to the ballpark!"

"First things first, Clarence," says Burns. "Tell us how you got here to Omaha and ended up all by yourself. We met Stuart Robson of your company earlier today. He said that Jarbeau and her troop were leaving town this morning. He looked mighty sharp, too, in that Astrakhan coat, silk hat, and patent leather shoes. You aren't looking so prosperous, Clarence. How come they left without you?"

"Well, you see, Mr. Burns, Miss Jarbeau just up and decided she didn't want me no more. She gave me my release this morning. I'm not that sad, though. She's treated me meaner than a poor dog, and turned me loose without a cent, and nothing to eat, either."

"Do I understand, then," the tall man, Tener, puts in, "that you've spent the past several months traveling with actors across the country? What did you do in their show?"

"Oh, I sang a little and danced around when they told me to. I didn't have much of a part, really."

Tener extends his hand. I hesitate for a moment, then shake it. He smiles.

Then I ask Burns, "Say, why are you and the boys here? I thought you'd finished playing ball for the year. I heard you got second place in the pennant race. How come you couldn't beat those New York boys?"

"New York had a fine nine this year, Clarence," Palmer says. "Just a little bit better than our boys. Moreover, they had a mascot, named Fred Boldt, who helped them win some games. When you

5

left us, and we didn't have a mascot anymore, we just couldn't match their luck."

I put my head down to contemplate this fact but look up again just in time to see the wink that Burns and Palmer share.

"Come now, men," says Tener. "It's clear that Clarence has had a rough day. Perhaps a little charity toward the young man is in order."

I look over Tener once more. While he's very tall, Tener is rather skinny. I'd bet he doesn't weigh much more than Ryan or Burns despite his height. He is also the only one of the four in our carriage without a mustache. Tener has intense eyes, and yet, he seems relaxed around other people. I don't know if I've ever seen him lose his temper, even when things don't go his way out on the diamond.

"Spoken like a true politician. Is that how you talk to your fellow Irishmen up in Pennsylvania?" Burns says.

"I'm not a politician," Tener counters.

"But you sound like one, and you want to be one."

"I'm not one, at least not today. I am, however, the treasurer for our little expedition. And if you don't ease up, I'll cut you off, and you'll go hungry tonight."

Tener says all this with a smile, and I perk up when I hear the word "expedition."

"What kind of an expedition?" I ask.

"Well, you see, Clarence," Palmer begins, straightening his back and sitting up straight as if about to meet someone important, "Mr. Spalding has made some very unique plans. With his characteristic pluck and daring, he has made special arrangements for these men here, along with the rest of the Chicago Club, to travel to Australia and show the people there all about the great American game of baseball. We're on our way there now. We play a game this afternoon here in Omaha, another tomorrow in Hastings, and then several more as we head west, until we get to San Francisco. Then we steam for Australia."

"Where's Australia?" I ask. "I've never heard of Australia before."

"Well, Clarence, if you go west by railroad far enough you get to San Francisco. You've never been to San Francisco, either, have you?"

"No."

"San Francisco is a city on the Far Slope, in California. It is right on a bay, which is part of the Pacific Ocean. Then, if you get on a boat in San Francisco and steam west some more, eventually, you get to Australia. It's a very big island. Big enough, in fact, it's considered its own continent."

"I don't know what a continent is, Mr. Palmer, but it sounds far away. You get to travel there with Mr. Spalding and the Chicagos?"

"That's right."

"Say," says Burns, "how about if we took you with us, Clarence? We can always use a mascot to bring us luck on the trip. You don't have any parents, anyway, and I'm guessing you have no place to stay this winter, do you?"

"I reckon I don't, Mr. Burns," I say, brightening immediately at the suggestion. But then, the cautious side of me forces me to ask, "Is it dangerous?"

Jimmy Ryan finally speaks. Like Burns, he's built solidly, and he's a little taller than average, but not much. Ryan appears to be in his mid-20s, and he's one of the longest hitters on the White Stockings. His mustache is a bit smaller than Palmer's or Burns's, and his hair is a lighter brown. He says, "I hear the native Australians can be quite dangerous. Cannibalistic, in fact."

"Where did you get that rot, Ryan?" Tener says. "Is that what they taught you at Boston College and Holy Cross?"

"Ease up, Tener. I jest. You can relax, Clarence, there's really no danger. Especially with someone like John to talk his way out of any problems with that refined vocabulary of his. So, what do you say? Will you go with us?"

"I reckon I've got nothing better to do, but it sounds really far. Are you sure Mr. Spalding will let me come?"

"It's not Spalding who's the problem," Burns says. "The problem is Old Man Anson. We'll have to talk him into it. Speaking of, we're arriving at the parade grounds now. You go see Anson, Clarence, and tell him that Burns, Tener, Palmer, and Ryan want you for our mascot."

While Tener pays the omnibus driver, I scramble down from the carriage into the street. It's dusty here, too, because the baseball grounds in Omaha are near the outskirts of town. Many of the buildings on this street are wooden, and have just one story instead of two. Most have a coat of whitewash but are dirty enough that they could use another.

I look down at myself and I'm embarrassed when I realize how ragged I look. My left elbow shows through a frayed hole in my linen shirt, and the right one will, too, before much longer. I can't do anything about it now, though, so I look around for Cap Anson, the captain of the Chicago baseball team. Sure enough, he's there, giving instructions to some other ballplayers in blue uniforms about where to stand. Then he sees me, and his smile instantly becomes a frown.

Anson is a very large, heavy man who easily weighs over 200 pounds, and he scares me. For that matter, I think he scares some of the Chicago players, too. His real name is Adrian, but no one except Mr. Spalding calls him that. To his face, they call him Anson or "Cap" because he's the captain of the Chicago ball team. Behind his back, they call him "Pop" or "Old Man" because he's starting to get old for a ballplayer. He looks to me like he's in his mid-30s. Some of the players on other teams even call him "The Baby" because he whines about the umpires so much during the games. My stomach churns in circles while he walks over to me because everyone knows how much he hates colored people, even little ones like me.

To my surprise, he offers to shake my hand. "Where did you come from, boy? How did you get to Omaha?"

"I came with Miss Jarbeau, but she let me go this morning."

"So, you did run off with Jarbeau, then, just like I suspected. What happened, boy? She flashed her diamonds at you, and then off you went? It'd be just like a nigger to do that."

"I'm sorry, Captain, but she said she needed me for her show. She changed her mind today, I guess."

"Well, we've blacklisted you from the Chicago Club. We don't want anything more to do with you, boy. I'm dead sore on you. Where's the suit of clothes we bought you down East? The ones you ran away in?"

"Those? They wore out, since they were the only ones I had. I reckon they aren't much use to anyone now."

"Well, you'll never get another one from this crowd. We want nothing to do with you, see?"

My heart sinks. I don't know if I can handle another rejection today, so I try to explain things to Anson. "I reckon I don't deserve anything better, Captain, but I've had a mighty hard time of things lately. Can I please have a chance? Mr. Burns, and Mr. Palmer, and Mr. Tener, and, and . . ." it takes me a moment to remember Ryan's name because I'm so scared, "and Mr. Ryan said they wanted me for a mascot again."

"You've had a hard time of things lately, is that right, boy? Yes, and you'll have a harder one yet, if you don't get out of here before our parade starts. Now, get!"

I slink away while the big captain glowers at me. I want to turn into a bird and fly. However, I can't, so I look around slowly, trying to think of what I'll do now. I'm stuck in Omaha, I have no money or food, and now I'll never get to see San Francisco, much less Australia. It looks like my days as a mascot are over, too. I sit down on the foot rail of one carriage still parked on the street, and for the second time today, I cry because I'm hungry and alone. A few of the horses look over at me. I wonder if horses ever feel like this when their owners lock them up in their stables and forget to feed them.

Chapter 2

October 25, 1888
Omaha, Nebraska, United States

While I sob, I bury my head in my hands, running them through my short, fuzzy hair. Then I think about how I got to be the mascot for the White Stockings in the first place. I was sweeping the sidewalk outside a Chicago barber shop back in May to get a little money for food, just humming a tune to myself, when Tom Burns and Silver Flint, the White Stockings' catcher, came out from having their hair trimmed.

Looking around, Burns said to Flint, "You know what we need, Flint? We need a new mascot. Ever since we lost Willie Hahn, we ain't been the same. Remember that time back in '86, when he stole the Newfoundland dog that Detroit brought with them as their mascot? That dog was bigger than he was, but Willie just snuck over there and grabbed its leash, then pulled it over to our bench. We need someone like that again."

"Yeah, Willie was a true mascot, for sure. How old was Willie? Six, seven maybe?"

"I think he turned seven last year. We could use him back."

"We could, but more than that, I'd prefer to have Mike Kelly back. He's worth about ten mascots."

Laughing, Burns said, "Well, he's in Boston now, and I don't think Spalding wants him back."

"I suppose not. Say, I'm thirsty. Let's go get a growler of beer."

"We gonna find a mascot in a saloon?"

"Maybe. Who knows?"

"I don't like the idea. You know, Flint, that Spalding has detectives follow us, and they report back to him if we go out drinking."

"Did you remember to check before we went in the barber shop? I don't see anyone around who looks like a Pinkerton."

"Nah, I forgot to check."

Then Burns looked down and noticed me for the first time. "Say, boy, did you see anyone who looked like a detective follow us into the shop? A man with a notebook? Short, wiry guy with a scrawny beard?"

"No, sir, I haven't seen anyone like that today."

"Say," Flint puts in, "you hum a pretty good tune. What's your name, boy?"

"Clarence. Clarence Duval, sir."

"You know anyone lucky around here, Clarence?" Burns asks me. "Our baseball team needs a new mascot."

"I like baseball, sir. Are you on the White Stockings?"

"We are. You know where West Side Park is, Clarence?"

"Yes, sir. I walk by it sometimes during the games, but I've never gone inside. I don't have much money to go to ball games."

"You like baseball, but you've never seen a game?" Flint asks me.

"Yes."

"You know, Tom, maybe this boy can help us. He's never seen us lose a game before, and sometimes that's lucky. Maybe we should bring him to the park today and see how much luck he's got."

11

"Couldn't hurt, I guess."

Then, looking down at me again, Burns asks, "Are you good at anything, Clarence?"

"I can sing a bit, sir. And I march real good. I've always loved parades."

So, I went to West Side Park for the first time, and the White Stockings won that day. Right after the game, the players voted to make me their mascot. That's what I did, until August when I made a bad mistake and joined Miss Jarbeau.

Between thinking back on my memories and being so sad and busy sobbing, I almost miss what happens next, but I look up just in time to see Burns and Tener walk toward Anson. Lucky for me, I have good ears, and I'm close enough I can just barely hear what they say to each other.

"That was low of you, Anse," Burns begins. "What would it hurt to at least ask Mr. Spalding if Clarence can go with us?"

"You know I hate that coon. He's great with his baton, but otherwise, he's a no-account nigger, that's what he is. He'll be more trouble than he's worth."

"Maybe," Tener counters. "But he's also twelve years old, homeless, and broke, and now he's stuck in Nebraska and it's almost November. What's going to happen to him when it gets freezing cold and the snow flies, would you say?"

"I won't say, and I don't care."

"That's hard, mighty hard," Burns puts in. "We all want him to come, and I'll bet you that Johnny Ward does, too. He's just as much a captain on this trip as you are."

Tener then says, "Cap, at least let him march with us today. That will lift his spirits, you know, and probably draw some attention. He's mighty good with the baton; you said so yourself. You know attention is what Spalding would want, if he were here, and I'll wager it's what you want, too, seeing that you have money invested in this whole operation."

"I guess it wouldn't hurt this once," the big captain finally gives in. "Go get him and tell him he's marching with us today. Although I don't suppose he still has his uniform? Look at the coon. Holes in the knees of his pants, and one elbow of his shirt, too. He's filthy. Although that's about right for his kind, I suppose."

"I'll let Clarence know," Burns says. "I'm afraid there's not much we can do about his attire today, Cap. What clothes he has will have to do. Meanwhile, John, you go tell Johnny Ward and the All-Americas and make sure they know we're gonna pass the hat for Clarence once we get to the grounds to play the game."

After hearing this, it's no surprise to me when Tom Burns walks over with a smile on his face. "Come on, Clarence, you're leading the parade!" He extends his hand and helps me up.

"Me?" I reply. "But I thought Master Anson said he didn't want me no more, and everyone was sore on me, and that he blacklisted me, whatever that means."

"He's changed his mind, Clarence. You've got your baton with you, right?"

I hold it up to show him I do.

"All the men are down the street there. Do you see them? The players in the blue uniforms are the All-America team. That's who we are playing on our tour. You just put on the best show you can once we start marching. The grounds here in Omaha are only five blocks that way. Can you see the grandstand and the field over there? That's where we're going. Jump to it, now!"

I can just see one edge of the grandstand because it isn't that far. Omaha has a few big buildings, like the hotel across the street that's five stories tall, so if you don't know where you're going, you can get lost. The hotel has a sign out front, of course, but I'm not good enough at reading to say for sure what its name is.

I walk over to where all the ballplayers are. I'm still very scared that Anson might change his mind again, but with Burns' encouragement I step to my spot in front. The Chicago team has white cotton uniform shirts and pants with black lettering on the shirts, while the All-America team's uniforms are light blue and have the word "All-America" in white block letters across the chest. Their uniform shirts lace up and have collars, just like the Chicago uniforms, and their pants are white. All the players have dark leather shoes with metal spikes on the bottom. That's what all the ballplayers use for shoes, I've noticed.

Burns gives me a nod to begin, then moves to take his place for the parade.

"Dress ranks there!" I shout, just as I'd done so many times back in Chicago. Burns, Tener, and a few of the All-Americas are grinning. Some of them aren't. Before I can see who they all are, however, someone blows a whistle, so I spin around, and off I go!

I toss my baton up into the air. I spin left, then hop right, and catch it perfectly. I twirl it while the band plays a march. We parade forward, and I loft the baton skyward again, in front of me just enough so that I catch it with a big jump a couple seconds later. I spin, and then I spin again, twirling my baton the whole time.

Then, something wonderful happens. We're about halfway to the ball field when the crowd, which had started out so quiet, starts cheering and clapping. I hope it's for me! I smile the best smile I've got, flick my wrist, and up the baton goes up one more time. I'm skipping along now, the spinning baton going from one hand to the other. I'm concentrating so hard that I don't realize we're almost there. I just know I don't want to drop it now! We get to the ballpark, the whistle blows again, and I've done it.

Several of the men pat me on the back as they trot by to warm up on the field. "Bravo, Clarence," Tener says. "You've still got your touch!"

"I try my best, Mr. Tener. You know I don't want to let the boys down again."

"Well, you go and see Burns after the game, you understand? He might have some good news for you." I think he says something else to me after that, but a streetcar rattles by, clanging away on its metal rails, and I don't quite catch the words. I hope they aren't too important.

Now, I'm so happy after such a hard day I almost want to cry again. This time, though, I won't. Can't let the players see that. They're all men, real professionals, and they would never cry at the ballpark. That means I can't, either.

I sit down on the bench of the Chicagos and dangle my legs while I watch the players toss the ball around and get ready to play. I look out on the field. Who is that talking to Anson? Wait, I recognize him. It's Johnny Ward, the crack shortstop of the New York nine. Ward is a dashing baserunner, and people say he's one of the handsomest men among all the ballplayers. He is a little larger than most in size, and people also consider Ward one of the smartest men in baseball. I guess that's why he gets to be captain. He and Anson are a fair distance away, though, and the spectators taking their seats in the wooden grandstand behind me make too much noise, so I can't hear what they're saying to each other.

After a few seconds, Ward holds his arms out at his sides and starts gesturing with them. Anson frowns a bit and says something back. Then, Ward points at him, then over at me, the muscles of his neck straining a bit. He's not smiling anymore, either. Anson shakes his head back and forth, meaning no. Ward gestures with his arms again, then shrugs his shoulders, while Anson continues shaking his head. Then Anson turns around and heads toward the Chicago bench where I'm sitting, grunting the whole way. After a moment, Ward decides to follow. When he speaks again, this time I can hear him.

"Hold on a minute there, Anson. Just let the kid stay with us for one day, won't you? We could use a mascot for good luck; you know that. Over in New York, we never play a game without at least one mascot, and it's not likely we'll find another before we get to San Francisco."

Anson answers, "Yes, I know all about your superstitions over in New York. Your manager, Jim Mutrie, is the most superstitious man I've ever seen. Is it true he spits over his left shoulder to ward off bad luck? He's got his fingers crossed, too, about half the time when I look over at your bench. About Clarence, though, the little darkey, I don't want him around. The boy's a good-for-nothing layabout, that's what he is."

"But you saw his performance today. His act is good, very good. The leader of any military band in this country would be famous for life if he could do an act like that."

"I figured you'd say that, Ward," Anson retorts. He's not quite shouting, but he's raised his voice a bit. "You always liked the darkeys, didn't you? I hear you even tried to get your owner, John Day, to sign that nigger pitcher George Stovey. You actually think your nine will play with a coon on the team?"

"George Stovey has an excellent reputation, you know that. After all, he struck you out twice in an exhibition game one time, as I recall. Regardless of what I think about colored people personally, I want to see the New York team win games, and I think we'd win more of them if we had him for a pitcher. Let's talk about Clarence, though. Now, your boys tell me he's broke, he has no parents to speak of, and his traveling minstrel company left him behind here in Omaha. Why shouldn't we let him come, if Mr. Spalding gives his permission? It won't hurt you, and both teams will feel better with a genuine mascot around."

Anson simply grunts again and walks away, muttering to himself. I don't think the argument is over yet.

I watch the game from my seat on the bench. As it turns out, it isn't much of a game. My Chicago boys lose, 12-2, against Ward's All-America team. Maybe I'm a little rusty at bringing people luck and being a mascot. Tom Brown and George Wood, two of the All-Americas, both hit the ball so far that they get all the way around the bases before the Chicagos can put them out. Home runs! The All-Americas sure have a fast pitcher. His name is Ed Crane, but most of his teammates call him "Cannonball." I don't know why, except maybe because his pitches are so fast. Ed sounds like a fine name to me.

While I watch the game, I'm supposed to bring the Chicago team luck, but that works best when they are up to bat. When they take the field and the All-Americas bat, I have some time to think things over. To my surprise, one of the players for the All-Americas comes over to sit by me when the game is in the fourth inning. He's one of the younger players, but still has a bit of a serious look about him. He's tall, too. Not quite as tall as John Tener, but tall, and just like Tener, he's rather thin.

"John Healy," he says, extending his right hand. He's got just a hint of an Irish brogue. Then I remember that Healy is a pitcher with the Indianapolis Hoosiers, so he can talk to me because it isn't his turn to be the All-Americas pitcher today.

I give it the best handshake I can. His handshake is quite firm.

"Some of the boys tell me you're to be our mascot. That was some fine marching, lad, back there before the game. The boys also tell me you're here all on your own. Tell me, laddie, how did you get here, and where are your parents? What do they say about a boy being off on his own like you are?"

I decide I might as well be honest with Healy, especially if I might travel to Australia with him. "I don't worry much about my parents, sir, because I haven't seen them in three or four years. I don't think I'll ever see them again."

"Really? You're truly on your own, then? How'd that happen, my boy?"

"We used to live in Kentucky, near the Ohio River, back when we were together. One day, though, I just woke up in our shack and they weren't there. No sign of where they went, or why they left, but they were gone. Because our shack was on a farm, we didn't have any close neighbors, so none of them saw what happened, either. My parents just disappeared. Then, later that day, someone came to the shack and told me it wasn't mine anymore, and I had to leave."

"Didn't you have friends or family to stay with?"

"I didn't know what to do then, but after a couple days of looking, I decided my folks weren't coming back home. I stayed at a neighbor's farm for a few days, but they were just as poor as we were, and the husband, Mr. Lewis, drank a lot. When he did, he'd rage in and out of his shack most of the night, and the fourth night I stayed there, he got drunk, got his shotgun, and shot a hole in the wall after he got mad. I left the next day."

"Then what?"

"I didn't know what else to do, so I hitched my first ride on a railroad. I didn't know where I was going. Didn't care. The conductor threw me off the train before I got too far, but after a couple more tries I got better at being sneaky, and eventually I got to Chicago. I feel bad that I had to steal from a couple farms along the way, so I wouldn't starve. I never liked the feeling of taking from other people, but I didn't like being hungry, either."

"So, then, what do you do in Chicago on your own, Clarence?"

"I've done just about every odd job that exists. Some business owners will give a bit of work to a colored person and some won't. Also, I've learned which policemen will move a person along while they work their beat and which ones have sympathy for a kid down on his luck. I know some restaurant owners who will give me a bit of food at the back door, and which bakers don't mind giving someone a loaf of bread that's getting old in exchange for a little work. Some others have a hard heart, though, and it's pointless to even ask them for anything, even if I'm willing to work for it."

"Go on, lad."

"The hardest part about living on streets of Chicago, though, comes during the winter because it's so very cold. The wind blows down from the north sometimes, and comes off the lake, and sometimes last winter I just couldn't get warm for days at a time. I just walked around and shivered for hours."

"I'm from Illinois, too, and I've been to Chicago in January. I know exactly what you're talking about, my boy."

"That's one reason why I decided to join Miss Jarbeau. She said her troupe toured all around the country, and I was hoping we'd spend the winter someplace a bit warmer than Chicago, if you follow me, sir."

"I heard some of the boys mention that, too. How you were the mascot for the Chicagos but left them in August, and they didn't know why."

"Yes, that's why I did it. Even when you have a small part like I did, at least you get to stay at a hotel when you travel, and you can be indoors at night. Except now I can't do that anymore because Miss Jarbeau let me go and gave me my release."

After I'm through, Healy strokes his chin for a moment. Like many of the ballplayers, he has a full mustache but no beard. "Well, my boy," he says finally with his slight Irish accent, "it'd be a pleasure to have a real mascot with us on this trip. I hope old Spalding will see it the way I do."

I look up, and notice that the inning is over, and the White Stockings are on their way in to bat. Healy sees it, too, and so, without saying anything further, he gets up, pats my shoulder, and heads back to the All-America bench.

After the game, I'm on the lookout for Tom Burns like I'm supposed to be, but Anson walks over my way instead. I fear he's going to send me away one more time, but I try not to show how scared I am.

"Boy," he growls, "most of the men want a mascot for our trip. Now, I can't make any contract with you, but Mr. Spalding will join us tomorrow, and if he says to take you to Australia, then I'll take you. Until then, here's a little money. Some of the men got up a collection for you. Come with us while we get some food. The men felt charitable today when they heard that the Woman's Christian Temperance Union runs a restaurant where they offer dishes for a nickel each. That's where we're going."

Anson hands a few nickels to me, then wipes his hands on his uniform pants. I can hardly hold them, though, because I'm so happy! I know I still must talk to Mr. Spalding, but I might go to Australia after all!

Chapter 3

We take our train west across Nebraska overnight. Mr. Spalding chartered a train with sleeping cars, the "Cosmopolitan," to take the teams from Chicago to Denver via the Burlington route.

"What does c-o-s-m-o-p-o-l-i-t-a-n mean?" I ask John Tener in the morning.

"That's a bit of a strange question. Why do you ask, Clarence?"

"I saw the word on the side of our train."

"It has to do with cities and modernity."

"Like Chicago?"

"Yeah, Chicago's a cosmopolitan place. Come, let's get some breakfast, Clarence."

"They serve breakfast on the train?" I've hitched rides on trains lots of times by now, but I don't get breakfast that way, for sure.

"Of course. Here's the dining car."

He opens a door and we cross into the car where you eat. We sit down, and a waiter brings us both a menu. I look at mine for a minute, then look up nervously.

"What's wrong, Clarence?"

"I'm afraid I can't read the menu, Mr. Tener. I know a few of the words, but not all of them."

"Well, they have just about everything on the menu. What do you usually eat for breakfast?"

"I don't know, Mr. Tener. I don't always get one."

At this, Tener, looks down at the table for a moment, and his mouth twitches. After a second or two, he says, "Well, what would you like to eat?"

"Do they have eggs?"

"Yes."

"And a piece of ham?"

"They do."

"What about an apple?"

"Sure."

"I'd like those."

"Didn't you ever order food while you were with Jarbeau, Clarence?"

"Not really. Most of the time, I just got the leftovers after everyone else finished eating, or someone ordered for me. When our shows had a good audience, we'd stay in nicer places with good food, but if our audiences were small, the places we'd stay weren't so nice."

"Well, here's your chance to do it for yourself."

"Really? I get to order myself?"

"Sure. When the waiter returns, just tell him what you want."

I think about things for a moment. "How much does it cost, Mr. Tener? I only have a couple nickels left from yesterday."

"Don't worry, Clarence. I'm the bookkeeper on our tour. Everything will be fine. The breakfast is part of our tour. We've already paid for it."

21

In a few moments our waiter returns. "Have the gentlemen decided what they'd like to order?"

"Go ahead, Clarence, tell him."

"I'd like two eggs, and a slice of ham, and an apple, please, sir. Oh, and may I have a coffee to drink?" I don't really like coffee, but I heard several of the players order it, so I do it, too. I'd like to fit in.

"Very good. And you, sir?" he asks Tener. He says something, but I'm distracted because I got to order my own breakfast and have someone serve me. I wonder if I'll get to do any other new things if I go to Australia?

When breakfast ends, things get better still. We arrive in Hastings, Nebraska, and I step off the train. I see glorious sunshine, almost like June, with blue sky from horizon to horizon. What a horizon! With all this open space, air, and light, it's so different from Chicago.

Some of the buildings in Hastings are very nice looking, and a lot of them look new. A few of the nicer ones have three stories, with a small rounded tower, one or two covered porches, and a whole bunch of glass windows facing the street. These big houses are set back from the street a way, and a few also have little white picket fences with gates. Most have brick foundations.

I wander aimlessly for a little while after breakfast, looking at the nice houses, while the players mill around trying to decide what to do before their game. I end up standing near John Ward. He's speaking with a man in a black suit and pants, a derby hat, and a tie. He seems to be from Hastings.

"Well, Mr. Ward," the man in the suit says, "we're mighty pleased to have you here in Hastings. We're quite a going concern here now; yes, we are. Just look at all these beautiful houses we've built. A bunch of our buildings burned down after the big fire we had back in '79, but thanks to Mr. Rittenhouse's designs, we just built them back all grand and new. My, what a growing town we have here. Almost 13,000 people live in Hastings now. Why, at this rate, we'll be the corn and wheat capital of Nebraska before long. You mark my words, Mr. Ward."

"I see," Ward says with a smile. "Very impressive, Mr. Osborne. I should say your town is very attractive, indeed. Why, you'll have paved streets and cable cars before long, I'll wager."

"That we will," the man says, not noticing Ward's gentle sarcasm. "We still draw our streetcars with horses, but soon, why, it'll be all powered, just like you have back East in New York."

"I look forward to the day."

"But that's not all. No, not by a long shot. See those buildings over there?" he asks Ward, pointing to a location east of the train station.

"I do."

"That's our new Presbyterian school, Hastings College. Been going since 1882. And there's our high school over there. Of course, you've noticed our county courthouse by now."

"Indeed. The three-story red brick building over yonder with the clock tower."

"That's correct, Mr. Ward. We're the seat of Adams County and proud of it. There's even talk of rebuilding our courthouse, so it's nicer and newer than ever. It's almost decided on. We've got an opera house, too, the Kerr, because those of us in the heart of the country, although we love our farming, why, we don't forget about culture and entertainment out here on the Nebraska Plains."

I look over at Johnny Ward while Mr. Osborne keeps talking. He's glancing off into the distance, then down at his feet, then he clicks his tongue once. He takes off his top hat and scratches his head a moment, but Mr. Osborne just keeps going on.

"We take care of our own here in Hastings. Just this year, we opened the Bethany Home for women and children, and a hospital, plus the Hastings Public Library."

At this point, Ward notices I'm standing nearby and uses my presence as his chance to change the subject. "Say, Mr. Osborne, where in Hastings might our boys find a fine clothing establishment?

23

I overheard a few of the men saying they might want a new suit before we head on down the line."

"Why, I'd say Main Street Mercantile & Clothiers should serve you as well as anything we've got in Hastings. It's just a block down this way."

"Thank you kindly, Mr. Osborne. I'll go and relay that to the men."

Then Ward turns to me. "Clarence, come with me. No mascot of the All-America team is going to lead us onto the field in those rags you're wearing. It's time to get you some new clothes!"

While we walk, I ask Ward, "Mr. Ward, how come Mr. Osborne kept going on and on about how modern Hastings was and telling you about all the buildings? This place isn't very big compared to Chicago or New York."

"No, it isn't," Ward says with a quiet laugh. "However, I suspect he is what we call a booster, Clarence. Do you know what a booster is?"

"No, not really."

"Boosters are people who want their town to grow, and so they try to publicize how great things are in their town so that more people will want to move there. It's true that Hastings is growing; you can see all the new construction as well as I can. But some people think it's their civic duty to let others know about how great their town is, or will be someday. Usually, what they have to say is a mix of facts and nonsense."

"You mean they don't have to tell the truth?"

"No, Clarence, no rules exist about that. I suspect that man, Mr. Osborne, was being more honest than most because we can see some of the buildings he mentioned, but not all boosters are very scrupulous about the truth of what they claim."

I nod.

"Ah, here we are, the clothing store," Ward tells me. "Let's go inside and see what they offer in your size."

Soon, I'm standing in front of the mirror in an honest-to-goodness clothing store. It's the first time I've been in one since Philadelphia in August, and that makes it only the second one I've ever shopped in. Several of the Chicago players have joined Ward to watch the tailors fit me out in a new suit of clothes. The man selling the clothes frowns, narrows his eyes, and glowers at me when I come in.

"What is *he* doing here?" the man says, pointing at me, when I come in with Captain Ward and Tom Burns. "He'll have to wait outside. We don't serve the colored here."

"Come with me to look at these clothes over here, Clarence," Burns says to me. We start browsing through some suits that are about my size. Meanwhile, Ward goes over and speaks with the salesman, talking to him too quietly for me to hear. The salesman eyes me darkly a few more times, but after Ward says something in his ear and shakes his hand, he gives a big huff and walks off.

Ward comes over and gives me a big smile. "No problem after all, Clarence. Now, which of these sets of clothing suits your tastes? Do you like dark brown, beige, or gray? This one here looks about your size, doesn't it? Do you want to try it? Oh, and let's get you a hat, too."

While I try on the clothes, I ask Ward, "Mr. Ward, what did you tell that salesman so that he changed his mind about me?"

"Oh, nothing to worry about, Clarence. I just mentioned how I was sending reports to the Chicago and New York newspapers as part of our baseball tour, and what a shame it would be if the whole nation learned of the poor service at this establishment. He had a change of heart after that."

Ward has a huge grin on his face, and I smile back. "Is that true? You write for the newspapers, too?"

"I do, yes. Honest. I'm not being a booster, either," he says with another big smile.

By the time everything is over, I have a brand new checkered suit, a Panama hat, new shoes, even a new bright blue handkerchief.

25

I've never looked so sharp before! I'm so pleased that I look nice once again. I am just getting ready to leave, smiling as wide as I can, when Harry Palmer comes in, along with Fred Pfeffer, the crack second baseman for the Chicago nine, and one of the All-Americas, the big pitcher Ed Crane.

Pfeffer is a rather tall man, although not nearly so tall as Tener. He has one of the largest, bushiest mustaches of any of the ballplayers, and his hair is brown. Ed Crane's build is like Tom Burns, powerful and muscular, except he is as tall as Pfeffer, almost six feet. Although he looks like he could cause a lot of trouble if someone made him upset, Crane wears a thoughtful expression today and usually is rather quiet. At least, he always acted rather quiet when I saw him playing ball this past season.

"Well," Palmer begins, "you're looking mighty spruced up, Clarence. If you're not careful, people will mistake you for a darkey dude from South Carolina. Won't they, Fred?"

"I can't understand it, Harry," Pfeffer says in his Kentucky accent. "Why do you want to bring this boy with us to Australia and back? Riding on a train with white folks is no place for the darkeys, you know. He ought to be picking cotton somewhere, I say. This expedition is no place for him, and I hope Anson tells Spalding so."

"Give it a rest, Fred," Crane breaks in. "It isn't his fault he's got no family and parents. You want to leave him here instead, in Nebraska? Where is he going to go?"

"He can go wherever he pleases, so long as it isn't with us. Although I'm not surprised to hear that nonsense from you, Crane, you hailing from Boston and all. We did the right thing when we got rid of that nigger catcher Walker and his brother back in '84. There just isn't room for any colored players in baseball, and that's a fact."

"That's right, I'm from Boston, but my family moved there from Tennessee. It hasn't caused them to hate colored folks."

"Now, men," Palmer interjects, "if I can get you to calm down, it's almost time to go to the ballpark for our game. Shall we proceed?"

The two men glower at each other for a moment, but then seem to call an unspoken truce, and they shake hands.

If the game is near, that means it's time for me to do my act. I look up and down the street to find the players, then head in their direction. The streets are just dirt, which means my brand-new clothes will get dusty, but I can't help that.

The streets of Hastings are a bit like those of Omaha. They are wide enough for carriage traffic and trees line them, although most of the trees look small, so I suspect someone planted them recently. One thing that's different, though, is the smell. In Omaha, there always seemed to be a rotting smell from the animal slaughterhouses, but maybe they don't have those in Hastings because the air seems fresher, other than the horse droppings in the street that I'll need to step around, anyway.

Because I come from Chicago, which is a big city, I'm not used to small towns like Hastings, but the streets themselves aren't that much different in size. The main street where we're standing, even with the horses and carriages parked on the side, is wide enough for nearly a dozen people to use it at the same time. Some of the stores on either side of the street are wood frame buildings, but others are brick. Most have an awning with a sign describing what kind of business the store owner deals in, and big, plate-glass windows so a person can see inside from the street. A few trees cast a bit of shade over the wooden sidewalks. However, a lot of dust hangs in the air here, too, so most of the awnings and white-painted storefronts are a dirty white color this time of year, and the bricks are a dusty red.

I get to the lines of ballplayers and step to the front. This time, my act will be extra special, now that I look more like a real bandleader.

"Form ranks there," I say, just like in Omaha, and we're off. I warm myself up, nice and slow, my arms pumping in and out with my baton, and then I use my best move, a move no one has ever seen me do yet. I toss the baton skyward, then do one, two, and three spins before catching it. I'm liable to fall over almost, I'm so dizzy, but I don't, and before long, we're at the ballpark. Parading in Hastings goes a lot faster than it does in Chicago because the ballpark isn't far from the main street. Again, Ward and Burns give me a friendly pat on the shoulder and a smile as they go to warm up.

I head toward the Chicago bench like always. The cranks (that's what all the players in baseball call the spectators) are piling into the wooden bleacher seats built around home plate. The field in Hastings has no grandstand, just wooden benches in rows. I can see that Hastings has never had a baseball game like this before because the cranks stand shoulder to shoulder, smoking their cigars and waving their top hats and derby hats excitedly, and everyone is talking all at once. The bleachers are extremely crowded. I see no room at all for more people, but more cranks keep trying to squeeze in, anyway. Other fans surround the field, standing in the outfield grass to watch the game from there because the field has no seats at all surrounding the outfield.

I'm halfway to the Chicago bench when I hear a loud groaning sound. In an instant, cracking and splintering sounds follow the groan, and before I can even move, right in front of me one section of the bleachers collapses! All the people in that section fall to the ground in a jumble of flailing arms, legs, hats, and splintering wood. People shout, curse, and yell. For a few minutes, chaos reigns. I drop my baton and run over to help.

"Here, sir, let me help you there. Are you hurt?" I ask the nearest person, offering my hand.

"I'm fine," the man snaps at me. "And you get out of here! I don't want help from no coon! Now move on, you. Don't you dare speak to my wife, either! How are you, dear, are you injured?"

While the angry man pulls his wife from the wreckage, I move on, like he said. Now all the ballplayers are there, helping people out of what's left of the bleachers, and wouldn't you know it, Anson is right next to me.

"Get away, boy," he says. "Let the real men take care of this. You've only been with us two days, and already look at the bad luck we've had because of you. Go play with the kids and stay out of the way."

I slink away and sit down on the ground, my head down. No one even seems to notice me, anyway. Maybe Anson is right, and this trip isn't such a good idea after all. I'm supposed to bring good luck, but it doesn't seem to be working so far. Since no one wants my help, I pull up a couple blades of grass and toss them back down.

Then, Pfeffer sees me and shouts out, "Boy, why are you just sitting over there? Get over here and help! Just like a nigger to sit and watch when there's work that needs doing. You people are such layabouts."

So, I stand up again and go over that way. Because no one will touch me when I offer my hand, I wrestle a piece of splintered wood from the pile-up and try to pull it away instead. I toss it on the pile of splintered bleacher boards someone's already started.

In fifteen or twenty minutes, things seem to be back in order. People stop yelling and cursing, the cranks wipe the dust from their bruised elbows and knees, and all agree that the game should go on. It seems that the collapse did not hurt anyone badly somehow. That seems a minor miracle to me, but I guess it's because the bleachers aren't more than ten or twelve feet high. Other than a couple men limping around on twisted ankles, it seems everyone is fine. I guess they don't want to miss seeing the Chicago and All-America teams play in Hastings, no matter what.

After the drama in the grandstand, I take my seat on the end of the Chicago bench like I always do, and as far away from Anson and Pfeffer as possible. Anson scares me all the time, but especially after today, I want to stay away from him. It isn't that hard to avoid Anson, generally, because he spends most of his time on the field, screaming and yelling at the umpires and the other team. People call what he says to the other team "coaching," and what he says to the umpires "bulldozing," although it just sounds like yelling angry insults to me. I don't even know what all the words mean, but from how the players on the other teams like to shout back, I assume most of the words I don't know aren't very nice ones because the ones I do know aren't very nice, either.

Today, however, Anson sits on the bench while his team is at bat and only goes onto the field when the All-Americas come up to bat, and it's his turn to play first base. I don't know why he's acting so differently now, so I ask Tener. It's Mark Baldwin's turn to pitch for Chicago today, so Tener remains on the bench when Chicago takes the field.

"These games are called exhibition games, Clarence. That means they don't count in the championship standings. We only play them to entertain the cranks and to make extra money. That's why Anson isn't doing much coaching. I guess he figures we're going to be traveling with the All-Americas for a couple months together, so it might be okay to lay off on the coaching for a while."

"Is that what this tour is for, Mr. Tener? To make more money for Mr. Spalding?"

"In a way, yes. Although Mr. Spalding and the players love baseball, and we want to help people in Australia learn about our National Game, we're hoping they'll take up the game and become ballplayers, too."

"So, we are going to teach people in other countries how to play baseball?"

"Not exactly, no. We are going to play games in a whole bunch of cities and hope our example of how to play inspires the other people to give baseball a try."

"How will that make money for Mr. Spalding?"

"Mr. Spalding, besides owning the Chicago White Stockings, also owns his own company that sells sports equipment. He plans to open stores in some of the cities we visit."

"They don't already have stores where you can buy bats and balls and scorecards?"

"Here in the United States we do. But over in Australia they don't have any. Most Australians like the sport of cricket instead of baseball, but we hope to change that a bit. Mr. Spalding thinks that if he can inspire the Australians to play more baseball, and he has the first stores in their country where people can buy baseball gear, they'll buy from him. As baseball gets more and more popular, he'll sell more and more supplies. That's how he plans to make money."

"I think I understand better now."

"Good, Clarence. I'm sure he hopes to make a little money selling tickets to Australians to come watch us play, of course. I'm sure he'd like to at least break even on our trip itself. But opening stores in Australia and selling them baseball supplies for years to come is the real prize."

That makes sense to me, I think, even if I don't understand how business works very well. Rather than try to figure it out today, I try to keep my eyes on the field and do my job as mascot, which is to bring the Chicago team good luck. Today, it's working. It's the fourth inning and the Chicagos are leading the All-Americas, 3-1. After a few innings, I hear Palmer's voice in what's left of the bleachers behind me, along with another voice I remember well from Chicago. It appears Spalding has arrived from Kansas City, and Palmer is filling him in on what happened before the game.

"Newton MacMillan and I were lucky and were sitting in the first row, so we are unscathed, Al. I believe a few people suffered sprained wrists, and the falling wood planks caused some cuts, but no other serious injuries took place. About 100 people were in the weakened section of the stands. You can bet they'll be talking about this in Hastings for months, if not longer. It might even top the blizzard they suffered through last winter."

"Well, I undertook this trip for the publicity, certainly, although this is not quite the publicity I had in mind. Still, if no one sustained any serious injuries, I suppose we can all be thankful. The boys are giving a good show on the diamond today. Tell me though, Harry, who is that little chap on the end of our bench? Have you and the boys found a new mascot?"

"We've found a mascot, yes, but not a new one. You'll never believe it, but that's Clarence Duval. Tom Burns found him in

Omaha yesterday. Burns, Ward, Tener, and several of the other players want him to come with us for good luck. I can vouch that his baton act is as good as ever."

"You don't say. Clarence Duval, indeed." Spalding pauses for some time, and then speaks more loudly, just to be sure I can hear him. "Clarence, come over and speak to us."

Al Spalding is the owner of the Chicago White Stockings. Even though he is about the same age as Anson, he stopped playing ball many years ago, although from the stories I've heard some of the players tell, people once considered him the smartest and best pitcher in baseball. Like almost everyone else on the teams, he has a dark mustache, and he is tall, probably over six feet, with a medium build. He wears a fancy, expensive suit, and a stylish top hat. His cane sits beside him, its tip resting near his new brown leather shoes.

"Yes, Mr. Spalding, sir?" I say as I trot toward Spalding and Palmer.

"Clarence, Harry here tells me that some of the boys would like you to accompany us on our trip to the Antipodes."

"What's an antipode, Mr. Spalding? I thought you were going to Australia."

He chuckles gently. "It's just another word for Australia, Clarence. I assume you are in favor of going with us?"

"Yes sir, Mr. Spalding, I am indeed."

"Well, while I am inclined to say yes because every team could use a good mascot for luck, I remain concerned regarding the little matter of how you left us at Philadelphia and ran off with that minstrel company. Miss Jarbeau's company, was it not?"

"Yes, that's so, Mr. Spalding. I wish now I hadn't done it." I look down and shuffle my feet. I'm scared he is going to say no and tell me to go away, just like Anson would.

Instead, a long pause. While I wait for the bad news, Palmer says to Spalding, "I'd like to see him come with us, Al, if you can manage to overlook his past lack of faithfulness. He is a coon, after all, so you can't expect him to have the same steadfastness and honor as a white person. Colored folks just don't raise their children to that kind of behavior, as you know. It's one of the many failings of his kind. Still, I think he feels sorry in his own way." Then, Palmer pauses and tweaks his mustache.

"Go on, Harry. I sense you have more to say. You seem to think he could be of benefit to our party. Moreover, you say many of the boys want Clarence to come. Please, speak freely."

"I think that, despite the shortcomings of his color, he is a great little nig. He can dance in a style that would turn a professional song and dance man green with envy. His little nut has so many funny Negro songs and sayings, and his drum major act is as novel as it is inimitable. I'd like to have him along, yes. If nothing else, having Clarence with us will give the men some entertainment while we're at sea."

"What you say is good sense, Harry, but still, I am uneasy with this idea. Some of the men may want him with us, but others, I assure you, do not."

Then, addressing me, "Clarence, if you are to be our mascot for this Australian adventure, we have to know that you still have your luck-bringing abilities. That is what mascots are for, after all. So, let's test whether you are still of any account as a mascot. If the Chicagos win today, I will prepare a contract for you to sign, and you may go with us. If the All-Americas win, I will take that as a sign that your lucky days are over, and you must go your own way. Are we agreed?"

"I suppose so, Mr. Spalding. I'll do my best."

It isn't what I wanted to hear, but I'll have to make the best of things. Seeing that I have no other choice, I trot back to the Chicago bench. Because it is now the fifth inning and the Chicago team is in the field while the All-Americas bat, I head straight to where the Chicago players stack their bats and try to give them all the luck I have. I rub Ryan's bat with my forehead. I tap Tom Burns's bat twice, once at the grip end and once at the thick end, then tap them

33

again, just to be sure. Bob Pettit is in right field today, and he has already made one error, so I figure he needs extra luck. I wave my hands over his bat, but I make sure I stop after exactly twelve circles. Thirteen would be bad luck. I've been a mascot long enough to know that. I pause when I come to Anson and Pfeffer's bats, which they stacked right next to each other because they bat one after the other in the Chicago batting order today. I shoot a quick look out to the field to make sure they aren't looking, and, as quick as I can, I do a circle around each one.

While I do all this, I hear Harry Palmer say to Spalding, "I'm a little surprised, Al. I know you don't believe in luck. What was that about, anyway?"

"You are correct, Harry. This mascot business is all bosh. Some of my men believe differently, however, even though they know I don't put any stock in such things. This way, you see, no matter what happens, I'll have something to tell the men who are disappointed. Anson, Pfeffer, Hanlon, maybe Fogarty, and several of the others, I'm sure, believe the boy a nuisance, at best. If he were to come with us, and if we are to have good morale throughout this trip, I must placate them somehow. The same is true for those like Ward, Burns, Tener, and a few others who like the boy. So, by letting fate decide, I take the decision out of my hands, and no one becomes resentful toward me."

"Al, you know I'm your friend, so perhaps you can forgive me if I say that seems awful calculating for something as simple as having a mascot."

"Perhaps it is, Harry, but you don't become a board member of five corporations without doing a little calculating now, do you?"

"And what would you prefer to see, if I may ask?"

"I'm willing to see the young man come with us, or not. It is immaterial to my intentions of expanding my sporting goods business in Australia. Still, it seems his odds are good. The score is 3-1 in favor of Chicago, and our pitcher, Baldwin, has terrific speed today, wouldn't you say?"

"He does, and the All-America pitcher, Van Haltren, is struggling to control his pitches, like he often does. He has allowed two batters their base on balls already. Why are you letting him pitch for the All-Americas when he is a member of your club?"

"Van Haltren is only going with us as far as California. He is from there, and he lives in Oakland. He needs the practice, so I figured why not let him pitch a few extra games against Anson, Ryan, and the rest of the boys? Perhaps he'll learn his craft better. He is only twenty-one, you know. He may have a career as a pitcher yet, but only if he learns to be more scientific while in the box."

"You mean a pitcher more in your own image. When I send my weekly letter to *The Sporting Life*, how shall I describe your decision to bring Clarence with us, should it come to that?"

"That it was all part of my plan, of course. Write that, upon encountering Clarence Duval, I immediately decided to take the little chap with the party because all the boys desired his presence to bring us luck."

That is all their conversation I hear because after I'm done working my magic on the bats of the Chicago players, the inning ends and it's their turn to hit. They come up to bat in the sixth inning, but they haven't scored off Van Haltren's delivery since the first inning, and I know they need my help to break the hoodoo. At first, it works. Anson comes to bat. As mean as he is, he sure can swing the ash when he means to, and this time, he means to. He strikes a sharp single to right field. Then Pfeffer comes up. Smack, another hit, and now Anson's at second. I knew that all that they needed was my help! Now Ned Williamson, the big shortstop, is up to bat. Oh no! He fans the air three times and returns to the bench, struck out by Van Haltren. Now it's Tom Burns' turn. I cross my fingers and turn around twice, then stand on my left foot. Burns already has one hit today, but this time, all he can do is a weak fly ball, and he is out. It's up to Marty Sullivan, the Chicago right fielder, if we are to score any runs this inning. I close my eyes, too nervous to watch. Crack! I open them just in time to see the ball sailing deep into the outfield, over the head of George Wood, who plays left field for the All-Americas today. The ballpark in Hastings has no fences, and the ball rolls into the crowd watching from the outfield, so Sullivan makes it all the way around the bases for a home run. Even though Mark Baldwin, the Chicago pitcher, makes an out next, the Chicagos now lead 6-1!

My good luck doesn't last long, however. The All-Americas score three runs themselves in their turn at bat in the sixth. Tom Brown, their speedy right fielder, hits a home run of his own, sending the ball between Marty Sullivan and Jimmy Ryan in the Chicago outfield.

Now it is the seventh inning, but my boys only have a 6-4 lead, and I'm nervous again. I toss some dirt in the air to see which way the wind blows it. I knew it! The dust drifts toward second base, which is a good sign. That means we should get more runs this inning. We always score when the wind blows dirt toward second base. It turns out that I'm right. The Chicago club scores twice in the seventh inning and now leads 8-4.

We still have the same advantage when the bottom of the eighth inning starts. Just six more outs, and I get to go to Australia. Baldwin, our pitcher, gets the first man out, but then the All-Americas start a rally. The next man hits a single, and then the next batter does as well. Williamson makes an error at shortstop, then Baldwin walks the next batter, letting in one run. Then, a fly ball to Jimmy Ryan in center field. He catches it, but the fly is deep enough that another runner comes home, and now our lead is only two runs. If only Baldwin can get one more out this inning, we'll still have the lead with one inning to go. But instead, another walk from Baldwin, which means the All-Americas have the bases loaded again.

I'm so scared I can't watch. I cover my eyes with my hands but then peek through my fingers. Now Jimmy Fogarty, the left fielder for the All-Americas, is at bat. Baldwin delivers. Strike one! Another pitch. Too low. Ball one. Then Baldwin sets and delivers his third pitch to Fogarty. He hits Baldwin's pitch deep into the outfield, and races all the way around to third base, clearing the bases. Now the All-America team has the lead. Even though Baldwin gets the next batter out, now Chicago trails, with only one inning left to go.

Then something terrible happens. With everyone in the crowd shouting and yelling in their excitement, Spalding walks out onto the field to address the crowd.

"My friends, I am so sorry to interrupt this tremendous exhibition of baseball. However, our train departs for Denver within half an hour. The ballplayers must have a chance to gather their things and catch this train, so we can continue our tour. Regrettably, that means we will not be able to play the final inning of our game."

Some of the spectators boo or mutter at this news, but only a few. I guess most people realize that the trains have a schedule, and Spalding has no choice but to call off the game.

He continues after a brief pause. "I, along with all the players, thank the people of Hastings for your great enthusiasm and hospitality today. In a gesture of goodwill and thanks, I have instructed our team treasurer to deposit a sum of money to help rebuild the bleachers that collapsed today. Farewell to you all, and Godspeed."

This second announcement brings a shower of applause. Spalding takes it in, waves to the crowd a few more times, and shakes a few hands on his way off the field.

I'm back on the Chicago bench, looking at the dusty ground between my legs. I know I shouldn't cry, but I want to. We had the lead, by four runs, with just two innings to go. But, we lost it. Maybe my luck is gone, and I don't deserve to be the mascot anymore. I hear people approaching. Without looking up, I can see that whoever the first person is, they have very nice leather shoes and a cane, so I guess it's Spalding.

"Clarence?" It's Spalding's voice.

I look up at him, my eyes glistening because I know what he's about to say.

"I am sorry, Clarence, but your luck was not with you today. By the terms of our agreement, that means you will not go with us to Australia. Let me give you a few dollars. They should be enough for a train ticket back to Chicago. Good luck."

Spalding walks away, and then I can see that John Ward and Tom Burns are there, too. They both pat me on the back gently. "Tough luck today, Clarence," Burns says. "Maybe we'll see you again at West Side Park sometime, okay?"

While the cranks leave the ballpark in Hastings, I think over my options. It was very nice of Spalding to give me money to go back to Chicago. Our agreement never said he had to do that. But, even though Chicago is my home, I don't really want to go back there. It will be very cold and windy there now because it's almost November. The wind blows a lot in Chicago all the time, but it's bitter cold living on the streets in the winter because of the icy air coming off Lake Michigan. Things are even worse when you only have one suit of clothes, like me, and don't even have a winter coat.

Then, I recall something I overhead on the train yesterday. Several of the ballplayers mentioned how much they wanted to go to California because Johnny Ward said he toured there during the winter once, and sometimes it was warm in California even in December. That sounds a lot better to me than snowy, cold Chicago. But, the ballplayers know I'm not supposed to go with them.

Quickly, I get up a plan. I grab my baton and my Panama hat and hurry off toward the railway station.

Chapter 4

October 26, 1888
Eastern Colorado, United States

I'm huddled against the night chill while I watch the miles roll by from the tiny rear platform of the last car of the train. It's too cold to sleep, not to mention dangerous, so I have plenty of time to think.

If I go to California, or even part of the way there, I'll have to learn a whole new city. That shouldn't be hard. From what the players said, though, San Francisco sounds like a big place, so it may take some time.

More than that, I'm worried about what I should do with myself when I get there. I'm twelve now, and I can't go around begging for food or a warm place to sleep my whole life. The problem is, I've never been to school for more than a few weeks here and there. I don't know how to read very well, and I can't do any math except to add by one, two, three, or four, because that's how you get runs in baseball. I suppose my first step should be to learn how to do those things, but how will I feed myself while I do, or stay in place long enough to get schooling?

I could get a job somewhere, I suppose. Many factories will hire children, from what I hear. But, I also know that factories are dreadful places to work. I've seen children my age and younger on the streets of Chicago who were missing fingers. When I asked them how it happened, they told me how they lost them in a machine at the factory where they work.

The one time I tried to work in a factory, I had a job cleaning the floor in a slaughterhouse. That's why I can recognize their smell anywhere. The smell was so vile, though. Standing in rotting chicken guts and heads with blood dripping from the severed veins that used to connect to other parts of the animal, it was just too much for me. My job was to sweep the severed chicken parts out of the way of the people who cut up the animals, but I kept slipping and falling into the bloody, slippery mess of chicken parts all over the floor. The shift went for twelve hours without a break, too. I tried to do that job for about an hour, but I couldn't take the stench, so I snuck out the door when the foreman wasn't looking. Not only did I hate that work, it ruined my clothes, too. I don't think I'd like to work in a factory again.

I know it's bound to happen eventually, but still, it takes me by surprise when one of the railroad conductors opens the door to check the rear platform and sees me.

"What are you doing here, son? Where's your ticket?"

"I have no ticket, sir."

"Then what are you doing, hitching a ride on my train?"

Quickly, I tell him about how I used to be the mascot of the Chicago team, and how I almost got to go to Australia, and why I don't want to go home to Chicago.

"So, you just decided to hitch a ride on my train and head for California to spend the winter there?"

"Yes, sir, that's about the truth of things. I have no family and no home in Chicago anyway, so it's all about the same to me where I spend the winter. I thought maybe I'd try California."

"Well, that is better than most of the stories I hear from the tramps and vagabonds who try to steal rides on my train."

At this point, I expect the conductor to frown and get angry. That's what usually happens when the conductors catch me on a train. He looks like he's near sixty years old, with a few wrinkles on his face and a bushy, bristling gray mustache. I can see a modest paunch showing through his conductor's uniform, and when he takes off his hat to scratch his head, it's plain that he's mostly bald. I wonder how long until he decides to toss me from the back of the train?

Instead, he gets a hint of a smile on his face, and he gives a little laugh.

"You say your job is to bring good luck to the ballplayers."

"Yes, sir."

"And are you good at your job as the mascot?"

"I was until today, it seems."

"Well, if you're good luck, I don't like the thought of just dumping you off our train, here and now. No use bringing down bad luck on us by treating someone like that. Railroading can be a dangerous business, so I don't mind having a mascot on board with us. However, I'm not supposed to let people hitch rides. Regulations, you know. So, my lad, here's what we'll do. Let's go and see your friends, the ballplayers, and ask them to reconsider. If they do, fine. If not, you'll have to buy a ticket to go the rest of the way to California, or get off at the next stop. Agreed?"

"I suppose so, sir."

He puts his hand on my shoulder firmly and leads me through the door at the rear of the train. I carry my baton with me, since it's the only thing I own besides the clothes on my back. We pass through a couple of sleeping cars before we enter the car where many of the players are still awake. Some play cards—poker, it looks like—others read, and some just watch out the window. I'm thankful I don't see either Anson or Pfeffer in the car. Spalding is there, however, reading a newspaper. He looks up when we enter.

"Clarence," he says carefully, "I thought you were headed back to Chicago."

I've been going over this story again and again to myself. Time to find out if it will work. "Mr. Spalding, sir, I decided to hitch a ride on this train because I wanted another chance to show you and the boys that I'm still lucky. I feel bad because I left you in Philadelphia this summer, and I want a chance to make it up to you and the boys. I know I did wrong, but I want to show how I've learned my lesson."

After a moment, Spalding answers. "So, you snuck onto our train, and have been riding outside all night?"

"Yes, sir, that's how things are. While the porters loaded the train, and everyone was finding their places, I snuck to the back and hid on the other side of the train, away from the platform. Since it was almost dark, no one saw me. When the whistle blew, and the train started, I just hopped on."

Spalding cups his chin in one hand and just stares at me for a few moments. Everyone in the car has stopped whatever they were doing, and they're all looking at us to see what will happen. John Ward and Ed Crane, the big pitcher, are there, sitting across the aisle from Spalding, but not Burns or Tener.

Spalding just stares at me for another moment with no expression on his face. Beads of sweat trickle down my back.

Finally, he lets out a big laugh. "Clarence, my boy, my personal motto is 'Everything is possible to him who dares,' and I'd say you've shown your share of daring tonight. Someone go find Jim Hart and have him bring Clarence a contract."

I get up all my nerve and sit down across from Spalding. Soon, a man comes in whom I don't know. That must be Jim Hart.

Then Spalding says, "Well, Clarence, we'll soon learn whether your mascotic talents are still potent. I suppose today was not really a fair trial in any case because we had to end the game one inning early, but we couldn't afford to miss our train. Regardless, given your pluck and courage, I'm prepared to offer you the position of official mascot for our Australia trip. Are you ready to sign on?"

I say, "Yes sir, Mr. Spalding," almost before he's done speaking.

He gives me a kindly smile. "Very well, then. This is an official contract. Please note that, should you violate it, we retain the right to keelhaul or draw-and-quarter you, or any other punishment that the men see fit to inflict."

"What does keelhaul and draw-and-quarter mean?"

"They are methods of torture."

My face blanches.

Another smile from Spalding as he says, "They are also mere figures of speech, Clarence. Adrian would never treat you in such a way, trust me."

I relax a bit. I was too excited. I couldn't tell he was joking with me.

"Okay, then. Where do I make my mark?"

"Right here at the end," the other man, Jim Hart, says.

I put an "X" on the line that Jim Hart points to.

"Now, that's settled," Spalding says. "Jim here will find Anson, and Adrian will show you which one is your sleeper car, Clarence. Congratulations on being a member of the tour."

Hart leaves again, and soon, Anson stomps into the car, and he makes a noise that sounds like a growl when he sees me. However, Spalding gives him a look and presents my signed contract, so Anson holds his tongue. For the moment. I follow the big captain to the proper train car. I feel like I'm just floating along, I'm so pleased, but it only lasts until Anson turns to speak to me.

"It won't surprise me a bit if you leave us at San Francisco."

"If I do, you can break my neck, Master Anson."

"That's what you said in Philadelphia, too. I believe you would desert us *now* for Jarbeau, if she asked you to."

"No sir. I'm not any such nigger, Master Anson. I know she *would* ask me. If she saw me now, she'd say, 'Come on, Clarence, come with me.' She'd say it, for sure."

"Well, what would *you* say?"

"I'd say, 'Go on, white woman. I don't know you.' No sir, Master Anson, I'm done with actresses, I tell you right now. I done learned my lesson, I promise."

Anson huffs at my answer and frowns again, but all the same, he turns to leave just as John Tener, the tall pitcher, and Captain Ward come in.

Tener says, "Clarence, we hear you are now a member of our party. Johnny Ward, me, and some of the other boys passed the hat for you during the game in Hastings, and we've put together a nice little purse of money. When we get to Denver, we're going to get you a real drum major uniform, so you can lead us in style. What do you think of that?"

I think I see Anson's eyes roll while he ducks out of the car, but I barely hear him slam the door because I'm happy once again. I get to have my own uniform!

A porter escorts me to my room where I'll sleep. I'm surprised when I find he's colored, like I am.

"Here you are, young sir. May I bring you any food before you retire?"

"No, thank you. What kind of wood is that on the seat backs?"

"It's finished mahogany. Do you like the carved flower designs? Pullman cars like this one used to have lacquered walnut, but the newer ones like this one have mahogany."

"It is very nice. The carpets make the floor very soft, too." As soon as I sit in one seat, I can see the plush cushions make the seats very comfortable as well. Each compartment has two bench seats that face each other and look out of a large window at the passing scenery.

"I'm glad you are happy with the accommodations, my young friend."

"But I don't understand; I thought this was a sleeping car."

"One moment, sir."

Quickly, the porter extends the leg cushions on each seat. They come together in the middle and make a perfect bed.

"Wow! Now I see."

Next, the porter pulls down the overhead compartment, and I can see that inside is another bed. He quickly puts it back up, however.

"Because you're the only one assigned this compartment, you won't be needing that, but I wanted to show you how it works. Did I hear someone say you are the mascot for the ball teams?"

"Yes."

"Well, I've been all over the country with this job, but I've never been to Australia. I hope the Australians treat you well."

"Thank you, sir."

"You're welcome. If you wish to retire now, I'll turn off the gas light before I go."

He does so, an exits the compartment. I lie down on the bed, put my head back, and fold my hands over my chest. I hear the hum of the train while it moves along, but it's not too loud. The bed beneath me is so soft compared to what I'm used to. The only time I've had anything like this was on Miss Jarbeau's tour, and even then, we only got decent beds sometimes. My eyes drift closed, and I finally relax.

It's hard to believe how lucky I am.

Chapter 5

October 27, 1888
Denver, Colorado, United States

Whew! I'm out of breath. Denver sure is a big place, at least compared to Hastings. I just finished leading our parade, and it took near on half an hour. There's something else, though. All the players seem out of breath, too, which I've never seen just from parading before. I heard someone say something about altitude and thin air. The air looks just the same as ever to me, but when I say so, Ed Crane just laughs at me.

"You don't understand, Clarence. When you are up in the mountains like we almost are, the air doesn't have as much oxygen in it. That's why it's thinner. You can't see it, though."

"Then why do you say it's thinner if it looks just the same?"

"That's just what people say."

"But how can they tell if you can't see it?"

"Science, Clarence, science."

Pfeffer yells out, "Crane, quit wasting your time trying to explain science to the darkey. You know darkeys are only a couple of generations removed from eating their own kind in the jungle.

How are you going to expect him to know about science? Come on, we got to get ready to play."

"Another time, Clarence," is all Crane says as he trots off. To Pfeffer, I hear him yell back, "Eating their own kind? Are you serious? We live in the nineteenth century, after all. Have you been drinking too much Kentucky bourbon again?"

I think about how something can be thin if you can't see it, but I just can't wrap my head around it. At least the cranks here in Denver are nice. They cheered the boys and me with gusto when we finally got to the grounds for the game. They don't cheer that much during the game, however, because the players on both teams are not playing a good game of ball. Several times, they miss easy fly balls that they nearly always catch. I wonder if the thin air is responsible for that, too. The final score is 16 to 12 in favor of Chicago.

I'm eating breakfast in the dining room of our hotel the next day, October 28, because we have one more game in Denver before continuing to California. I liked my breakfast of eggs, ham, and an apple so much I decide to have it again. I pass on coffee this time, though, because I just don't like it much, so I drink milk instead. Jim Fogarty of the All-Americas reads a newspaper after he finishes eating. He's already got his uniform on for today's game. Fogarty is another tall, well-built ballplayer who plays the outfield. He is very fast and covers a lot of ground. Fogarty is also younger than most of the men; he looks about twenty-five or so to me. The thing that stands out about him most, however, is his sense of humor. He is always outgoing and joking with the other players.

This morning Fogarty says to Jimmy Ryan, "Hey, Ryan, you and Burns made the local papers this morning. Here you are in the *Rocky Mountain News*."

"Yeah? What did I do?"

"There's an article here that mentions the two of you, titled 'Baseball in Australia.' You're on the first page."

"Well, go on, read it for us," Ryan says while he and a few other players gather around Fogarty.

Fogarty reads, "Baseball in the bush! The American national game played by its ablest exponents before the Zulus, the bushmen and kangaroos of Australia! Kelly the beauty, Anson the irrepressible, Ward the intellectual, Pfeffer the statuesque, Burns the lady-killer, Ryan the Adonis of center field! What incredible wealth of brains, manly beauty, and athletic talent Manager Spalding lavishes on the hitherto benighted antipodeans! What a time the boys will have! They will be in danger from the aggressive female population from the time they first appear in their snow-white jersey suits in all the vigor of their virile powers. Travelers who have traversed the wilds of the inland continent say that one of the favorite ways of expressing love practiced by the dark-skinned but intensely affectionate maiden of the bush is to offer her accepted lover as a toothsome tidbit to her cannibalistic chieftain father.

"What a fricassee Ryan would make! How the tears would well up into the eyes of some dusky beauty of the forest as she sharpened her teeth on his femur, or how her ring-nosed papa would swear in choice Zulunese as his teeth fastened in one of Jimmy's old-time Charley horses. Burns will mightily deceive any cannibal who tries to convert his stocky muscular form into pate de foi gras. Tommy is rather tough. His rounded limbs, which, swelling beneath his tight-fitting suit, captivate the ladies in the grandstand back of third base, would be wearisome picking if done upon the festal board a la spring chicken. It's a good bet that Tommy will never return. Some aboriginal princess will become stuck on him, and she will make him a royal dude in her father's halls as it were. He will wear rings in his nose, and, clothed in a necklace and his royal dignity, he will umpire at all the games he organizes and runs for his royal pleasure. King or subject, Tommy will always play ball."

Fogarty looks up from reading. "There's more, about Pfeffer and some of you other boys. It says you can have whatever woman you want in Australia, but first you must chase her, overtake her, choke her senseless, and carry her off to your cave. That's how it works in Kentucky, too, right, Pfeffer?"

Everyone laughs at this last joke, except Pfeffer, who scowls and almost barks back his answer. "That's how the niggers do it. We Kentucky gentlemen have a more refined approach of courting our women. You know that. However, this newspaper is right about one thing. See? Look at that picture there, of the cannibals cutting up Ryan and stewing him in a big pot. Crane, didn't I tell you that the niggers here in this country were just a step removed from eating their own kind in the jungle? There's your proof that they do it in other countries, yes sir. I fear it will take some time yet for us good white folks to properly civilize them, so they won't fall back to a more primitive state."

At this point, John Ward can hold back his disdain no longer. "Hmpf," he snorts, "what a load of rot. You men should know better. For one thing, Zulus don't live in Australia. They live in Africa. We aren't traveling to the bush, either. Our itinerary clearly calls for us to play in towns and cities, not the middle of the Australian forest. Which is another absurdity, because most of their land is desert, rather than forest, once you head inland. Can't you men see that this whole article is written in jest?"

"Now, this piece may be off in its particulars," Pfeffer answers. "But the general truth of the thing is dead on. I'll bet you'd feel right at home with those kangaroos, chasing them with your shield and spear, wouldn't you, Clarence?"

"I don't fancy running with kangaroos, Mr. Pfeffer. I'm only twelve, and I'll wager they're too fast for me."

"Maybe we should do what this article suggests at the end," Fogarty breaks in. "It says we should obtain a bushman as a mascot. What would you do then, Clarence? Maybe we should leave you there and trade you for a bushman to come back to the States with us. I'll bet you'd like it in the bush, chasing women and hunting kangaroos."

"I've never hunted anything, except my next meal," I answer, and a few of the men laugh. "I'd rather be back in Omaha than stuck in the bush with kangaroos and spears."

"Would you just let the kid alone," Ward says to the group. To me, he continues, "Don't worry, Clarence, we aren't going to meet any cannibals or hunt any kangaroos. Some of the boys just can't tell a joke when they read one, that's all."

"Can I ask you something, Mr. Ward?"

"Sure, Clarence."

"How come you decided to come on this trip? I'm glad you did, so that I have someone to help stick up for me."

"Well, I think that everyone deserves decent treatment, Clarence. If any of the All-America players give you too hard a time, I'll try to straighten them out. As for why I decided to join Spalding's Tour, or whatever we're calling it, I got married just a little while ago, and I wanted to show my new wife part of the world, and this tour seemed a great chance to do that."

"Where is your wife? I've seen Mr. Spalding's mother, and Captain Anson's wife, and one other lady, but she always stays right beside Mr. Williamson."

"That's because the other woman is Ned Williamson's new wife. My bride, Helen, well, I don't know if she's going to come with us after all, Clarence. You see, she's a well-known actress, and her stage engagements may prevent her from joining our tour."

"Is your wife Helen Dauvray, Mr. Ward?"

"That's right. Helen Dauvray Ward, now. How did you guess?"

"Well, because I'm an actor myself, and all the actors know who she is. She's famous. And now she's your wife?"

"She is."

"I've never seen her perform, but everyone talks about how wonderful she is on the stage."

"I can only say I agree, Clarence."

"Well, I hope she can come with us, after all. I'd like to meet her someday."

"Me too, Clarence. Me too. Now, please excuse me, so I can get ready to play ball today."

Denver

One thing about Denver—you can see mountains almost wherever you look. Chicago has no mountains at all, and these ones are so tall and huge. I wonder if they get that tall because of the thin air in Denver. In fact, I'm riding through the mountains right now. The boys are taking a side trip to a mountain called Pike's Peak before their game today, and I'm along with them. They're all traveling on horses, but because I'm smaller than they are, I only have a pony. Suddenly, I hear an awful howling sound. *Awoooooo.* Wolves!

Tom Daly, the catcher for the Chicago team, is riding at the head of our column, and I hear him shout, "Quick, boys, the Manitou Resort is just up ahead! Ride hard!"

They all take off, but my pony can't keep up, and I'm falling behind. Now I can see the wolves leaping down the mountainside on our left, and I can see they'll get between the other players and me. No one looks back or turns around to help me because they're all riding as hard as they can. The sagebrush rushes by as my pony runs ahead, but it's all a blur of brown, green, and gray. All I can focus on are the gray and black shapes leaping downward toward us, moving faster than I am. The last of the other riders, Jim Fogarty, the All-America outfielder, disappears around a bend some ways ahead. I shout for help, but he doesn't hear me. Before I can get any farther, two very big wolves leap down onto the trail.

My pony rears up, and I fall to the dusty ground. Just as I sit up, the two big wolves leap at my pony. I'm almost on my feet when another vicious wolf springs from a large rock at the side of the trail, right at me. Its yellow eyes get bigger and bigger, and I can almost count its teeth while its jaws open just a foot from my face.

My eyes open and I sit up with a yell. What a vivid dream! I wipe a little sweat from my forehead, but then I hear the howling sound again. This time it's real, or so it seems for a moment. Then, I remember the howling is the same thing that gave me nightmares last night. Two of the players, Tom Daly and Jim Fogarty, got the idea of starting something called "The Order of the Howling

51

Wolves," and just about every night, they let forth with a slew of howls that just might wake a dead person.

It was Fogarty's idea first, I think. He is one of the youngest players on the trip, and he never stops moving or talking. He loves a good joke, like when he read the newspaper to everyone in the hotel this morning. I don't know if he likes me or not, because he never seems to stay serious long enough for me to tell.

Daly, the other Howling Wolf, is also rather young, even younger than Fogarty, I think. He is of medium height and has a stocky frame, probably because he can eat so much. At breakfast this morning, he kept the waiters practically running to the dining room and back. He's been with the Chicago club for the last two years, which is only a little longer than I have, and he has a strange way of playing catcher. When the pitcher winds up and is almost ready to throw the ball, Daly squats down and gets ready to catch each pitch from a crouch. Most of the other catchers stand behind the batter and lean over to catch the pitch when it comes in, but not Daly. All the other players remark on his unusual stance as a catcher.

At this moment, however, I don't really care how Daly catches the pitches, because he and Fogarty won't stop howling. Last night it was just the two of them, but now, it seems, two new wolves are in their pack. I'm not sure exactly who their two new recruits are, but they sound like Marty Sullivan, the Chicago outfielder, and Fred Carroll, who plays catcher and outfield with the All-America club. Or, maybe the other voice besides Sullivan belongs to Mark Baldwin, the pitcher. I'm not sure. So now there are four wolves, the group is louder than ever, and I don't think I'm going back to sleep for a while. I'm not sure I want to, anyway, because I don't want another dream about wolves eating me. Therefore, I put on the shirt the players bought me in Hastings and, dodging Daly and Sullivan on my way, head to the rear of the train, where I find Harry Palmer standing and taking in the night view.

"Good evening, Clarence. It would seem we drew the short end of the stick as far as traveling company goes. When they split our train into two sections to make it easier to ascend the Continental Divide, we ended up with the Howling Wolves in our party. I take it you couldn't sleep any better than I could?"

Palmer is right. At first, I was happy that I wasn't on the same train as Anson. However, if he were on our train, I have a feeling he would strangle one of the Howling Wolves rather than stand all this noise.

Rather than mention that, instead I say, "I dreamed of getting eaten by wolves. We were on our ride this morning to Pike's Peak, and they almost ate me before I woke up."

Palmer smiles at me. "Fortunately, our real trip was not so dramatic. How would we ever make it to Australia and back without our faithful mascot? I'd ask you for one of your charming plantation songs, but I don't know that I could listen properly with the Howling Wolves going on so." He pats me on the head when he says this.

"Did Mr. Spalding hire you to go with the players and write for the newspapers about our trip?"

"He did. I'll be sending dispatches to both the *Chicago Daily Tribune* and *The Sporting Life* as we travel. It's once-in-a-lifetime opportunity, and I didn't intend to turn down a chance to see new parts of the world. Now, tell me, Clarence. How should I describe the present view in my next letter?"

I consider the question a moment, and I'm about to respond when another round of howling commences. After waiting for Daly to finish wailing, I haven't thought of anything good to say, so I answer, "Well, it is hard to say because it seems awful dark, Mr. Palmer, and the moon isn't out yet. Do you know where we are?"

"A conductor told me a short time ago that we are soon to arrive at Marshall Pass, which is 10,850 feet above sea level. Next, we'll pass through the Black Canyon of the Gunnison River, which the conductor also mentioned was a sight we should not miss, even at night. From there, we'll soon be in the territory of Utah. Watch out when we get there, Clarence, or you'll have six wives before we leave."

"I'll have six wives? Why will I have so many? I don't even have one right now, because I'm only twelve, and I don't reckon I'll get one until I'm a bit older, at least."

"It's just a joke, Clarence. When we reach Utah Territory, we'll pass through Salt Lake City, where the Mormons live. In their religion, it is permissible to have more than one wife. Some men have several. Some people say that is why Utah is still a territory and not a state of the United States. It is a barbarous, heathen practice from a strange group of people, if you ask me."

The Howling Wolves begin to serenade the night sky again, as loud as ever. Eventually, it gets quiet enough for me to say, "Well, I don't think I want six wives. One will do for me, I suppose."

"And me, too."

"Say, Mr. Palmer, what's that red light up ahead of us?"

"That is the other car, the one with Anson, Ward, Tener, Burns, and some of the others. The trains we're on burn coal to power their engines, and when the coal burns out, they dump it behind them. The coal is so hot it glows red."

Just then, another man steps out onto the rear platform of our train. It is Ned Hanlon, who captains the Detroit Wolverines and is one of the outfielders for the All-America team. He is another man of medium size who, like Fogarty, covers lots of ground in the outfield. Sometimes, I hear the players talk about how smart he is and how much he knows about baseball strategy. Maybe that is why he is the captain of the Wolverines. He does not have his hat on this evening, so I can see he's parted his dark hair right down the middle. Like Pfeffer, his bushy mustache really stands out.

"Good evening, Captain Hanlon," I say in greeting.

"Mmpf," is all I get in response.

Then Hanlon says to Palmer, "Say, Harry, you told me there's some mighty good scenery that we're passing through tonight, so I guess I'll sit with you and take it in. Maybe we can catch Daly while we're at it and throw him into one of these canyons. How would that suit you?"

"Capitally, although I'll wager we could still hear him no matter how far the drop," Palmer answers. "And I'm pleased to take in the view with you, Ned, wolves or," and here he pauses while yet another chorus of howls assaults our ears, "no wolves. Clarence," he says to me, "I see insufficient room on our platform for the three of us, so why don't you retire so that Hanlon and I can watch the sky and come up with some ideas of how to describe the experience to my newspaper readership?"

"But you said it would be pretty. I'd like to see the canyon you told me about."

"Maybe we'll throw you over the rail instead of Daly, then," Hanlon says to me.

I take that as my cue to leave and slink back to my sleeping car, even though I know it will be some time before I get to sleep again. I guess it's all right. It is rather cold up here in the mountains, anyway. It takes a long time for me to sleep, but I finally do. The last thing I remember thinking about is where in the world I would ever put six wives if I had my own house.

Chapter 6

November 1, 1888
Salt Lake City, Utah Territory, United States

"Come on, Clarence," shouts Jimmy Ryan, the Chicago outfielder, as he slaps his leg rhythmically. "Give us a good, old-time plantation shuffle."

"Step lively, now," Fred Pfeffer adds in his Kentucky drawl, clapping his hands in time with Ryan. "Where's your Uncle Sambo with his banjo? Come on, boy, you got to earn your keep on this trip. Maybe you could dance better if we put some chains on you. Would that help you keep the rhythm? Or maybe the lash would help." Pfeffer calls out to the onlookers, "Who here has a horsewhip?"

I'm liable to drop dead any minute now. Dinner is over, it's getting dark, and I've been dancing on the train platform outside the Walker House in Salt Lake City for the amusement of some of the players, who cackle with delight at seeing me jump, stomp, shuffle, and caper while singing at the same time.

"Let's have a real plantation song, boy!" shouts Ryan. "Just like from before the war."

"I'm sorry, Mr. Ryan, but I'm from Chicago. I don't know any plantation songs." Because I'm almost out of breath, it's all I can pant out in response. I don't know why Ryan seems to be angry toward me so suddenly, but he sure has become meaner lately.

"Of course you do," Pfeffer breaks in. "All you darkeys know them. It's in your blood. Let's have a real one, now."

I don't know what to do, so I try to sing a few notes about sunshine and picking cotton, since it's warmer in the South, and I think that's where cotton grows. I don't get further than a couple lines, however, before I accidentally trip over my own feet because I'm so tired.

The people on the platform clap loudly after they finish laughing at me, and then some of them throw pennies at me.

Pfeffer and Ryan collect the money and put it in a hat they next pass among the onlookers. I pick up the few coins that land right next to me. "We'll give this to Tener for you," Pfeffer drawls again. "Since you gotta do something to pay for yourself on this trip."

I end up with a bruised right knee that trickles a bit of blood, a few pennies jingling in my pocket, and a lot of confusion in my head. While we waited on the platform, Pfeffer and Ryan told me I needed to do my drum major act to entertain the people after dinner, and I did, but they never said anything about a plantation dance. I've never lived on a plantation, and I have no idea what a plantation song sounds like or how to dance to one. All I know is I've only been the mascot on this trip for five days, and I'm getting tired of the boys picking on me when no one like Johnny Ward or Tom Burns or John Tener is around to watch out for me.

Besides what just happened, I think about the ball game in Hastings where the stands collapsed, and no one wanted me to help them. Or the time this morning when I tried to get a newspaper someone left at the breakfast table, so I could practice some of my words, but Pfeffer just snatched it away from me, claiming he was still reading it, even though he wasn't even in the room when I first picked it up. And then yesterday evening, Jim Fogarty, the prankster, and another of the Howling Wolves, Mark Baldwin, came to my sleeping berth on the train and howled right through the door and woke me up, then laughed all the way back to their own beds.

I'm still thinking about these things when the big train arrives at the platform. Because our party is rather large and plans to travel so far, we have a small mountain of baggage to load, which will take the porters some time. Well, everyone except me has baggage. I have the suit of clothes in my knapsack, my uniform, which I'm wearing, and my baton, although it looks like one leg of my uniform needs patching after taking my tumble.

The train porters busy themselves loading all the suitcases. I'm getting ready to board when I hear Jim Fogarty call out, in a low, growling voice, "We are the howling wolves, and this is our night to howl."

Instantly, he, Daly, Sullivan, and Baldwin let out a cry that seems to echo off the slopes of the Wasatch Mountains for several minutes.

The howls take everyone by surprise, and for a moment, panic rolls across the platform. One of the porters, another colored man, drops the baggage he has in hand and tries to leap aboard the train.

Another of the passengers on the platform, a well-dressed woman with a hat case in each hand, screams out, "Injuns, we're under attack by Injuns!" She drops both her hat cases and runs for cover inside the station house. "Where's the manager? Sound the alarm, we're under attack!"

The station manager, a graying man of fifty or so years, knows what is afoot and keeps his head. He calmly says to her, "It is only them durned baseball people, miss, no need to panic."

The woman turns and sees that all the Wolves have ceased howling and started laughing. Soon, everyone else on the platform is as well, except for her.

"Why, the nerve of some people," she huffs. "You all are meaner than my husband's third wife!"

Having spoken her mind, she retrieves her hat cases and stomps off the platform. The last I see of her, she's outside the station, calling for a carriage.

Eventually, our baggage stowed, we get on the train and roll down the line, but we don't make it far, only traveling an hour and a half, or maybe two hours, before the train stops in a town named Ogden. In Ogden, just like when we left Denver, we board two separate trains for the trip west across the rest of Utah and Nevada. I manage to avoid the car with Anson and Pfeffer, just like I always try to do, but this comes at the price of being in the same car with the Howling Wolves again. By now, it is nearly 11 p.m., but for some reason the train is not yet ready to resume, and the Wolves are on the prowl.

I go to my assigned berth and try to settle in. I'm feeling pleased with myself for getting through Utah and avoiding getting a wife, let alone six of them, when the Wolves let forth with another round of howling that the people back in Salt Lake City can probably hear. Then comes a knock at my door.

"Clarence, come on out," Tom Daly, the Chicago catcher, says.

I open the door to see Daly and the other Howling Wolves. Somehow or other, they've gotten hold of several bottles of whiskey, and by this point, none of the bottles are full. I'm afraid to ask if these are the first bottles they've had tonight, or if they are already on their second round with John L. Redeye.

I'm very nervous now because I know from experience that white men and alcohol can mean real trouble for colored people, especially on trains. I grimace and take a step back. Daly, however, claps his hand on my shoulder and says, "Not to worry, my boy. The Order of the Howling Wolvess hass descided to dine late thiss evening, and while our beautiful Pullman ssleeping carss are being loaded, we require your company in our quesst for victualss."

When he finishes speaking, the rest of the Wolves bay in agreement, and before I can protest, they pull me along with them into the Ogden train station's waiting room. After hearing how much

Daly slurs his words already, this looks like it might not end well, but the Wolves aren't giving me a choice, so I go.

Ogden is on the Union Pacific railroad line, and the Union Station in Ogden is much bigger than I thought it would be. It's made from red and brown bricks, has two stories, and a clock tower that rises two or three more stories into the air. From one end to the other, it looks like it's almost the distance from home plate to the left field fence at West Side Park, which means it's over three hundred feet long.

The Howling Wolves lead me into the dining area of the station. Fogarty is in front. "Good evening, miss," he says with exaggerated politeness while bowing deeply to the woman serving coffee near the door. "My men and I are in search of repast. What does this fine establishment offer in the way of refreshment?"

"Well, you're a little late for that," she replies. "Our cook has gone home for the evening. But we still serve coffee, and there are some ham sandwiches and apple pies I can get for you." The woman is in her mid-20s and, to my eyes, rather homely looking, but the boys don't seem to see things the same way.

"That will do nicely. We thank you, ma'am." Another deep bow from Fogarty follows, although he loses his balance and stumbles a bit this time. I wonder what joke he's thinking of now?

Then Daly says, "I, for one, am famisshed. Famisshed. Two piess, pleasse, and five ssandwichess. Now, what will you boyss be having?"

Then I remember. Daly has the largest appetite of anyone in our party. He can eat any amount of food when he's hungry, and he's hungry often.

"Come on, Clarence, take a seat with us," Marty Sullivan says while Daly slurs out his order and the rest of the men ask for sandwiches.

Sullivan is a player who just joined the White Stockings last year. He is in his mid-20s and is a large man who can hit the ball a long way. He just doesn't hit it that way as often as Anson, Ryan, or

Ned Williamson, so he bats near the end of the Chicago batting order. Sullivan is clean-shaven, a rarity among the ballplayers. Most of the time, he's rather quiet, but when his temper is up, well, I've learned to just stay clear of him for a while. I still remember the time this past season when he collided with Dude Esterbrook, who played first base for Indianapolis, and got in a fight with him. Esterbrook is a large, husky man, but Sullivan gave as good as he got.

"Thank you, Mr. Sullivan," I say to him. "But since I have no money on me, I don't guess I'll get to order anything and eat with you boys."

It's not quite true. I do have a little saved from the platform this evening, but I decide to save that for when I really need it because that could be at any moment.

Sullivan replies, "Don't worry, the newest member of the Howling Wolves, Pettit here, will be paying for our meal as his initiation to the Order."

"There are five Howling Wolves now, Mr. Sullivan?"

"Yep, and Bob here is like a brother to us."

"Awooooo!" all the Howling Wolves howl in unison.

Great. Now there are five of them. I'll never get to sleep again if this keeps up.

I look at Bob Pettit who, like Sullivan, is one of the newer members of the White Stockings. He is one of their substitute players and doesn't have a permanent position in the field. He is of medium build and, at least when he's sober, rather quiet like Sullivan. Tonight, however, his bottle of whiskey contains less liquid than anyone else's, except for maybe Daly's, and Pettit howls again in agreement. Then he stammers, "Thaas rright, m'boy, have a sseat now, Clarrence. Drrink up, lad."

He offers me his whiskey bottle. I know this is a bad idea, but I want to fit in with the boys if I can, so I do as Pettit says and take a gulp. Wow! I cough and spit some of it back out.

No one told me that whiskey really burns the throat. I've had alcohol before, of course, but only beer. Even beer is tough for me to get sometimes, because I'm barely even five feet tall, and some of the bartenders won't serve people a beer unless they are taller and look older than I am. I expected the whiskey to be like beer, but boy, am I wrong. I cough a bit more, and the men are already laughing.

"Easy now, boy," Sullivan says. "You'll never learn to hold your liquor taking drinks like that."

It takes several seconds before I finish coughing and spluttering, and the Wolves finish laughing at me. Once I recover from the shock, I notice that the other waitress went out the door and is talking to the station manager outside on the platform instead of getting food. I wonder if that means something important, but before I can think about it too much, Sullivan starts speaking loudly once again.

"A queer place Utah is. Someone told me we wouldn't be able to get any liquor in Utah, but Jimmy here, you learned them a thing or two."

Meanwhile, the first waitress returns with the pile of sandwiches the Wolves ordered and two apple pies for Daly. She sets them on the table and walks off. I noticed that her hands shake a bit when she set the plates down, and she glances over her shoulder while she walks away from our table. All the men drink again and wish her good health.

"Cheers, boys," Fogarty says as everyone takes yet another gulp. "To the All-America team, the Chicago club, and the Order of the Howling Wolves. May our voices never grow weaker."

The players spend the next couple of minutes chewing contentedly on their ham sandwiches, and then they stop to watch Daly devour his food. He is already about to tackle the apple pie after finishing off three of his five sandwiches. If he were a real howling wolf, he could hardly eat more quickly.

"I'll wager four bits," Sullivan begins, "he finishes in less than ten minutes. Both pies."

"I'll take the bet," Pettit blurts out. "But I'll ssay he doess it in eight."

"You're on."

The men spend the next several minutes cheering Daly while he stuffs two entire pies into his gaping mouth. It takes him just over nine minutes according to Fogarty's pocket watch, so Sullivan wins the bet. A couple quarters exchange hands.

Jim Fogarty applauds heartily. Loudly addressing anyone who can hear him, which is everyone in the station's dining room, he says, "Wonderful performance, wonderful. You truly belong amongst the Howling Wolves. But, Tom, you disappoint me in one respect."

Turning to Daly, Fogarty continues, "You bet us you would have twelve wives before we left Utah and, if my count is correct, you still have twelve to go." Of the handful of people still in the station at this late hour, a few laugh. One or two grumble something I can't quite make out while they frown or gesture toward Fogarty. One slaps his palm on his table. I don't think Fogarty notices any of it because he is so far from sober.

"I'sse working on that. Now, how about thiss waitresss here; sshe'd do now, wouldn't sshe?"

"Ay, a sprightly lass, she is," says the final member of the Order present, Mark Baldwin. He is a pitcher for the White Stockings who can really toss the sphere. His fastball might be the speediest in the National League. I heard a story that once, when he was with St. Paul back in '86, he struck out twelve batters in a row. Baldwin is about the same age as the other Howling Wolves, twenty-five or so, and stands a clear six feet tall. He's also a good friend of John Tener, although Tener is not one of the Howling Wolves. Yet. Baldwin takes a swig, then continues, in his somewhat high-pitched voice, "Whad'ya say we go an' talk to 'er, ay Tom?"

Another drink follows, and then Daly and Baldwin stand up and stagger over to the woman, whose eyes have gotten very wide by now, and she is already backing away when the station manager barges in and confronts the ballplayers.

"You there! You leave my waitresses alone. Go back to your seats or get out of here."

"You 'ear that, Tom?" Baldwin says. "He ain't takin' a likin' to the Order of Howling Wolves now, is he?"

"And what will he do about uss?" Daly slurs in response.

The two parties exchange a few curses, and Baldwin leans in and bumps the station manager's chest. The station manager gets red in the face, and he's clenched his fists, but Daly and Baldwin have him so distracted he doesn't see Fogarty sneak over behind him, hiding behind the tables. Then Fogarty gets down on his knees and crawls on all fours, grinning the whole time. Just at that moment, Baldwin gives the station manager a little shove. The man takes a step backward, trips over Fogarty, and tumbles to the ground, banging his head on a wooden chair in the process.

He is dazed for a moment, but not for long, and quickly, he's back on his feet. The waitresses run for the kitchen while Daly takes a swing at the manager. Sadly for Tom, he punches awkwardly and with poor coordination, and he strikes only air. He lunges over with the momentum of his swing and lands on a table on his stomach, cursing again. He knocks a pair of drinking glasses to the floor, breaking them.

The manager, who is the same man who had been on the platform earlier, has a little blood trickling from a slight cut on his head, but otherwise seems okay. He looks around, slowly backing away from his three opponents. The other people in the dining room have all gotten up and backed away from the fight. I see two families hustle their children out the door.

Seeing that no one in the station appears ready to rally to his cause, and that the other two Wolves, Sullivan and Pettit, are on their feet now and stumbling his way, the manager breaks for the door to the kitchen. The waitresses inside throw the door open when they see him outpacing the staggering, drunken ballplayers, and then I hear the click of the lock as soon as he passes through. While all this happens, no one is looking at me anymore, so I sneak two more drinks of whiskey, but smaller this time.

Just at that moment, the colored porter from the train walks into the dining room. "I just came to get a cup of coffee for one of the ladies . . ." he begins, until he sees three chairs knocked over, broken glass in the middle of the dining room, a splatter of blood on the floor, the five drunk ballplayers, a handful of other travelers, and no station employees in sight.

Before he can do anything, Fogarty is on him. To my surprise, however, Jim takes him by the hand and says, "Let's dance, shall we?"

To my amazement, and the amusement of everyone else, Fogarty proceeds to lead the porter in a waltz around the dining room. Except, instead of music, he waltzes to the yowling of the Wolves, now more off-key than ever. The poor man's eyes go wide open when Fogarty grabs him, and then he starts turning his head to look around in all directions, almost like a scared animal does, once Fogarty starts prancing around the dining room. It barely registers, because the scene is so bizarre, and I can't look away, but somewhere at the edge of my hearing I think I hear a train whistle. More clearly, I also hear the station manager rummaging around the kitchen.

"I need some ammunition for my pistol."

The crazy scene continues for another minute or two. The Wolves start clapping while they howl, so Fogarty dances faster. Then John Healy, the tall pitcher whom I spoke with on the bench in Omaha, opens the door.

"All aboard, men," he says. Then, everything registers, and he asks, "What on earth is this now?"

"Awoooooo," is the answer he gets from the Wolves.

"Good Lord," is all Healy says as he puts his head in his hands. Fogarty and the porter are about to waltz by for another circle around the dining room when Healy grabs Fogarty by the wrist, halting the dance.

"Let's go, Jim. Get the boys on board the train. It's about to leave."

Fogarty bows one more time, to the porter, nearly falling over as he does, and then extends his arm toward the doorway. "A fine time we've all had here, but men, we must remove at once to our car. Wolves, right this way."

While all this happens, I hide one of the whiskey bottles inside of my bandleader jacket, hoping no one will notice. It doesn't taste so bad when I pace myself. I don't manage to hide it very well, but in the hurry and rush to get to the train, none of the Wolves seem to care. The train whistle sounds again, and this time everyone hears it.

The porter is out the door first, probably scared out of his mind, so he reaches the train easily. Healy, being fully sober, is next. Fogarty, Sullivan, and Pettit make it aboard just when the train starts into motion. They might be drunk, but they still run faster than I can. Sullivan turns around and grabs Daly and Baldwin by their arms, hauling them on board one at a time, but because I'm shorter and can't run that fast, I'm last in line, and now I'm running to keep up with the train. To make things even more desperate, from the corner of my eye, I see the station manager emerge from the station's main doors. He's waving his pistol and shouting curses at us while he, too, starts running after the train.

"Jump, Clarence, we've got you, boy," shouts Baldwin from the third step of the entrance door. Sullivan crouches on the bottom step, arms extended to me, while Baldwin holds onto Sullivan from behind, so he can lean out without falling.

I know they're drunk, so I'm not so sure they'll catch me, but my short legs can't keep up with the train, which is gaining speed now and will edge away from me if I wait any longer. If they miss, I'll probably fall underneath the train wheels, and that surely will be the end of me. It's that or nothing, however, so I jump with my arms out.

"Got him!" Sullivan exalts as he yanks me onto the train.

"Hooray!" cheer the Wolves.

Pettit gives me a slap on the chest in congratulations. Oh no, that's where I hid the whiskey!

"What's this?" Pettit asks, pulling open my jacket and finding the bottle. He yanks it out. "This is Jim's bottle."

I'm ready for the worst, and from behind me, Daly and Baldwin clap hands on each of my shoulders. I think they're about to toss me back off the train, and if I survive that, maybe the station manager will shoot at me, too. I just hope I land in the grass instead of the gravel. Maybe I can get away in the darkness before I'm shot.

"What are you doing, men?" Fogarty says. "Can't you see that Clarence is a hero? When I went to help you in your fight, he was smart enough to save my liquor for me and bring it with him. Isn't that right, Clarence?"

"Yes, Mr. Fogarty, that's so," I manage to lie.

Fogarty bows low again, sweeping his derby hat through the air while taking an extra wobbling step to keep his balance. "At your service, my liege. To Clarence!"

"Awooooo," the Wolves bellow into the night. Daly and Baldwin hoist me off my feet, all right, but instead of tossing me off a moving train, now the two ballplayers have me on their shoulders, and they start prancing around in drunken celebration, only stopping to drain their bottles amidst the howls of their fellows. I can't keep my balance, however, mostly because Baldwin is about half a foot taller than Daly, so I'm soon back on my own feet.

Fogarty extends his bottle to me. "I am in your debt, good sir. Please, have another drink on me."

I do, and remember to keep it small, so I won't choke this time. Just then, Healy comes back into the corridor of the sleeping car, hands on his hips, chin jutting out, and frowning. "For goodness sakes, men, it is now nearly one in the morning. Can't the rest of us have a bit of peace?"

Pettit and Sullivan exchange looks, then leap for Healy, and soon, they've managed to wrestle him to the floor of the sleeping car. His body makes a soft thump when he lands on the plush carpet. Healy is quite tall, over six feet, but he is thin and wiry, and with two opponents, he gets the worst of the wrestling contest.

"Holler 'nuf!" shouts Sullivan, who has Healy in a kind of chokehold from behind. Healy now gets a few playful slaps from Pettit.

"All right, I give," Healy manages to gasp out.

While the men untangle, I try to slip unnoticed to my sleeping berth before any of the ballplayers have second thoughts about how I ended up with a bottle of their whiskey. Because all the bottles are empty now, I don't try to steal another.

The howling continues for another hour or so. Since I don't have a watch, I can't tell for sure, but it seems to take an awful long time. Eventually, though, it stops, and things get quiet. I'm surprised when, about half an hour later, when my heartbeat has calmed down and I've just about gotten to sleep at last, I hear a soft knock at my door. I open it to find Healy standing outside. I have no idea where it came from, but he has a small bowl containing a blackish paste in his hands.

"Come on, Clarence, I've got a job for you," he says to me, the Irish brogue softening his words just a bit. "I've still got some of the money from this evening on the train platform, and there's a quarter in it for you if you'll help me."

Surprised that Healy wants anything to do with me, I ask softly, "What for, Mr. Healy?"

Healy grins. "Well, you see, Fogarty and Daly finally are asleep, lad, and given how much whiskey they've downed, I don't think they'll be wakin' again for some time. I plan to pay them back for their incessant howling tonight, but I want to do it quick and quiet, just in case. Are you with me?"

Realizing it's more a command than a question, I answer, "I suppose so, sir."

"Good. Very good. Now, here's the plan. See the pot I have? Well, I got some soot from the coal car, mixed in some water, and now we're going to paint Fogarty and Daly until their faces look as black as yours does. That's why I want your help; we need to get it done before all the water dries up. I have another bowl for you in my room. Are you ready?"

Again, it's a command, not a question, so I nod. It is my job to paint Daly. He is fast asleep, snoring loudly, when I enter his sleeping berth. Moreover, he smells funny. When I get close to his face, it hits me. Whiskey mixed with vomit. Yuck! I almost retch myself.

I hold my nose with my left hand while doing the deed with my right. My hand shakes the whole time, and I can barely breathe, but I get it done without waking him from his drunken slumber. He's so out of things, he doesn't even stir. Healy is waiting for me when I slip back into the corridor, grinning. He flips me a quarter, just as he promised, then another, just for good measure.

"There's a good lad, Clarence. Now, let's wash up and get some rest. I'm sure we'll know when Daly and Fogarty wake up in the morning," he says to me with a wink.

I'm not so sure I want to be around when that happens. If they find out I had a hand in things, I might find myself walking home from the middle of the Nevada desert.

While I wash the black coal paste off my hands, a thought occurs to me that hadn't before. During my years on the streets of Chicago, I've seen many white people color their faces black and pretend to be colored people. Usually, they do it because they think it's entertaining. They caper around, act clumsy and stupid, speak in very poor English, and all the white viewers cackle and applaud. I'm not sure if I should feel bad for doing this, or pleased because I helped Healy pull a prank and got away without anyone seeing me.

I want to feel bad because I know this is something white folks do to make fun of colored people. I probably shouldn't have done it. But what choice did I have? I already have enough ballplayers who don't like me. If I said no to Healy and didn't help him, that might make him just one more, and I don't think I can afford that.

But I still feel ashamed, just a little bit. Sometimes, I think that white folks think of all colored folks as people wearing blackface. Like everyone's white underneath, but colored people have something on top of their skin that makes them different, and if they could get rid of it, wash it away, they'd be as good as white people.

I don't know if that's a very good way to put it, but that's how it seems to me. Maybe when I learn to read better, I'll have more words to describe how I feel about it. It's hard to understand white people sometimes because colored people need to follow all their rules. I don't look them in the eye too long when they talk to me, and I never talk to white women. I always stay on the proper side of the street, or the right part of the beach at the lake, or wait for the next streetcar if white people want on and there aren't enough spots. I stay away from certain parts of town where the wealthy people live. There are so many rules, and things get confusing sometimes, as if it wasn't hard enough being a homeless kid.

Maybe I just need to be more careful and avoid some of the players better in the future. I'm not sure how I can do that, but I guess I'll try. It's all so much for a twelve-year-old to think about and worry about every day.

As it turns out, I have nothing to fear in the morning, but Healy does. I wake up to the sound of him yelling, but it sounds like he's far away. I open my door and walk into the smoking room of the big Pullman sleeping car, and there he is. I think it's Healy, anyway, judging by the sound, but the Howling Wolves have wrapped him up in several blankets, so I can't see his face, and he's on the floor receiving a good stomping. Daly and Fogarty have cleaned their faces, and they laugh while Healy takes the punishment.

Luckily, he's been true and hasn't told them about my role in the affair because when Daly sees me, he says, "Clarence, come get your licks in, if you want to."

"No thank you, Mr. Daly. You're doing a pretty good job of things on your own, I'd say. Is that Mr. Healy?"

70

"It sure is. He got the nerve to paint up John and me last night, so the Order of the Howling Wolves must exact retribution."

"You just go on, I'm okay."

After a few more seconds, Fogarty says, "That's enough, men. I'd let you go on for a good while yet, but I vaguely remember that Healy helped warn us to get on the train at the station last night, so perhaps we should let him be for now." Then, with a final howl, the Wolves lay off, and Healy frees himself from his cotton prison.

We keep traveling all that day. The boys tell me our next stop is Sacramento, in California, and then we go on until we reach San Francisco. After that, we leave for Australia.

Chapter 7

November 3, 1888
Sacramento, California, United States

We have an enormous meal this morning in our Sacramento hotel. Since we arrive in time for a real breakfast, there are waiters and everything. They bring me food, and what food it is! There are fresh fruits of all kinds—apples, pears, peaches, and grapes—the type of food I get only once or twice a month back in Chicago, and there are eggs and breakfast rolls with jam, besides. The waiter who serves me is polite, calling me "my young sir." I don't know if anyone has ever said that to me before, until the porter on the train just a couple days ago. I end up sitting by Harry Palmer, the newspaper writer.

"Good morning, Clarence, my boy, how was the trip from Salt Lake City?"

"A bit noisy, sir, with the Howling Wolves and all."

"The boy is right," says the man seated on the other side of Palmer. I've seen him before. He rode in our railroad car, but I don't know his name, and no one has introduced us. Today, the man wears his top hat and a dark gray overcoat. It covers a starched white shirt with a stiff collar, and he wears a bow tie. The man appears about the same age as Palmer does, somewhere in his later 30s or early 40s, and he walks around with a cane like Spalding. I think it's for style, though, rather than because he needs help walking.

The man says, "Fogarty, Daly, and the rest have been at it non-stop for most of the past two days. I hear that, as of this morning, they have a pair of new recruits to the order, as well."

Palmer says, "Well, when I parted ways with you at Salt Lake City, they had five men, correct? Daly, Baldwin, Sullivan, Pettit, and of course Fogarty. Who has succumbed to their lupine charms now, pray tell, Newton?"

"If you join us for the ride to San Francisco, you'll find out soon enough, I'll wager. "Until then, I'll let you speculate. But tell me, who is your young friend here? I don't believe we've met." He extends a hand to me.

I shake it, and he gives me a kindly smile.

"This is Clarence Duval. Clarence, this is Newton MacMillan. He is a sportswriter, like me, and like me, he'll accompany us to the antipodes as a reporter. He writes for the *Chicago Herald*. We are rivals in the newspaper business, but he's a good man all the same and a friend of mine."

"A pleasure, Clarence," MacMillan says. To Palmer, he asks, "Now it is my turn to ask you for a revelation. How did Clarence here end up with you? He was the mascot for our nine this past season, or most of it, that much I remember. As I recall, however, he disappeared for the final two months of the schedule."

"Quite right, Newton, but we rediscovered Clarence when our train passed through Omaha about a week ago. Sad to say, the minstrel company he took up with in August turned him loose, and so when we crossed paths, several of the boys demanded that he go with us on our tour. His skills with the baton are second to none, and the boys wanted a mascot for good luck on our trip."

"So, you are to be our mascot, then?" MacMillan says to me. "I think the boys have made a wise choice," he says with another kindly smile. "I missed seeing you at West Side Park after you left us."

"I'll do my best, sir. I think I still have a bit of luck in me."

Then Palmer points across the dining room. "Speaking of doing one's best, check out Daly. I've never seen a man who can feed at the rate that he can. My goodness, before long he'll look like an alderman or a Dutch brewer."

"I dare say," MacMillan chuckles. "The man waiting on his table is practically out of breath, the boys have him running to bring more food so often."

I'm not sure if I should say it, but I decide to add, "In Ogden I watched him eat two apple pies in nine minutes."

Both men guffaw. "Nine minutes, not bad, not bad at all," Palmer opines. "He is certainly the champion feeder of this combination. If there is a lunch counter between here and New York City that he can't clean out, why, I'll pay for what he does eat!"

MacMillan then offers, "So Harry, you'll join us, then, for the train ride to San Francisco? You wouldn't want to miss out on the identity of our new Wolves, would you?"

"I'll be there. The temptation is just too much, and because we won't require more than a few hours to get there, it should not impinge on my need for further rest."

Turning back to me, Palmer adds, "Clarence, I hear that, upon reaching San Francisco, we are to play tomorrow, and you'll lead our parade to the grounds on Haight Street, as is customary. The next day, however, the boys will take a day off from playing ball, and our hosts have planned an expedition to Chinatown. Would you like to accompany us?"

"I thought we were going to Australia," I reply. "Now we are going to China instead?"

Another guffaw from the two men. "No, Clarence," says MacMillan. "Chinatown is a neighborhood of San Francisco where Chinese people live. It is part of the city. It won't take us long to visit. I may not go myself, but Harry here wants to see it."

"Quite right. Before we finish with San Francisco, Clarence, we'll pass through areas simply overrun with Mongolians, or so I'm told. We plan to visit their section of the city, so I can describe for the readers of *The Sporting Life* their hideous savagery in firsthand detail."

Palmer turns and addresses MacMillan once again. "Well, Newton, breakfast was excellent today. I'll catch up to you in a few moments. I do burn with curiosity over the identity of the newest Howling Wolves."

When we pull out of the station at Sacramento, fueled by their generous breakfast, the Wolves let loose another barrage of howls so demonic that every remaining person on the station platform looks our way. Soon, the identity of the mystery recruit is clear to all because we hear a clear female voice amongst the group.

Again, I'm standing next to Harry Palmer on the rear platform of the train car. He seems to like standing there and taking in the scenery, and I don't blame him. All these Western mountains sure are pretty. There's a better word for them than that, however, so I ask Palmer about it.

"Mr. Palmer, when you write for the papers, how do you describe these mountains to people who haven't seen them?"

"A good question, my lad. For Midwesterners like us, words hardly do them justice, do they? Picturesque, towering, sublime, majestic, I've tried them all, but I'm still not sure they convey the reality of things. With the sky so clear, and the colors so vivid, we'd need a Thoreau or an Emerson to get the words just right, I think."

"I agree, sir. It's all very fantastic and strange to me, too. Are Thoreau and Emerson newspaper writers like you?"

"No, my boy, they are famous American authors. Or, perhaps I should say that they *were* famous authors. Thoreau died during the War Between the States, as I recall, while Emerson passed on just a few years ago. They lived in Massachusetts."

"Did they live in Boston? Were they fans of the Beaneaters?"

"I don't know whether they thought much about baseball, Clarence. But they lived in the town of Concord, which is near the city of Boston."

We fall silent for a moment while the terrain rolls by. It is mostly orchards.

"Well, Clarence, I believe I've solved a less vexing problem than how to describe the Sierra Nevadas for my readership. Do you agree that the newest additions to the Howling Wolves are Mr. and Mrs. Ned Williamson?"

"I suppose so, Mr. Palmer, seeing that we don't have very many ladies traveling with us. There's Mr. Spalding's mother, but she isn't with us on this car, is she?"

"No, she is with the half of our party traveling on the other train. Johnny Ward's new wife, Helen Dauvray, was supposed to join us for the trip, but I hear that business relating to her acting career has recalled her to the East, and she will not travel abroad with our company. Too bad for Johnny. I believe he expected her to be by his side the whole way. I think Mrs. Williamson is the only other female candidate for membership in the order. Anson's wife is also with us, but I can't see Old Man Anson allowing her to become a Howling Wolf."

Ned Williamson is the Chicago shortstop, one of the most athletic players in baseball. He is a large man; I think he weighs more than 200 pounds, but he's very fast in the field and powerful when at bat. When he keeps his weight under control, that is. He often drinks a lot of beer and gets rather fat, or at least he used to. But since his marriage this last year, it looks like he's changed his ways because I can really see his muscles when he plays now.

I've also heard stories that Williamson was a good friend to the last mascot that the Chicago team had, a boy named Willie Hahn, who was even younger than I am. Willie was the team's mascot for two years before they found me. I've never asked what happened to Willie. Maybe no one knows.

It makes me worried, though. If Willie was the mascot for two years, does that mean I can only be mascot for two years before the White Stockings get rid of me, too? If they do, what will I do? I add this to my list of reasons why learning to read and do math is a good idea.

I consider this, and Palmer's last remark, for a minute. Then as I ask him, "Will they ask you to join, too, Mr. Palmer?"

A hearty laugh. "I think not. I'm rather too old for such things, and even worse, Spalding, Ward, and Anson would probably stop talking to me if I did. A newspaperman without contacts isn't much of a newspaperman, I'm afraid. Still, it is a bit surprising that Mrs. Williamson wants to join the Howling Wolves. I've always found her husband, Ned, to be one of the whitest men I know. But then again, he does enjoy a bit of the foaming amber from time to time, so perhaps she has a bit of his wild streak in her as well."

"What does it mean when you say he is one of the whitest men you know? Aren't all the players white men?"

"Yes, they are, but that isn't what I mean. When you call someone a white man, it is a way of saying that they are honest."

I stop to think about this statement. I am honest, other than drinking some of Jim Fogarty's whiskey when he wasn't watching, so does that make me white? Or, if I'm not white, does that mean I'm not honest even though I think I am? This is very confusing to me. I thought that honesty depended on the person, not on the color of the person's skin.

I consider asking Palmer about this, but he already has his head down, scribbling something in his notebook, and he starts humming a tune I don't recognize. This means he's done talking with me, so I decide that I'll ask him another time. I wander back to my berth to watch out the window, but what Palmer said about white meaning the same as honest sticks with me. It's hard for me to understand how that can be true.

Chapter 8

November 3, 1888
San Francisco, California, United States

The trip to San Francisco astonishes me. To get there from Sacramento, we get off the train at the San Francisco station, but we still must cross a large bay to get to the city itself, which we do by steamboat. I'm standing on the deck of the steamboat, and the wind is fierce today, although when the breeze lets up, the temperature is very pleasant. Little whitecaps are all around us on the water while we approach the docks downtown. I'm trying to keep away from Cap Anson and Fred Pfeffer, which leaves me watching the approaching city with the newspaper writer I met earlier in the day, Newton MacMillan.

"Astounding, isn't it, Clarence?" he says to me. "San Francisco is indeed as modern a city as its boosters claim. I've read that 350,000 people live here now, or thereabouts."

I have no idea how many people 350,000 really stands for, but I can see the city is quite large. I look at the docks, and then my gaze drifts up the hill behind them. I see row after row of houses packed almost on top of each other.

"Is that as many as in Chicago where we live?"

"No, not by a sight. Chicago has nigh on one million residents, so it is equal to about three San Franciscos. I hope you are feeling robust because we are going to have quite a march from our hotel near the waterfront to the grounds where the ball game takes place tomorrow. As you can see from the view before us, we must climb many hills on the way. I've been to the grounds here in San Francisco once before. They are laid out rather nicely, but it will take some walking to get there."

It takes us about fifteen minutes to reach our hotel, the Baldwin, by carriage from the waterfront. What a hotel, too! It is right where two streets meet, Powell Street and Market Street, and stands five stories tall. Its wings overlook both the streets, and each wing has about 30 big windows on each floor. I try to think how many windows that makes total, but I never learned to count that high, so I can't. But that isn't all. On top of the five main floors where the guests stay, the hotel's roof has a large dome, with a smaller dome stacked on top of that larger one. I just stand there looking at it for a time while the players unload their luggage with the help of the hotel porters. The whole thing just looks massive and solid, like nothing could ever knock it down.

"Rather grand, isn't it, Clarence?" MacMillan says to me. "The mansard roof just adds to the grandness of it all. The dome reminds one of Brunelleschi's dome on the Florence Cathedral, does it not?"

I've never seen the Florence Cathedral, of course. In fact, I don't even know where Florence is, or who Brunelleschi is, so I just nod and agree.

"The owner of the hotel is Mr. Elias Baldwin, a gold rush millionaire. There is also a theater attached to the hotel. Perhaps we'll get to see a show there during our stay."

Once MacMillan finishes telling me about the hotel, word comes to the ballplayers for some of the men to hurry on to a formal dinner. All the rest of the party receive invitations to a show called *The Corsair*, which plays later in the evening at the Baldwin Theater that

MacMillan mentioned to me. All of this takes place while we mill around in the hotel's lobby, waiting to learn where our rooms are.

When John Tener walks by me, I ask him, "Is the owner of the theater the same person who owns the hotel?"

"Yes, Clarence, I believe that he is."

"Wow, I'll bet he could show Miss Jarbeau a thing or two about running a theater!"

Tener smiles broadly. "I suppose Mr. Baldwin could, yes, although I hear he's had a bit of luck along the way. I believe I heard Mr. Spalding say he survived the most recent financial panic by sheer good fortune rather than by shrewd business practices, but all the same, here we are in his fine hotel, going to a show and, from what I hear, with more fun yet to come tonight. Although . . ." and here Tener's voice trails off.

"What is it?"

"Well, my boy, I didn't want to tell you this, but you are not invited to go with us to the show. Jim Hart, Mr. Spalding's business manager, told me to give you some money," and here he hands me some quarters, "so you can dine at the hotel tonight. The manager assures me that your color will be no obstacle to obtaining service here, so you needn't worry about that, but you may have to dine alone, I'm afraid. I am sorry, Clarence. I think you deserve better than this, and of all our company, you are better equipped than most to understand the finer points of a dramatic performance, but all the same, it seems enough of the men complained that Mr. Spalding decided that only the adult members of the party would get to see the show tonight."

I don't know what to say, so I mutter a "thank you" that might have been loud enough for Tener to hear, then mope away in the direction of my room. I know it isn't his fault; he's been rather nice to me compared to many of the players, but all the same, my spirits sink at the news. I've eaten dinner by myself many evenings over the years, most evenings, in fact, when I even get dinner, but why can't I go with the rest of the party?

Well, I know the answer, but I don't understand why that's the answer. Like Tener said, I know how plays work, and I can tell when an actor is good or not. Why am I so valuable when it's time to lead parades, but no one wants me around the rest of the time? Why am I so great when we march, but nearly everyone in our party is embarrassed to go to a play with me along?

I spend the evening alone in my room. I did go downstairs for dinner, but I don't have much to say about that, since I ate by myself. At least the roasted chicken tasted good. I pull out the one other personal possession I always carry with me, a pair of dice, and practice shooting craps. Then there comes a soft knock at the door. I open it.

"Good evening, my young, um, sir," says a hotel employee in a suit, who fidgets and adjusts his tie when he sees who I am. "May I, um, offer you a newspaper for your reading pleasure? Compliments of hotel management, of course." The bellboy adjusts his tie again, and then glances down the hallway, then down at his shoes, before taking another look down the hallway and finally back at me.

That sounds good, except for one problem. I can barely read. "No, sir, I'm not much for reading newspapers."

"Can you read a newspaper?"

"I can read some, thank you. Nothing against it, but when you have no parents and you need to fend for yourself every day, it doesn't leave much time for schooling, I guess."

The man's look softens visibly. "My apologies, my young friend. I'll be on my way." He turns to leave, but then turns back and says hesitantly, "You are with Mr. Spalding and his baseball players, are you not?"

"I am. We're going to Australia."

At that, his face perks up, and his voice becomes much more excited. "I wanted to be a ballplayer, too, once. A real crack second baseman like Fred Dunlap. I proved a little short on talent, however. Now I think I'd like to maybe be an umpire someday."

"If you do get to be an umpire, don't let Captain Anson bulldoze you. He gets pretty mean to the umpires." I've seen so many times where Anson abused umpires until they wilted and just gave up. He'd shout at them, or tell them they didn't know the rules, or get right up in their face and curse them out. I don't know how he always says the right thing and gets his way, but I know he scares most of the umpires in the National League almost as much as he scares me.

"I thank you for your advice on umpiring, Mr. . . . ."

"Clarence, my name is Clarence Duval."

"Thank you, Mr. Duval. Enjoy your evening."

It's almost 10:00 p.m., according to the clock in my room, and I'm getting ready to go to sleep when I hear a noise building outside my window.

From my room on the fourth floor, I can see people start lining the street below me. I sit and watch longer, wondering what they are doing, until it becomes clear they are lining the street on both sides, which means a parade. Well, I'm not going to get to sleep right now after all, so I grab a chair and watch from my window. At least I understand parades.

After a time, the marchers come into view. It's a parade, all right, and a big one, with banners, torches, three military bands, floats, and men in suits sporting canes and top hats and waving them to the crowd. I sigh when one parade leader drops his baton.

I can't tell what the parade is for at first, but I soon learn. A banner comes into view reading "California Republicans." I'd seen similar banners on our way to the hotel earlier in the day and asked Tener what they meant, so I know how to read this one.

After telling me what the banners read, Tener added, "Our next national election is only a few days away, Clarence." Then, in a low voice meant just for me, he said, "I hope to go into politics on the Republican ticket someday. Promise that you'll vote for me when I do?"

"Sure, Mr. Tener. How old must I be before I can vote?"

"Twenty-one, Clarence, so you've got a little time ahead of you."

"Why does a person want to go into politics, Mr. Tener?"

"Why, to serve their country, of course, and to improve the lives of people in America."

"If you win, will you do something to improve my life? Like find out what happened to my parents, or help me find a place to live, so I can go to school?"

A sad look came over Tener's face. "I wish I could, Clarence. I wish I could."

Now that I know what the parade is about, and when I see it's bound to go on for a good while, I decide to walk around my floor of the hotel a bit because I have nothing better to do. I make it to the other wing of the building when I see a door cracked open and hear muttering voices beyond the door. Creeping closer, I recognize the voices inside. One belongs to Spalding, another to Anson, and the third, Harry Palmer. As quietly as I can, I sit down and listen.

Anson is speaking. ". . . good fortune that we are sleeping on the side of the hotel away from this parade. Now, I can speak without shouting and still be heard."

Spalding answers, "Yes, I saw to it personally once I learned that the parade was in the works. Now, regarding why I've summoned the two of you to this private conference, while the rest of the boys are out in the streets living it up and enjoying themselves. I've decided to change the itinerary for our trip."

"Indeed?" Palmer says. "How so? Did your representative in New Zealand not arrange for us to play according to our original schedule?"

"Or did incompetent old Jim Hart simply fail to arrange things properly?" Anson chimes in.

Spalding answers, "Now Adrian, I know you and Hart don't always see eye to eye, but he knows his work, and I have faith in his abilities. No, gentlemen, I have something much grander and more spectacular in mind. You see, after we finish playing in Australia and New Zealand, we are not coming back to the United States immediately, like I've led all the men to believe. Instead, we will travel onward to India, Egypt, Italy, France, and Great Britain and return to Chicago by way of New York and an Atlantic crossing."

What? We're going around the world? I can't believe I'm so lucky!

No one speaks for several seconds while the news sinks in. Then Anson says to Spalding, "Why this change of plans? Surely, you don't believe that the Egyptians are going to pay to see us play baseball. The feeble and backward Arab mind could never fathom the greatness of our National Game. How will we ever make money there?"

"And there is also the matter of contracts," Palmer adds. "I've seen the contracts all the men have signed, and the contract calls for them to go to Australia and New Zealand to play ball. It says nothing about these other locations."

Spalding replies to Palmer's question first. "The contract question is simple enough. The contract that all the men signed does indeed call for them to accompany us to Australia and New Zealand. That is true. The contract does not specify, however, the route by which we will return to the United States after playing in those locations. Nor does it specify the date by which we must return, although of course we must finish touring and be home before Opening Day of the 1889 championship season. So, I am free to take whatever route home as suits my fancy, within that one constraint."

Both men give a bit of a laugh. "Al," Palmer says, "you do tend to see things from every angle, my friend. I should not have doubted you'd have thought of that already."

"That is not all, however," Spalding adds in reply. "The men seem to be having a capital time of things so far, and so I do not anticipate that many of them will object to extending our trip and going all the way around the world. Just to be sure, however, you must not reveal this plan to anyone until we are already at sea. I've spent significant money already on promotional materials and the like, and we can't afford to have anyone back out on us like Mike Kelly did. That only costs me more money. In addition, we can hardly spare a man and still have both sides field a full complement of players."

"Kelly," grumbles Anson. "That boy is a terrific player and would have made a great addition to our party, but we all knew how chancy it was to depend on him going with us. He is a great companion, and few men alive know how to have fun as well as he does, but he is utterly unpredictable and undependable. If he were dependable, he'd still be playing ball with us in Chicago, and you never would have sold him to Boston. Even if the sale was for ten thousand dollars."

Mike Kelly, I didn't know he might go with us! Mike Kelly, the player some people call "King" Kelly, is one of my favorite players in the whole world. He was an outfielder and catcher on the Chicago nine in 1886. During the next winter, though, he got into some kind of argument with Spalding—over money, I think—and refused to come back to Chicago. Spalding sold him to the Boston Beaneaters before the 1887 season because of it. All the cranks love Mike Kelly, and he loves them back. He's one of the most fun, most outgoing, kindhearted, and popular men in baseball. He also drinks a lot, however, and I think that was the other reason Spalding sold him to the Beaneaters. You never knew which Mike Kelly would show up at the ballpark, the sober one or the drunk one.

"Yes," Spalding goes on, answering Anson. "I have not fully abandoned hope that he won't just turn up one day here in San Francisco and decide to join us after all, but having had no communication from him for several weeks, that seems unlikely. Still, with Kelly, anything is possible."

"Other than Kelly staying sober," Anson replies. "Can you picture how much worse Daly, Fogarty, Pettit, Sullivan, and Baldwin would be with Kelly around to lead them? Both of you, I'm sure, remember the time in New Orleans last fall when he came drunk to the grounds for an exhibition game. While his so-called friends spewed profanity at the New York players he was with, he defended the hoodlums when the police came to remove them. Then, when his team was to take the field the next inning, he stayed in the stands drinking beer instead. I can only imagine the bad influence he'd have on some of our men."

"And can you imagine how much larger our crowds would be if he were here to excite people?" Palmer says. "Sober or not, the man is a prodigy, and the people love him. Especially the laboring classes."

"You mean the mules," Anson snaps back at Palmer. "They are good for working, but little else. If they wouldn't waste their money on drinking and gambling, they might not have to labor so hard."

"Spoken by a man who will take any bet at any time," Palmer retorts. "Although I must give you credit on the drinking issue. Your prohibitionist ways would serve some of the younger members of the nine well, if only they would be wise enough to follow you and take the blue-ribbon pledge."

"Gentlemen, that is enough about that," Spalding interrupts. "You both know my feelings on why we must cater to the respectable element of the population first and foremost when it comes to drawing spectators to our home grounds. And unless Kelly does appear, let's have no more talk of Mike Kelly. I have one more thing I want to discuss with you two tonight, however, which is the real reason I've called you here. If it were merely a matter of extending our trip, I could have told you that news at the same time I told everyone else. No, something of much greater importance is going on, and the two of you must help me manage the news."

I was about to creep back to my room after hearing the incredible news that I was going to travel around the world, and possibly with the great Mike Kelly, no less, but just as I start to get on my feet, I hear Spalding drop this last piece of information.

The two other men saying nothing, Spalding eventually continues. "While I was downstairs before dinner this evening, I received a telegraph from John Brush in Indianapolis. He has agreed to lend his name to my plan for a salary limit scale for the 1889 baseball season. I've clandestinely canvassed the other owners and sworn each of them to secrecy on this issue until they are sure we've left the United States. Then, and only then, will they make public my plan to classify players into categories A, B, C, D, and E, and pay the men in each category a set salary."

"So, you did convince the other owners to go through with it, then?" Anson says.

"When were you going to tell me about this plan?" Palmer asks.

"Ah yes, Harry my friend, I was going to get around to it as soon as all the details became final. The essentials of the plan go like this. You know very well how the growing salaries in baseball stand to impair the profitability of the game. Not for us in Chicago, of course. The spectators of the city patronize our games rather liberally, and the Chicago Club does not lack for income. Our average crowd this past season was 3,366 people. The same is generally true in Boston and New York, as you know. Those teams get even more spectators at their games than we do.

"However, consider some of the other cities of the National League, like Washington or Indianapolis, for instance. How many games have we played in those towns where over 2,000 spectators attended? Very few. The average crowd last year in Indianapolis was a mere 1,182 people, while in Washington it was 891. That paltry figure even includes all the members of the national government whom the Washington management admits for free to make sure that Congress stays favorably disposed toward baseball. Even in Detroit, when they won the World's Championship in 1887 with that wonderful team of slugging hitters they had, only 1,557 people attended their home games, on average.

"It is those cities we must help, if baseball is to continue growing and prospering as a sport. They cannot survive unless salaries go down. That is why I came up with my salary plan. Like I just said, we'll divide all the players into five categories. We will tell the public that the classification of the player depends on two things, his playing ability and his comportment off the field. In the process, we strike a balance between rewarding good players whom spectators will pay to see and rewarding upright men with good morals who will bring respectable people to our games. Salaries will go in increments of $250. A man in Class A will get $2,500 for the 1889 season, a man in Class B gets $2,250, and so on down to Class E at $1,500." At this point, Spalding pauses to allow the news to sink in for Palmer.

"Do you think the public will really believe this?" Palmer finally says. "You know as well as I do that every team in the National League made money in 1887. *The Sporting Life* confirmed this in one of its issues. You also know that when the Detroit Club closed its affairs just a month ago, it declared a profit of over $50,000 and paid every one of its investors a dividend of almost 250% on their stock in the club. The public will never believe it. Besides, who will classify the players? Will every club in the National League employ Pinkerton detectives like you do to follow their men around and watch how they behave?"

"To take your second question first," Spalding replies, "we will tell the newspapers that National League President Nick Young classifies the players. However, that will be only a cover story, of course. While my detectives keep me well-informed of what transpires after each game, not all clubs are wise enough to keep track of their men at all hours of the day like I do. So, of course, their assessment of the conduct of their players off the field would be a mere guess. In practice, the other owners will simply inform Young where to classify each man, and Young will make up some way to rationalize what they tell him to the public."

"I see," the sportswriter replies.

"Now, as to your first question regarding the profitability of the teams. Detroit was foolish to make that information public. It was a mistake by Fred Stearns, pure and simple, and I'm sure he regrets it now. It is likewise true all the clubs made money in 1887, although some much more than others.

"However, Harry, my friend, you forget certain important things when you say the public will never believe it. For one, 1887 was more than one year ago. Very few members of the public reflect backward that far when forming judgments. Furthermore, do not underestimate the willingness of people to believe information coming from established authorities, whether that information is true, false, or somewhere in between. To convince the public of the lie that high salaries are killing the game, we simply must repeat that lie, often and with conviction. If we do so convincingly enough, most people will believe."

Palmer is silent for a moment, then finally says, "I thought it was John Tener who wanted to go into politics after he finished with baseball, but I'd say you might make a good politician yourself. You could teach him a thing or two, it seems."

"It really is all quite simple. Lie about how much money the teams make and use the press to brand the players as greedy for wanting too much. The working man on the streets who makes $800 in a year will look at a player asking for $3,000 and side with us, as often as not, out of jealousy that someone playing a sport for a living makes four times as much as he does. Furthermore, we continue pointing out that players only work six months out of the year to earn that sum, and the average man's jealousy rises further."

Anson breaks in at this point. "It is wrong to say that ballplayers only work six months of the year. Many of us train year-round to stay in top condition, or nearly year-round."

"Are you not listening to me?" Spalding says, his voice rising in volume and intensity just a bit. "That doesn't matter. The facts don't matter. Appearances matter. The public does not see you, or any other ballplayer, working out in the gymnasium in January. They only see you in June playing first base at West Side Park. Therefore, we say that players work only six months of the year and say it repeatedly and with conviction, and the public believes it. We deal in appearances, not facts, and we manage the appearances to portray the image we want."

Anson says nothing in reply, and while I cannot see him through the door, I'd like to imagine that he has a sheepish look on his face right now.

After a moment, Spalding goes on. "To conclude this lesson on appearances, that is why we will call my salary plan the Brush Plan and not the Spalding Plan. It must seem as if the other owners originated the plan without me, and you both know why."

"Because of Johnny Ward," Palmer says.

"Correct. Now, let me explain where I need your cooperation, and the most important reason why I've brought you two here this evening. The reason no one must know of this until after we've left San Francisco is obvious. We have two officers of the Brotherhood of Professional Baseball Players with us in our party—Ward and Ned Hanlon. Ward is the president of their union. With Ward and Hanlon out of communication with their Brotherhood for several months, it is my hope that the organization will be powerless, or at least disunited enough, to resist my plan. If Hanlon and Ward find out about it before we leave, however, they likely will desert our party, and then we would have real trouble fielding a complete team for each game. Not to mention all the problems they might cause over the winter in stirring up the Brotherhood to resist this new plan, which is so necessary to save ownership's profits in baseball."

Palmer breaks in, "So that was your plan in inviting Ward and Hanlon all along, as I suspected it might be."

"A major part of it, certainly. Although both are good men, sober and articulate, and will represent our National Game well abroad, the chance of getting both out of the country at once was too good to pass up. I do not think Tim Keefe and Jim O'Rourke possess enough organizational ability to carry on the Brotherhood's affairs without Ward around to lead them. At least, I am betting they do not. Time will tell if I am correct, but it seems well worth the risk."

"So why are we here, then?" Anson asks.

"What I need from you, Adrian, since I know you'll never join the Brotherhood, is to keep the boys' minds off legal issues and keep them as focused on playing ball as possible. We want to offer the spectators a good show, and rumors about money and legal affairs will detract from that effort. Should any reporter ask you for your thoughts on the Brotherhood, and they might, simply tell them you disagree with its efforts for the same reasons you always have, but that we are here to play ball and show the people of Australia what America's National Game is about. Under no circumstances will you acknowledge having any information about the plans for salaries in 1889.

"Harry, you also should continue following the script we've laid out. In your writing for the papers, continue painting the Brotherhood as an organization of questionable tactics and ethics, one in which the leaders manipulate the rank and file for their own selfish purposes. You've done a good job of this so far. You must deny any knowledge of my salary plan until it appears in the newspapers, and you must always deny my involvement in getting the other owners to accept it, even after we get back to the States in the spring. So, from now on, I will simply call it the Brush Plan. You must do so as well. Not only do I want to flatter the vanity of John Brush a bit and allow him to take credit for this measure, but also, there must be no charges of duplicity against me. The sporting public must not know I brought Ward and Hanlon with us for this purpose. I do not know all the plans of their Brotherhood, or what it might choose to do in the future, but if trouble ever arises, the sporting public must be on our side. Keeping my name above reproach will be important, if that time ever comes. This will, not incidentally, also help ensure that we have harmony on the present trip."

"Agreed," both of Spalding's companions say in unison.

"In return for your cooperation, the two of you will continue to receive the bonuses previously agreed upon, with a little extra to sweeten things. Adrian, you'll get a share of whatever profits we might make on this trip. For you, Harry, there will be access to inside information, so you can continue getting the scoop on your fellows at *The Sporting Life* and keep your eminent standing amongst the sportswriting fraternity. Additionally, I have something special for you planned on our trip to Chinatown tomorrow that I think you will appreciate. Our police escort, Sergeant Burdsall, is your contact.

"Now that we've settled these things, let us return to enjoying our present situation. I believe the parade is almost over now, or should be soon, so feel free to spend the rest of your evening as you choose."

I take this as my cue to leave as well and tiptoe away as fast as I dare. I've just turned the corner to my hallway when I hear the door to Spalding's room close behind me and two pairs of footsteps echoing off the brightly polished wooden floors in the hallway.

I make it back to my room and close the door silently. What do I do now? Johnny Ward has been very nice to me, but if I tell him about Spalding's plans and Anson finds out, will he keelhaul me or throw me overboard? Or, will I have to stay here and miss my chance to see Australia? I don't even know what the Brotherhood is or how a union works, let alone whether it is a good thing, but I now know that all is not what it seems for this trip. I also know that I should not trust Spalding, Palmer, or Anson if I can help it. Anyone who makes secret plans against their companions should not be my friend.

I also wonder if they might have secret plans about me. Do they plan to leave me in the bush in Australia to hunt kangaroos, like Pfeffer suggested? Or, might the teams leave me on the dock at San Francisco? I can't lead any parades while we're at sea, and that seems the only reason I've traveled with the teams this far.

I get to sleep much later than I thought I would because I just lie there thinking and worrying about everything that might happen to me, and then weighing that against how great it would be to see the whole world.

Chapter 9

The teams played a game of ball yesterday, and MacMillan was right about how far it was from our hotel. We started the parade on Market Street and walked uphill until reaching Haight Street, where we turned right and marched to the grounds. Just like MacMillan said, these were the best grounds for baseball that we'd seen on our trip—perfectly level, trimmed grass in the outfield with no ruts, and very few rocks in the infield dirt to cause bad hops for the fielders. So many spectators came to see the teams, I couldn't believe it. I'm not sure if I've ever seen that many before, even at West Side Park in Chicago where the White Stockings play their games, or at the South End Grounds in Boston. I led the march, like always, and pumped my arms, but didn't toss the baton much. I don't have much practice catching it while marching uphill, and I couldn't let the boys see me drop my baton, or else they might decide I'm not lucky anymore and leave me here.

Today we visit Chinatown, and as promised, I get to go along. I'm still a little confused, however, about why it's okay for me to go to Chinatown with the players and see things there, but it's different when it comes to going to plays and other fancy events. It seems that I'm worthy for showing to people in the streets but not in nice places.

Chinatown isn't far from our hotel, and it takes us only a few minutes to walk there, so before long I need to pay attention to what's happening around me. A good number of the players decide to see the sights; there are about fifteen of us in all, including the escort from the San Francisco police. Spalding is there, along with Harry Palmer, Jim Fogarty, Ned Williamson, Fred Pfeffer, Cap Anson, John Tener, Ed Crane, John Ward, a few baseball officials from California whom I don't recognize, and Newton MacMillan.

"Couldn't resist coming after all," MacMillan says to Palmer. "This may well be my only trip to Chinatown, so I might as well make the best of it and see what there is to see."

Our party starts the tour marching south on DuPont Street, at which point things get interesting. We pass about a dozen businesses on each side of the street, where Chinese merchants sell any number of things. There are street vendors offering rice, various vegetables, and live chickens. I also see merchants selling clothing, dry goods, tools, and hats. Some of the shops have their signs in English, others don't. Most are two stories tall, although some are taller, and built from brick.

The streets are very crowded here, just like they are in the neighborhoods of Chicago where I spend most of my time. It's not only Chinese people in the streets, although most of them are. The streets themselves are dirty, noisy, and chaotic, just like most of the other streets in the San Francisco. Adults hurry this way and that while children play, darting in and out from behind the stalls selling vegetables and fruit. There are also containers for some of the food—pottery bins, wicker baskets, wooden packing boxes, glass jars—depending on the item.

The people of Chinatown dress in many styles, some of them strange to me. Some of the Chinese dress in business suits and look just like anyone else, except for their long hair. Many of the Chinese braid their hair in the back, and it sticks out from the back of their hats, gently bouncing off their back while they walk around. Other people, who I judge are workers, have on a cloth jacket that is loose in the sleeves and buttons up in the front and at the neck. Most of the jackets are either dark gray, brown, or black. A few people, including some of the women and the children, wear embroidered jackets, some of the nicer ones made from silk, with bright colors and fancy patterns woven into the fabric.

In the first alley on our right, just past Pacific Street, half a dozen hogs root through the garbage dumped down from the three-story buildings that stand shoulder to shoulder on either side of the narrow alley. Luckily, it hasn't rained lately, so the alley is dusty rather than muddy, but I smell quite an odor of decaying garbage nonetheless. I've slept in my share of alleys with pigs back in Chicago, and I know the smell of spoiled cabbage mixed with the rotting innards of chickens and pig manure when I come across it.

"Hey, you, come away from there. Keep up." The gruff, commanding voice of the policeman startles me. I must have been standing and taking in the scene too long for his tastes. "That alley is no place for decent folks."

"It's okay, he ain't decent, anyway," Anson replies. "If he gets lost, no one will miss him." Pfeffer laughs.

The policeman, whose name is Sergeant Burdsall, does not laugh. Through his frown, he barks, "That ain't what I mean. These Chinamen ain't decent folks, and that alley ain't no decent place, unless you fancy spending your time and your money to check out the foreign women."

"There's a brothel here?" Fogarty asks, with a barely noticeable tone of hope in his voice.

"No, there ain't one brothel here," Burdsall responds. "There are sixteen brothels just down that alley. If that ain't enough for you, I'll take you to the alley on the other side of the street where there are twenty-one more."

"Find Tom Daly. He might have a chance at twelve wives after all," Fogarty jokes. Some people laugh, but not Sergeant Burdsall.

"Most of the girls in the brothels are between ten and sixteen, if you fancy that," Burdsall tells him.

"Ten to sixteen? Where's Clarence? Clarence, are you with me?" Fogarty says to the group. He gets more laughs.

I'm scared. I hope Fogarty is only joking. I know what happens in brothels. Chicago has lots of them, but I've never gone in one. For one thing, it takes money to go in, and I rarely have enough for food, let alone for brothels. My fear must show in my face because Spalding walks toward Fogarty and points at him.

"Enough," he says, raising his voice a little. "There will be no visiting brothels, Chinese or any other kind. You men all know that. Now, Sergeant Burdsall, I'm told we are to meet someone for our tour?"

"Right up ahead, there he is." Burdsall sighs and rolls his eyes while he points to a short, middle-aged man standing in the doorway of a mercantile house at the corner of the next block.

Unlike many of the Chinese whom I've seen, this man dresses in American style, with a suit, tie, rounded glasses, and bowler hat. When I get close enough to him, I see something glinting in his tie pin. Is that a diamond?

Burdsall speaks again as we approach the man. "This is Li Qiang, a local merchant. Or should I say, *the* local merchant. He is the head of the Chinese Consolidated Benevolent Association, which we usually just call the Six Companies. He has agreed to show us some of the sights of Chinatown. Here he is."

"Good afternoon, my friends," Li says. I see a few members of our party blink in surprise when Li speaks formal English, with only a slight accent. Although he dresses in a business suit, wears leather shoes, and sports a stylish bowler hat, his dark hair is long and braided in the back. Li bows and cordially shakes the hands of Sergeant Burdsall, who only gives him a quick glance before looking away, exhaling loudly, and sighing again, and Spalding.

"Mr. Spalding, Sergeant Burdsall tells me you and your men would like to see our wonderful section of San Francisco. I've arranged a special tour for you, which includes one of our finest temples in America, the Lung Gong Taoist Temple. By the way, can I interest you in a complimentary copy of the *Chung Sai Yat Po*? It is the finest Chinese newspaper in America." He extends a copy of an eight-page newssheet in Spalding's direction.

"I'm afraid we can't read your language, Mr. Qiang, so I must decline."

"Understandable, certainly. I know our characters seem unusual to those who speak English as their native language. Did you know that back in China, drawing our characters is an art form? Chinese calligraphers have been perfecting the art for centuries."

"That's nice, Qiang," Pfeffer breaks in with his Kentucky drawl, "but why do you think good Christian men such as ourselves would want to see your pagan temples? We aren't interested in devil worship or idolatry."

"Easy, Fred," I hear Palmer say. "Let it go. You wanted to see Chinatown, didn't you? Let him give his little speech."

"My friend," Li replies, "we have a minor misunderstanding. In China, we use our family name, what you call a last name, first. This means I am Mr. Li, not Mr. Qiang. That is a small matter, however. I take no offense. If you do not desire to see our temples, you will be perfectly safe waiting outside, I assure you. The Lung Gong is, however, a most peaceful, tranquil, and beautiful place."

"He's a cheeky little man, isn't he?" Pfeffer twangs to Sergeant Burdsall, his voice rising while Pfeffer crosses his arms over his chest. "If a nigger talked to a white man that way back in Kentucky, it would be the last anyone heard of him."

"Well, you ain't in Kentucky. So just settle down."

"Why do you good white people put up with these Chinese, anyway? Why not just burn this whole district to the ground and run them into the bay and let them swim home?"

"Fred, that will be all," Spalding interrupts. "Sergeant Burdsall assures me that although the people of Chinatown enjoy a fair measure of autonomy from the city authorities, the situation in Chinatown is under control. If you really are the Kentucky gentleman you want everyone to think you are, you should be able to tolerate the mere presence of the Chinese in San Francisco. Now, my friends, let us begin the tour. Please, Mr. Li, carry on."

Li bows low. "This way."

We turn right and walk up Jackson Street, passing a drug store, a pawnbroker, a boot and shoe store, another hardware store, and several cigar and tobacco shops on the way. Just like on Pacific Street, each building immediately borders the next. The buildings have no spaces between any of them. It seems to be that way in all of Chinatown, as far as I can see, at least. A quick left takes us to a street called St. Louis Alley, where we pass various lodging houses and restaurants. The streets are quite busy here, too. Merchants sell fruits and vegetables outside, pigs roam freely, and I see few chickens kept in wire enclosures. Barefooted or sandaled children run here and there. A few of the children wave at us. Most of the adults keep their heads down and attend to their own business.

Once we turn into the alley, I notice one business on our right does not announce its goods. A strange and overwhelming smell comes from the door, however, one I am not familiar with, but it even overpowers the stench of the pigs nosing around the garbage dumped outside by the restaurants. Newton MacMillan walks next to me, and he notices me sniffing the air.

"Take it easy there, Clarence," he tells me in a very low and quiet voice. "Unless I am quite mistaken, we just passed what people commonly call an opium den."

"What's opium?" I almost whisper back as we make another left turn. I've never smelled anything quite that strong before.

"It is a drug that, they say, produces both relaxation and mildly disorienting effects." I frown and bite my lip a bit. When he realizes

I don't know what disorienting means, MacMillan smiles and says, "That means you can't think properly if you smoke opium."

"That doesn't sound very good to me. Do we have any opium dens in Chicago?"

"Yes, we do, although not, apparently, in your neighborhood. I wouldn't worry too much about it. Ah, here we are, back on DuPont Street," MacMillan says as we come out into the wider main street of Chinatown.

That is not the end of the tour, however. We turn right on DuPont Street, then right again up Washington Street. Our party passes a bunch of stores on each side of the street selling more food, clothing, and tools, all jammed together like on the last street, just before we get to Stockton Street and arrive at the temple.

"Ah, my friends, we have arrived at the Lung Gong," Li Qiang says. "All who wish to see the inside, please continue with me." Even Pfeffer goes in.

The courtyard, unlike the streets we've just traveled, is quiet and clean. After passing through the doorway of the temple and entering its sanctuary, I see five lifelike faces made from fabric against the back wall of the temple, with the one in the middle set on a special pedestal, so it's taller than the others. Each of the five faces also has a fake body resting beneath rich robes of multicolored silk. All the faces have beards and mustaches several inches in length, and on their heads, they wear large square hats. At each of the four corners of the hat, there are rounded cones pointing upward. The end of each cone features the brightly colored feathers of some bird I do not recognize. Each face has a different expression. One looks calm, one stern, one surprised, one thoughtful, and the last, happy. I notice two monks sweeping the floor beneath the fake people.

A low table standing about a foot above the ground runs in front of the group of dolls, and on the table rest five large brass urns with markings etched around the outside. The markings don't look like English letters. Maybe they are the characters that Li mentioned. Several paper lanterns hang from the ceiling, and their light produces an odd, yet pleasing, glow indoors. It's hard to describe the light, except that it's not so bright as a gas lamp and certainly not as bright as that recent invention I've seen once or twice, the electric lightbulb. Instead, the light is softer, like it's supposed to be easier on your eyes, or like it wants to calm you down, so you can just sit and think quietly.

The group looks around in silence, taking in the scene, when Pfeffer makes his move. Just when Li starts describing what the five pretend people are for, Pfeffer bends forward, as if to look into one of the urns, then, without warning, he traces his fingers across his chest like a cross, grabs one end of the table, and topples it over, the urns clanging to the floor and making quite a racket.

Pfeffer shouts, "No more pagan idolatry, for only the Lord is true and righteous. Who'll help me destroy these abominations?" He then starts for the figures on the back wall, apparently wanting to tear them down as well, but before he can, the two monks cut him off and try to wrestle him away. I hear shouts outside, and Fogarty runs to the door of the sanctuary.

"The people outside heard what happened. I have a feeling that in a couple of minutes there'll be a horde of Chinamen coming this way! What now?" he shouts as he shuts the heavy wooden sanctuary doors.

Li Qiang, undaunted, starts to motion our party toward the side wall of the temple. When he steps on the floor in a certain spot, the wall slides open revealing a hidden door, and he motions the party inside. Not waiting for a swarm of angry Chinese to attack us, we go through. Just as Li Qiang hustles me through the hidden door and down some stairs, I hear him say something to the two monks in Chinese.

"They will say it was an accident to buy time while we escape," Li says quickly to Sergeant Burdsall, who has drawn his pistol. "Follow me."

Li slides by everyone to the head of the party and leads us through a secret underground corridor. It is narrow and dusty, and the floor of the passage is wooden planks on top of packed dirt. We see side passages and doors to rooms on either side of us. The tunnels have gas lighting, so we aren't traveling in the dark.

Li Qiang says, by way of explanation, "We use this passage as protection against raids by police or angry Christians. I will lead you back to the streets by a safe route."

We follow Li while he trots ahead, although I can't tell what direction we're going because we are underground. Li does not hesitate and seems sure of where he is and where he is going. We pass by several tunnels branching off from ours, all propped up by mining support timbers.

We've only been walking through the tunnel for a little while when I get a weird feeling I've never had before. I notice my breathing comes in gasps rather than being normal. We aren't running, so I should not be tired, but my heart pounds like I'm at the end of a parade. Even though the gas lamps give plenty of light, it seems to me like things are growing dim and the walls are getting closer. Next, I stumble a bit.

Ed Crane, the burly pitcher from New York who pitches for the All-Americas, is next to me, and he notices. "Clarence, are you all right, lad?"

I try to be brave, so I tell him, "Yes, Mr. Crane. This is my first time in a tunnel. I'm just not used to it."

"To be honest, Clarence, you don't look too good."

While I'm trying to think of what to tell Crane, without warning, the gas lights go out. Because it's unexpected, several people crash into the person in front of them, and most of us topple to the wood plank floor. Someone bumps into me from behind, and I fall over, too. I think it's Fogarty because he was near the back of our line, but I can't say for sure in the dark.

Then someone in our party screams out, "It's a trap. They mean to kill us all and hide our bodies underground!"

Several people start speaking all at once.

"Li!" roars Sergeant Burdsall, and then I hear the click of his gun.

Shouting in the hope we can hear him over the commotion, Li starts to say something, but before he can get out more than a few words, an explosion rocks the tunnel right in the direction we'd been walking. Dirt from the ceiling falls on me in large chunks, and right in front of us, where Li and Spalding were leading the way, there's a huge roaring sound, followed by the rush of dust and dirt sliding around and filling the passage.

Either the ceiling or the wall must have collapsed from the explosion. I hear some of our party choking on the dust. A few more chunks of dirt fall on me. I try to scream, but all that comes out is a strange gurgling sound because I'm so scared. I don't even know if anyone else heard it above all the commotion. Someone brushes by me in the darkness, and I try to scream again, but the same pitiful noise comes out of my throat instead.

Then, from right behind us, a small crack of light appears. I see Li standing in the increasing light as he pulls a doorway open. He's lost his hat, and dust covers his nice suit from head to toe.

"This way!" he shouts at us, motioning with his left arm for us to enter while he holds the door open with his right.

Some of the men continue arguing or trying to get their bearings, but John Ward starts for the door, and then the others follow. Except me. I can't seem to move because I'm too scared and I'm not sure what to do. Ed Crane gets to his feet and heads for the door, but then sees me just kneeling on the ground. He grabs my arms and pulls me toward the light. Crane sure is strong. He tugs me along like I'm barely any weight at all.

We no sooner get through the door, however, when the smell hits me again. I go down on my right knee as soon as Crane lets go of my arm. A couple other of the players are choking, too, their hands on their knees bracing themselves. Through my watering eyes, I look around at the room we've entered.

In this new room several mats cover the floor, and on some of them, grown men lie on their sides with long pipes in their mouths. I thought they might react with anger, or at least surprise, to see us barge in on them, or that they might be panicking because of the explosion that just happened, but they just lie there, inhaling from their pipes. Most of them have calm expressions on their faces, almost like this was normal and they expected it, or like it wasn't worth worrying about. A few look up at us as baseball players start filing in. One man has a goofy grin, then passes his pipe to the man beside him sitting cross-legged on the same mat.

On the other side of the room, the exit door opens, and a Chinese man looks through. Li says something to this new man in Chinese, and he gives a quick reply, also in Chinese, frowning and scowling when he sees all of us. Li waves us through this next door. I still feel very dizzy and gasp for breath, but I manage to crawl forward a bit and finally get to my feet. After walking down a short hallway, we pass through one last door and into a shop selling dry goods. I gasp a sigh of relief. I can see daylight once more and breathe some fresh air.

Once we're all in the street, I see Spalding counting heads. "All here," he says after a moment.

"Well, damn it," I hear Pfeffer drawl from somewhere behind me. "A tunnel collapses, and there's an explosion, and we still couldn't get rid of the Chinaman or the nigger."

Before anyone can say anything to him, the discussion that Sergeant Burdsall and Li Qiang are having off to the side becomes heated. Burdsall shouts some insults, and Li shrugs his shoulders and holds out his arms from his side while raising his own voice. This goes on for a bit.

Finally, Burdsall storms over to us. "A gas explosion. That's why the tunnel caved in. Li claims that the room just ahead of us was also an opium den, and someone must have left the gas on in that room."

103

"How did that cause the explosion?" a confused Harry Palmer asks.

"Easy. The people inside were out of their wits, just like in the room we just passed through. Someone forgets to turn off the gas, then they light a match to light their pipe, and you get an explosion and a cave-in. The department will have to investigate, I suppose, to verify and to see if the explosion killed any Chinamen, but you saw what those opium addicts were like. Fifteen of us appeared from nowhere and marched through their den, and they didn't even bat an eye."

"Can you direct us back toward our hotel?" Spalding says to the policeman. "I think we've seen enough of Chinatown for one day."

The sergeant grunts his assent and points his arm. "That way," he growls.

Fortunately, it looks like we are already right on the edge of Chinatown. A street sign says Stockton Street. Things are busy here, like they are everywhere in Chinatown, but no one takes any special notice of us, as if seeing a group of white men emerge from a dry goods store and stand arguing in the street is an everyday thing in Chinatown. The people passing by on this street are a mixture of Chinese and white. At least the smell from the opium den is gone. I inhale several times, only to get the stench of more rotting garbage instead. After how badly I felt just a moment ago, I'll take it.

Li Qiang, despite breathing a bit heavily, is still in command of his wits after his argument with Sergeant Burdsall. "We had best leave soon, I think. I am sorry your tour turned out to be so dramatic."

Most of the players are still recovering their senses after everything that just happened, but Jim Fogarty seems excited. He walks over and pumps Li's arm with a vigorous handshake. "That was bully!" he says. "Can we have another tour tomorrow?"

Most of the players look at Fogarty like he's nuts, but even though he jokes around a lot, he seems sincere this time because he's looking Li Qiang right in the face and waiting intently for answer. If it were a joke, I think we'd have heard the punch line by now.

"Pagan temples, secret passages, a gas explosion, a cave-in, and then an opium den, and look, here we are, back on a busy street with all this action! We've gotta go again tomorrow!"

"That is enough, Jimmy," Spalding tells him. Fogarty frowns in disappointment, then looks down at the street. He draws his right leg back to kick the dirt in frustration but then thinks better of it.

Turning to Li, Spalding says, "Mr. Li, on behalf of the Chicago and All-America teams, we thank you for your hospitality and regret that everything did not go as planned. Thank you for a most unusual tour. I assume we can keep things quiet about what happened back at the Lung Gong?"

"Of course," Li replies. "It is just good business. If the people had mobbed you, all the whites in San Francisco would clamor for revenge. Although I do not understand your game of baseball, I know you are famous because you play it, and that it would make people even angrier if something happened to famous baseball players. Violence would ensue, business would go down, and whites would hurt or kill Chinese. There would be more anger against the Chinese, and the white people of San Francisco would never believe that a white person started the whole thing. I do not suppose I can convince you to keep the knowledge of our tunnels to yourself?"

"Don't worry about that," Burdsall breaks in. "The San Francisco police know all about them, anyway."

When we prepare to leave and return to our hotel, some of the players start directing hostile stares at Pfeffer and saying things to him, blaming him for wrecking the whole tour, and the second baseman seems unsure of whether he should apologize or try to defend his actions. He scowls, clenches his fists, and folds his arms over his chest.

Before he can think of exactly what to say back, however, Jim Fogarty suddenly shouts out, "Hey, it's my friend, Charlie Gagus."

105

Then I remember that Fogarty is from San Francisco and knows most of the local ballplayers of any quality, and Charlie Gagus is a local pitcher with a good reputation. Earlier, I overhead someone say he might pitch for the local nine, the Greenwood & Moran team, in a game with the All-America team tomorrow, so I recognize his name when Fogarty says it.

"Fogarty!" Gagus shouts back to the fun-loving All-America outfielder. "You and your friends got here just in time."

"Just in time for what?"

It is only then that I become aware of what has been building up for the few minutes while everyone was talking. The street is getting more crowded, the street noise is getting louder, and there are some angry shouts. Once again, I start to think we are in danger of a mobbing. Out of the corner of my eye, I see Sergeant Burdsall hand something to Harry Palmer. It looks like an envelope, but I can't tell for sure because people are in the way. Burdsall then turns and makes his way up the street and away from the crowd, leaving us there on our own. That can't be a good sign.

Gagus, however, almost bounces up and down with excitement. "For the hanging, of course! Watch this."

The group crowds around Gagus now.

"Who is that?" Ed Crane says.

"What did he say?" John Ward asks in surprise.

"Did he say a hangin'?" Pfeffer drawls.

"How do you know that?" Fogarty asks Gagus. Now Fogarty shakes his arms and bounces from one foot to the other, too, like he needs to get ready for action.

"Oh, it's simple, Jimmy. You know I have my contacts among most of the young men in this city. Everyone wants to have a good time, right? Doesn't matter if it's a hoodlum ball or a hanging, ol' Charlie knows something about it. Come on, let's watch the fun and see what happens."

We turn and face south, looking down Sacramento Street, and see many people running south, away from us. When I turn and look to the north, I see a few Chinese running away in that direction, and then a horde of hostile white people stomp through the intersection of Sacramento and Stockton streets and cross into Chinatown. Most of them carry bricks, two or three at least, while some have lead pipes or some other improvised weapon or have drawn knives. All look furious, with brows furrowed, eyes narrowed, and mouths set.

Trying to stay out of the way of this white mob, the people in our party scamper to the edge of the street and try to move northward toward the intersection. Once we get there and the mob passes by, Fogarty gives me a wink, picks me up, and puts me on his shoulders, so I get a good look at what happens next.

A tall man with dark hair, a plaid suit jacket, and an enormous mustache that droops off his chin stops in front of a large brick building with three stories, including balconies facing the street on the second and third floor, on the east side of Sacramento Street. It appears he is the leader of the mob. From the outside, the large building appears to be a hotel, but there are no lights or signs of movement inside. Ascending a short flight of brick-and-mortar steps and standing in front of the double doors that allow entrance to the building, he holds up his hands, palms open and facing outward, for quiet. After a few seconds, the crowd obeys.

He shouts out, "Where is the owner? Where is Wang Chao? We understand that this has become a house of prostitution where American women work for Chinese pimps!" The crowd shouts, jeers, and curses.

The speaker waves his arms again, the shouts die down, and he continues. "We, the good Americans of San Francisco, will not stand by and see our American women degraded and enslaved by a race of degenerate foreigners!" More cheers and threats from the mob.

The speaker bangs on the doors with his fists. "Come out, and see justice done, Wang Chao!"

While this is going on, I can see from my perch on Fogarty's shoulders that two members of our group, Anson and Pfeffer, have wound their way through the jeering crowd and are now near the speaker. The rest of us stay put. The speaker continues his banging on the door, but I still can't see any movement inside the building.

It doesn't take long for the speaker to lose his patience. "Bring him out!" he shouts to the crowd. "You know what our man looks like!"

The crowd explodes. A hail of bricks shatters every window on the first two floors of the building, and then people continue throwing more bricks through the jagged openings. People surge toward the doors, but whoever is inside has locked them, so several members of the mob climb through the broken windows first, then unlock the doors from the inside. The crowd, including Anson and Pfeffer, now pours inside. This also thins things out on the street a bit, and Fogarty moves in closer, so we can get a better look.

"Charlie was right, Clarence, look at all this action! You don't see this every day!"

I'm not sure what to say. I don't like what's happening.

While the sounds of breaking furniture and shouting men filter out from the building, I look around to see what the rest of our party is doing. Gagus is there, bouncing up and down right next to me and Fogarty, with a grin on his face. He gives me the impression that the fun is just beginning. Palmer and MacMillan stand at the rear edge of the crowd, as far from the action as possible. Both have notebooks out and scribble down notes rapidly while they watch what is going on. Spalding is nowhere in sight, while most of the others seem unsure of what to do. Some of them, including Ward and Crane, stand in a small circle near Palmer and MacMillan, obviously unwilling to join the action but also unwilling to abandon Anson and Pfeffer and leave the scene.

Soon there are high-pitched screams coming from inside the building. Moments later, a few of the mob come back out, escorting a handful of women. Pfeffer and Anson are among them. The women are white, and they exit the building with eyes wide, gasping in fright. A few have on gowns or robes of some shiny material. I think it's silk. The rest wear petticoats or long dresses of various colors that nearly touch the ground.

Their rescuers hustle them up the street, away from the scene. Three of the women try to free themselves and go back, obviously not feeling in need of rescue, but most whimper or cry while about a dozen men lead them away.

Another roar from the remaining crowd redirects my gaze back to the front door. Another handful of men come out, hauling a Chinese man by the arms. The Chinese man, who must be Wang Chao, drags on the floor behind his attackers. They yank him along, cursing and spitting on him. Already beaten and bruised, he's hardly moving at all. Wang Chao has no hat or shoes and only half a shirt because his captors tore away the rest. Blood streams from his nose, and his left eye socket already swells from a punch.

The leader with the dark hair and mustache screams in triumph. The crowd roars back. Then the leader shouts, "Set up the rope! String him up!"

Someone tosses a rope to one of the mob standing on the second-floor balcony of the building. Quickly, the man secures the knot, ties the noose, and tosses the rope back down to the street. The noose dangles about seven feet from the ground. Two men emerge from the building with chairs while others land a few more punches and kicks on Wang Chao, just to make sure he can't resist. I hear his ribs crack after one of the punches, but being only semi-conscious, he just moans in pain with his head down.

Four men, two for each arm, prop him up on one chair, while the mob's leader stands on the other, tightening the noose around Wang Chao's neck. I see Wang's right eye open and give a pleading look, but his left is almost swollen shut. He gurgles a few sounds, but the man tying the noose backhands him when he does. Blood sprays two of the men below, but they don't seem to mind.

All is ready. The four men propping Wang Chao in place kick away the chair, and he dangles for a few moments, gasping helplessly, but before long he just swings slowly back and forth, not moving.

He is dead. Wang Chao hangs lifelessly in front of his own building, murdered by a mob without a trial or any attempt at justice. The man leading the mob waves his arms for quiet once more. It takes a minute or two, but the crowd complies eventually. He shouts, "This fate will come to any Chinaman in San Francisco who dares to defile true American womanhood! Today, we have justice!"

Everyone in the crowd cheers. "Justice! Justice!"

Then, with a final flourish, the speaker pulls a large knife from his belt and stabs it into the heart of Wang Chao. Blood spurts onto the dirt street. He spits in Wang Chao's face, raises his arms in triumph and, for the final time, the crowd explodes in exaltation.

I haven't said a word the entire time. I can't. When the scene is over, and we're walking back to our hotel, I silently follow behind everyone, just looking down at the street.

Chapter 10

November 6, 1888
San Francisco, California, United States

This time, the bloodstains are all over me. I recoil in horror, but the billy club swings again, and more blood spatters my ragged, patched overcoat. Quickly, I turn and run, ducking while another swinging club whizzes by my ear. Heart pounding, I run past a blur of faces and the mingled shouts of onlookers that all blend into one jumbled roar while I try to get away.

From the side, a body slams into me, even as I try to duck and dodge. The desperate man scrambles back to his feet, saying nothing, and I try to do the same. Then, gunshots.

The man who just knocked me down falls flat on his face. He doesn't move, but a pool of red spreads out from his neck as he lies there. I run again, barely remembering to breathe, anything to get away.

"Clarence, over here!" a voice shouts. Somehow, I recognize my name through the chaos. It's Tommy, my friend.

I run to where he is and dive into the side alley, gasping and heaving for breath. I just kneel there, trying to draw in some air. Tommy peers around the corner.

"We've got to go, Clarence. The police are coming this way!"

My legs shaking and quivering, I get up, and we run again, down the street, away from the onrushing police. Unfortunately, some have horses, and they're gaining on us.

More gunfire crackles in the air. A bullet whines past my ear. Then I see Tommy go down on my right. He gets up and starts hopping on one leg into another side alley, but blood pours from two gaping wounds, one in his right leg and one in his back. I grab his left arm, drape it over my neck, and help him.

While I do, the police on horseback gallop past, chasing down some of the others fleeing through the Chicago streets. I look at Tommy. Blood now runs from one corner of his mouth, as well. It covers my hands from where I helped him.

"They got me, Clarence, they got me," he gasps, the words struggling out of his mouth.

"No!" I say. "Don't die, Tommy, you're my only friend. You can't die!"

He looks me straight in the eye, but his eyelids start trembling. Tommy reaches into his coat pocket with one shaking hand. "Here, take these, Clarence. They're all I have."

When Tommy pulls his hand out of his pocket, it's shaking so badly, he drops his craps dice on the street. They clatter away a couple feet before coming to rest.

"No!" I say again. I scramble over to pick them up to give them back to Tommy. When I try to hand the dice back, Tommy's already closed his eyes. I can't see him breathe anymore.

Ten years old, I sit at the edge of the street in Chicago and cry while the blood dries on my hands, watching my only friend die.

From somewhere, I hear another horse gallop toward us. I look up just in time to see a club swing down, arcing directly at my face. It connects, and I go down. As I do, my vision blurs and fades. The last thing I remember is my head hitting Tommy's body and seeing his face, his brown eyes staring blankly at me.

Tonight, I sit on the bed in my San Francisco hotel room, seeing this scene again and again. I stare at the wall waiting for the vision to fade, but it won't. I don't know why it's all coming back to me tonight, as vivid as it was on May 3, 1886, when it first happened, except that what I saw today in Chinatown must have triggered the memories in my mind. Another tear drops off my cheek and onto the bed.

I think it over and realize that Tommy died almost exactly two-and-a-half years ago. May 3, 1886. I've learned that date by heart. When I got to Chicago after my parents disappeared, I met Tommy on the streets when we were both looking for a place to sleep one night. He was homeless, just like I was, and a couple years older, but he helped me learn how to survive. Tommy showed me what places gave out soup on holidays, which bakery owners were friendly and would share food in exchange for some work, and which police officers to stay away from.

Again, the memory starts over. We were just walking along the streets when we passed the McCormick Reaper Plant on that fateful May afternoon. A bunch of workers were there, striking, when the police showed up and started attacking everyone with their clubs. When the crowd of strikers fled in panic, some of the police charged on their horses and opened fire with their pistols while the rest moved in on foot with clubs. That's when the police nearly shot me twice and murdered Tommy while he tried to run away. Later, I learned that a riot happened the next day, and a bomb exploded. People in Chicago call May 4, 1886, the Haymarket Square Massacre, but for Tommy, the massacre happened the day before.

Tommy was the only real friend I had in Chicago, and I've never had a better one since.

I take out the craps dice he gave me and roll them over in my hands. The bloodstains wore off a long time ago, but the dice are the same. Corners rounded, the numbers scuffed and almost worn away, they were Tommy's favorite thing in the world. They're all I have left to remind me of Tommy.

I do not sleep at all until the night ends, and I can see dawn creep into the sky. I lie down and close my eyes even while my room gets lighter, and sleep finally takes me, but I feel like I'm awake again as soon as my eyes close.

When I stumble down the hotel's red-carpeted stairs to the hotel lobby two hours later, I'm still very tired but hoping my lack of rest doesn't show too badly. I blink my eyes again and again, but they still hurt a bit no matter how many times I do it. I'm supposed to lead another parade today, and I don't want to make any mistakes now, when I'm so close to going to Australia.

Several of the players, especially the ones who didn't go to Chinatown yesterday, gather around Harry Palmer and Newton MacMillan, our reporters, and my seat for breakfast is just close enough that I can hear what everyone says. Fogarty begs Palmer to read to the group what he plans to write in *The Sporting Life* about the trip to Chinatown.

"Come on, Harry, tell us what you are going to report. The 45,000 subscribers to *The Sporting Life* need to hear about what happened yesterday. And tell them about our escape, too. There must have been, what, 400 or 500 Chinamen armed with machetes and butcher's knives after us when we disappeared into the tunnels? We were down there wandering around for a least three hours, too. We probably walked five miles underground. And then that mob in the streets almost mistook us for Chinamen, because we smelled like they do after going in the opium den, but then they recognized Anson and Ward and knew we were ballplayers instead."

Everyone looks at Fogarty because everyone who went to Chinatown yesterday knows that nothing he just said is anywhere close to the truth.

"What, it's only exaggerating a little, isn't it?" he says in defense. "Won't that make better reading for your audience than what really happened? Everyone loves a good story, right?"

It appears that the men have been pleading with Palmer for some time before my arrival because he says, after sighing deeply then exhaling loudly, "All right, but only once. Not because you all need to hear it, but because I need some breakfast, and it appears I'll only get a chance to eat once you all stop circling like vultures."

Palmer clears his throat and begins, "It would take a cleverer pen than mine to describe the scenes through which we passed, and I feel I am safe in saying that no pen, however clever, could adequately depict the revolting and fascinatingly hideous sights we witnessed. The illustrations of vice, crime, and bestiality, so prevalent in the Chinese quarters of this city, which have appeared in our illustrated publications from time to time, have not been overdrawn or exaggerated. Indeed, they have fallen far short of depicting the horror of it all.

"Chinatown is, perhaps, six blocks long by three wide, and it is steadily growing. A moneyed Chinaman will lease a building four stories high, and, by deepening the foundation will make a six-story building of it. Then he will construct partitions in the rooms and hallways, until he has secured accommodations for between 400 and 600 Chinamen in a building that could not accommodate more than 30 or 40 Americans comfortably. Although revolting, a trip through Chinatown is intensely interesting. The streets swarm with Mongolians. They have run all white people out of the district and have established their own government, their own mercantile houses, their own water works, their own courts, until, although they are under the surveillance of the city authorities, they nevertheless, to a great extent, live independently of the municipal laws. It is almost impossible to apprehend a criminal among them, and equally as difficult to convict him if apprehended. They have established their gambling houses within walls of heavy steel plate. Sentries stand at the outer and inner doors, and these give the signals that lock and bar the massive barriers in the very faces of intruders.

"Into vile-smelling lodging houses; into opium joints, thick with the sickening vapors that issued from the over-crowded compartments, down through underground passageways, where it would be death for a white man to go alone; into Joss houses, with their hideous idols; into the din and through the fantastic surroundings of the Chinese Theater, with hordes of almond-eyed, villainous-looking and, at times, murderous faces peering at us from every nook and corner, our little party threaded its way, until we grew dizzy from the overpowering odors and anxious to again breathe the air of a Christianized and civilized community. Chinatown knows no religion save idolatry. Virtue has never had an abiding place there. The people have brought the heathenish customs and horrible practices of their barbarous country with them to San Francisco and cling to them with a tenacity that shows the hopelessness of their conforming to our views of life and religion, or of their ever becoming desirable citizens."

"Sounds about right to me," Anson says.

"Yes, you've said it just right, Harry. No religion save idolatry. Couldn't have said it better myself," Pfeffer chimes in with his Kentucky twang.

"Enough. What's written is written. Can I eat now?" Palmer shuts his notebook with a dramatic flourish and walks the short distance to my table.

"You look a bit the worse for wear, Clarence. Yesterday was quite a day, wasn't it?"

"Yes, Mr. Palmer. I confess I didn't sleep much last night."

"Sometimes life isn't very kind. If I may confess something myself, I'm sorry you had to see everything that you saw."

I don't want to tell Palmer about Tommy, so instead of that, I say, "Well, I've seen plenty of people fight on the streets of Chicago, but nothing quite like that. How come the police officer went the other way when the crowd showed up? I thought they were supposed to help control the crowds, just like they do at West Side Park in Chicago for our games."

Palmer lets out a deep sigh. "Sometimes they do, Clarence, but other times, the crowd is just too large and there aren't enough police officers. I don't think Sergeant Burdsall could have done anything against so many people, do you?"

"I guess not. Why didn't you write anything about that in your news dispatch? I heard what you said to the boys, and I don't remember anything about steel plates, or gambling houses, or some of the rest."

Palmer heaves another deep sigh. He looks around, and then he speaks in a low voice, so only I can hear. "I had to write those things, Clarence. The police in San Francisco only let us go to Chinatown on the condition that Newton and I write something unflattering in our letters to our Chicago newspapers. It's true we saw no gambling houses or steel plates, much less bestiality, nor did we see any Chinese theater, but it appears the white people of San Francisco do not want the Chinese around, and they've started a public campaign to discredit the Chinese as a public menace. That is why my letter reads as it does. I haven't spoken to Newton this morning, so I have no idea what he plans to write."

"I don't know what bestiality means. Does it have something to do with wild animals?"

"You don't want to know, Clarence. It isn't something you talk about in polite company."

"So, it's another thing you made up about the Chinese."

"Yes."

"What about Mr. Li? He helped us out of trouble, and you didn't mention him."

"Mentioning the incident at the Lung Gong Temple would not have meshed with the tenor of the rest of the piece."

I consider asking Palmer about the envelope that Sergeant Burdsall handed him, but think better of it. At this point in our conversation, however, I remember another conversation I had with

Palmer about a week ago. I ask him, "Does this mean you aren't white anymore?"

"Whatever do you mean?"

"Well, on the train a few days back, you said that Mr. Williamson was one of the whitest men you knew, and that calling someone white means that they are honest. If the police made you write something that was untrue, does that mean you aren't white anymore? Or that they aren't white?"

"No, Clarence, I'm afraid it doesn't work quite like that. Calling someone white is just a figure of speech. Now, can I eat my breakfast?"

All this talk about being white and being honest still confuses me because it seems to mean one thing in some cases and something else at other times. Clearly, though, Palmer doesn't want to talk anymore, so I finish my eggs and bacon and go to dress up in my bandleader's uniform for today's parade. I just need to stay awake long enough to finish the parade.

Chapter 11

November 18, 1888
Pacific Ocean

While I look out over the blue water, it's hard to imagine that I'm going to see nothing but water for several days. Johnny Ward, the captain of the All-America team, comes and stands next to me while I watch.

"Quite a sight, isn't it, Clarence?"

"Yes, Mr. Ward. Have you ever been at sea before?"

"A couple times, yes, but that was on the Atlantic Ocean. This is my first time sailing the Pacific."

"Why do people say we're at sea when we're sailing the ocean?"

"That's a good question, Clarence. I confess I don't know for certain. I suspect that, in years gone by before people sailed the ocean very often, they stayed closer to shore, and sometimes those waters are known as seas, and the term just stuck."

"And why did you say we were sailing? I don't see any sails on our ship."

He laughs a bit. "The same reason, I think. Until recently, ships did have sails. But now we travel by steam power. Our ship, the

Alameda, has a big engine room where workers shovel coal into a steam engine to make the ship run. Words like sailing, when you call something by a name that doesn't really fit anymore, are called anachronisms."

I nod. "Is that why, when I saw some sailors walk by a little while ago, they looked all hot and sweaty? Because they have to shovel coal and it's hot in the engine room?"

"Probably, yes. It's not a job I'd ever choose to do, for sure."

"Did your wife get to join us for our trip, Mr. Ward? Someone told me you have a wife now."

"No, she is not with us, Clarence. Her acting career required that she stay behind."

"I'm sorry to ask so many questions, Mr. Ward, but someone also told me you were the leader of something called a brotherhood. What does a brotherhood do?"

"I am the president of the Brotherhood of Professional Baseball Players, yes. A brotherhood is an organization that seeks to benefit its members through cooperative action. You see, in many ways, Clarence, baseball is an unfair system. When players sign to play for a team, they are subject to something called the reserve clause. I don't suppose you know what that is?"

"No, sir, I don't."

"It means that when we sign our contract to play baseball, our team can reserve us. That means that, at the end of each season, our team decides whether it wants us back the next year. If they do, they offer us another contract for one year, with the team holding the option to reserve us again the next year. And it goes like that, each year the same, until the team decides it doesn't want us anymore."

"What does the player do if he doesn't want to play for that team anymore?"

"The player can do nothing. Because the team he plays for holds the option to reserve him every year, the player cannot get away unless his team decides to part with him, or sells him to another team."

"So, you must stay with your team, and you can't leave, even if you want to?"

"That is correct, Clarence. The only ways to escape the contract are if your team sets you free by releasing you, like what Jarbeau did to you, or if they sell you to another team."

"The players get bought and sold, too?"

"Yes. It is a sports version of the slavery our country used to have before the Civil War. The team can end the contract with the player with ten days of notice, but the player cannot escape his contract with his team at all, even with ten years of notice."

"That doesn't sound fair to me."

"It isn't. My brotherhood is trying to put an end to some of the abuses in baseball, like buying and selling players without their permission."

Now I have some idea what a brotherhood does. It sounds like a good thing to me. But I don't tell Ward about Spalding's plans yet. I'm not sure why I don't, but the time doesn't seem right. Instead, I ask another question I've been thinking about.

"Do you know Mike Kelly, Mr. Ward? Somebody told me that he might come on our trip, but I haven't seen him."

"Yes, I know Mike. I believe he planned to go with us at first but then changed his mind. I think that made Mr. Spalding angry because he'd planned on having Kelly with us, and even printed some promotional materials with Kelly's name and face on them."

"I've met Mike Kelly once. He's one of my most favorite ballplayers."

"Well, he is quite a character, Clarence. Many of the fans love Mike Kelly. It would be fun to have him here, no doubt. Well, I need to move along now, Clarence. It was good to speak with you."

"And you too, Mr. Ward. Good luck with your brotherhood."

Although I'm thrilled that I'm finally at sea and on my way to Australia, I'm feeling a little blue because Mike Kelly did not turn up in San Francisco. It is true that he drinks about as much beer as any two normal men combined, but when he's sober, Kelly is one of the nicest and most generous men in the world. I still remember the day this past season when Boston came to Chicago to play some games. Kelly was chatting with his old Chicago teammates when he spotted me carrying the bats for the players and getting them in place for the game. He came over and helped me, asked me my name, and then gave me a quarter, so I could get some dinner after the game. The next day was a Saturday, and after he watched me lead the parade of players like I always do on Saturday, he rubbed my head and gave me another quarter. That's what kind of a person Mike Kelly is.

Other than no Mike Kelly, however, everything is going great, and I'm in high spirits as our ship passes through the Golden Gate and into the Pacific Ocean. The teams played a few more games in California after the trip to Chinatown, and I marched in the parade for most of them, but nothing special happened, at least nothing special compared to all the things that happened in Chinatown.

I should have seen it coming, maybe, but when the *Alameda* blows its whistle and the ship pulls away from the San Francisco wharf, the Howling Wolves, all seven of them, let forth one final *awoooooooo* to the crowd of onlookers. The crowd howls back, and it is even worse at imitating wolves than the ballplayers, but everyone takes things in good spirits, and just like that, we are finally on our way.

Quickly, I learn one thing about traveling on the ocean that no one told me about when I decided to go on this trip: getting your sea legs. I find that once a ship is out on the ocean, the waves never stop. Your ship goes up and down, up and down, and it never ends. Getting used to this is hard for many of the passengers. After we've been at sea only an hour, I'm walking across the deck when I come across Jimmy Ryan and Tom Burns. Normally, Burns would greet me or at least look in my direction but not today. Their heads are down, and they look almost green in the face. Instead of talking, they hurry past me and stumble below the deck and disappear. I, however, feel just fine.

I walk calmly all the way to the front of the ship. I've learned that sailors call the front of the ship the bow. Our ship, the *Alameda*, is very long, with walkways on both sides of the main deck. In some places, a canvas awning covers the walkways, but at either end of the ship the deck opens to the sky. In the middle of the ship are three black smokestacks that belch out dark smoke nonstop. The ship does have masts, but not for sails. The only thing flying from our masts are flags. The hull of the ship is black, like the smokestacks, but the rest of the ship, including the railings and lifeboats, are white. The deck itself is wood.

When I reach the bow, John Healy, the one everyone calls the Egyptian, is there, along with Billy Earle, who is a catcher on the All-America team. Even though he is big, Earle is one of the youngest people on our tour besides me. I'm not sure if he is even twenty years old. He also likes dressing sharply in the latest fashions, but today that isn't what draws my attention to him. Instead, he and Healy are so pale, they look like they've seen a ghost.

"Afternoon, Clarence," Healy says without much spirit, his gaze downcast and his voice a constant, quiet volume. "You're looking in the pink of condition today, if I may say so. Being at sea doesn't seem to bother you in the least."

"Yes, Mr. Healy, I think that ocean travel agrees with me a little more than with some of the others. Maybe they should have stayed in San Francisco."

"My hat is off to you. Or it would be, except I worry the wind will blow it away if I take my hat off. I'm feeling rather poorly myself, but I'm glad you've joined Billy and me here at the bow. You see, it is our belief that once we get sick and vomit, we'll get over being seasick, and everything will be normal."

"Did Captain Morse tell you that's how it works?"

"No, it is a theory only. Billy came up with it himself. It sounded logical to me, so here we are, putting it to the test. How are you, Billy, my lad?"

"I'd almost rather be shot," is all Earle manages to croak out. He's rubbing his forehead, and even though it's clear he hears us, his eyes stare at something far away. "This isn't quite like fishing on the Delaware back in Philadelphia."

"Not even the mighty Mississippi, on which I've traveled many times, can quite compare," Healy says in agreement. "Still, I don't think it will be much longer before we find out if we are correct. This is worse than traveling in a railroad sleeping car with the Howling Wolves."

"John, how far is it to Australia? Will we be there tomorrow? I don't know how long I'll live if this keeps up," Earle puts in.

"No, Billy, Australia is thousands of miles away. It will take a couple weeks at sea before we get there."

"It takes weeks to reach Australia?" he whines pitifully. "I think maybe I should swim back to San Francisco."

"We're stopping in the Sandwich Islands first. It should take us a mere five or six days to get that far. I heard the captain say it is 2,100 miles from San Francisco to Honolulu."

"I'm liable to die by tomorrow, I think, based on how sick I feel. If that happens, will you men make sure someone says something nice when they bury me? And make sure they know I'm sorry for leaving Philadelphia. That was a mistake."

They stop speaking to deal with their misery in silence for a while. Although I'm feeling down to see these players in such sad shape and so unsteady on their feet that I'm not sure they could walk away without stumbling now, I really don't want to be around when Healy and Earle get sick.

Therefore, when Healy finally asks me if I would stay with them until both men finish vomiting, I answer, "No, sir, I think I'll try to make my way to my room. Please let me know if your idea works out."

I amble back toward the stairway that takes me below the main deck. I'm almost there when I hear a gong sound. That is the signal for a meal.

124

Now I'm in a pickle. I've learned over the last four years, as a homeless person, you never pass up a free meal. Ever. Instead, you eat as much as you can get and don't ask any questions. Today, however, I've heard several people say that, on your first day at sea, you should take it easy and only eat lightly. Since I've never been at sea, and some of them have, I'm considering breaking my rule for the first time in my life.

I come across Al Spalding, Johnny Ward, Ned Williamson, and Harry Palmer heading toward the dining room. Ward says to me, "That's the signal for lunch, Clarence. Are you coming with us to eat? If you aren't prompt, Daly might eat your share."

I join them, although when we reach the dining room, they sit with each other talking while I eat off to the side. I try to pace myself at first, but I can see that many of our party have not come to eat at all. It looks like quite a bit of food will go uneaten. Even Daly is absent. Apparently, he is seasick, too. In the end, my rule holds. I eat, and eat well, and several of the travelers compliment me on my appetite and ability to travel in good health.

That night, however, I dream of marching in a parade, but the street rolls toward me in waves like the ocean, and I drop my baton. I don't know what that means, or if it even means anything, but it worries me.

The next day, November 19, is better for most members of our party. I feel great again, and very few of the others skip any meals.

The *Alameda* is a large ship. If you walk from the bow to the stern and back nine times, you've walked one mile. I am happy our ship is large. Among other benefits, it means I have plenty of room to stay away from Anson, Pfeffer, and the Howling Wolves, and I try my best to avoid any run-ins with them on the first leg of our sea voyage.

My good mood only lasts a few hours on the second day, however. About noon, John Tener locates me and says, "Clarence, I have bad news, lad. Mr. Spalding and the captain tell me they want you to report to the kitchen. It's over that way."

I get to the kitchen to see why the cooks want to see me. When I arrive, the head cook who is in charge notices me right away. "You are Clarence Duval, correct?"

"Yes."

"Mr. Spalding and Mr. Anson inform me that you will be assigned kitchen cleanup and dishwashing duties to pay your way on this voyage. Come over here, lad, and I'll show you how it's done."

I look around to see if any of the other players are on kitchen cleanup duty to pay their way, but I'm the only one. No one told me about this, or mentioned washing dishes when they asked me to be the mascot. I'd felt very good because I wasn't seasick, but now my spirits sink while I scrub soup bowls. I try to fake getting seasick to get out of washing dishes, but everyone saw me eating lunch today, and no one believes me. I know perfectly well how to wash dishes, too. I've done it many times to earn a meal from a restaurant in Chicago. I pretend I don't know how at first, though, so I can get away with working more slowly for a while.

Washing dishes is not my only chore, it turns out. I also must sweep a section of the deck each day. Neither job is hard. I've washed dishes and swept floors hundreds of times back in Chicago. The supervision out on the deck isn't very tight, either, so I spend as much time watching the other passengers as I do sweeping most days, but still, I'm the only one of our party required to do work. The players spend quite a bit of time lounging in their deck chairs while I sweep around them.

For some reason, having not given things any thought, part of me believed our party would be the only ones on the ship. I am mistaken, of course; many others travel with us. To my surprise, one of the other passengers is colored, like I am, and on our second day at sea, he notices me sweeping and introduces himself while I clean the deck in his area.

"How are you, my boy? William Miller."

"Clarence Duval." He reaches out to shake my hand, and I notice that his hands are enormous. In fact, all of him is enormous. His shoulders seem as wide as a horse's, and his muscles are massive, bigger muscles than any ballplayer I've seen as the Chicago mascot. Even Ed Crane or Ned Williamson would look puny if they stood next to William Miller.

"Are you a ballplayer, Mr. Miller?"

He gives me a friendly smile. "No, son, I am not, although I do enjoy the game. I particularly enjoy watching the Cuban Giants of New York play ball. My sport, however, is wrestling."

Just by looking at him, it's easy to believe it. "Is that why you are going to Australia?"

"Yes, I plan to debark at Melbourne and test my abilities against the finest wrestlers in Australia. I plan to bring home my share of prize money, too." he grins.

"I'm the mascot for Mr. Spalding's tour."

"Are you, now? What does the mascot of a ball team do, besides sweep the deck while the players lounge around, gamble, and play cards?"

"I bring the men good luck, of course. I also lead the parade before every game. If I weren't finding my sea legs still, I'd show you how I do it. I have a uniform and a baton and everything."

"And are your parents here, too?"

"No, sir, I don't have any parents. At least I think I don't. It's been years since I've seen them, so I don't rightly know."

"Then how did you end up here, steaming for Australia?"

"Well, you see, I was the mascot for the Chicago Club this past season, so the boys all know who I am. A couple weeks ago, we crossed paths in Omaha. They asked Mr. Spalding if I could come and be the mascot, and he agreed. So here I am."

He strokes his chin and puts his lips together while thinking a moment. "And how do the boys treat you? Do you get a square deal from them?"

"I suppose I do. Some of them don't care for me much, like Captain Anson or Pfeffer. Some treat me nicely, though."

"Well, Clarence Duval, let me show you some tricks just in case they ever try to do you wrong." A friendly smile on his face, Miller looks around, and seeing that no one nearby is paying much attention, shows me some of his wrestling moves. We spend about fifteen minutes while I practice on him.

"That's a good one, Clarence. When you get behind someone, you wrap your arms around their neck, one in front, one in back, and squeeze. They can't breathe when you do that, and sometimes they'll give up."

Then he takes me by the arm. "Here's a simple move. If you get someone by the arm like this, and give their arm a sharp twist like so, sometimes you can throw them to the ground. I won't try it on you, though. You'll need your arm in good condition to keep leading parades."

"I'll show you a few more tricks tomorrow morning if you meet me up here before breakfast, my lad. You never know when they might come in handy. In return, I want to see you lead a parade at least once."

I promise to be there tomorrow morning. Before I go, however, I ask William Miller, "You said you were a fan of the Cuban Giants in New York. Are they part of the New York Giants?"

"Not quite, Clarence. The Cuban Giants are a team of colored players. All the colored players must team together because the whites won't let them play on white teams. I'm not sure why they call themselves the Cuban Giants because none of the players come from Cuba, but that's what they call themselves."

"Are they a good team?"

"They are. They win about two games for every one they lose. I've seen them play major league teams in exhibition games before. Sometimes they win, sometimes the white teams win."

"Is George Stovey one of their players?"

"He is. How do you know about him?"

"I heard Johnny Ward say he struck out Anson twice in a game once."

Miller laughs a deep, rolling laugh. "I wish I'd been there to see that. Okay, Clarence, you'd probably better get back to your chores now. Remember, I'll see you again tomorrow."

Chapter 12

November 20, 1888
Pacific Ocean

Because of the size of our ship, a person on deck can do several things besides just look out at the waves toward the endless horizon, fascinating as I find that to be when I get a break from sweeping. The afternoon after I practice more wrestling with Mr. Miller, I walk toward the stern of the ship, where I see some of the players putting up a large canvas tent. Ward is there, so I decide to ask him what's happening.

"You see that man over there, Clarence?"

"Yes. I don't think I've met him before."

"That is George Wright. Even though he's too old to play ball now, he's one of the best ballplayers to ever live. I only played against him a little bit when I was a young player just starting out, but Anson or Spalding will swear to you he's the greatest shortstop to ever play baseball."

"Aren't you a shortstop, too?"

"I am," Ward says with a smile.

"Why are you putting up a tent?"

"George Wright is going to show us how to play cricket. But we can't just practice on the deck, because if the batter hits the ball, the ball will fly over the edge of the ship and we'll lose it. So, we brought a tent, so we could learn to play on our way to Australia. Wright holds practice each day, and anyone who wants to learn goes into the tent for a while to practice striking the ball."

"Can I go in the tent and watch?"

"Have you finished sweeping?"

"Mostly."

"I suppose so, then."

I ask one more question while I set down my broom. "I thought we were going to Australia to show the people there how to play baseball, so they'll play that instead of cricket. How come you and the other boys are practicing cricket when you are going there to play baseball?"

"Although giving the Australians an exhibition of the grand American game is our first task, Clarence, we must be ready to reciprocate and play the Australian National Game to show our appreciation for our hosts."

"I see. That makes sense to me. Is cricket hard?"

"It is different, certainly. The ball comes toward you much differently than in baseball. It takes some adjustment to gauge its speed and location, and then strike it."

"Can you beat the Australians?"

"We shall see, my boy, we shall see. I believe that, with a bit more practice, we stand a fair chance."

I consider asking Ward something more about his brotherhood but decide that now is not the time because lots of other people are around, including Spalding. If Spalding ever finds out that I overheard his conference with Anson and Harry Palmer back in San Francisco, he might use that part of my contract allowing him to keelhaul me or throw me overboard against me. So, I wait and don't say anything more to Ward yet.

While I think about this, Ward points toward the rear of the boat. "See those large birds, Clarence? The ones with the dark backs and yellow bills?"

"Yes, sir."

"They've been following us ever since we left San Francisco's harbor."

"How many miles have we traveled so far?"

"At least 300, I would guess. Is that about right, Al?"

"Yes, 300 or thereabouts," Spalding says, looking up from a large sheet of unrolled paper he's spent all day studying. "With fair weather, the ship should make about 300 miles a day I'm told, perhaps more. Some of the men have started a contest to see who can guess the exact number. They've marked tickets with the numbers 290 through 340, and they buy and sell each number depending on how many miles they think the ship will make in 24 hours. They call it the Calcutta Pool, if I'm not mistaken. Are you in the pool yet, Adrian?"

I realize that Anson is there now, standing outside the tent, swinging his arms back and forth across his chest, and then swinging them in circles. He must be about to practice in the tent.

"Not yet. I'm going to get a feel for what the ship can do before I enter the game."

Turning back to me, Ward continues, "The birds are a kind of albatross, I'm told, but the men call them molly-hawks. It means something like, 'the foolish bird.' The sailors say the molly-hawks will fly with us all the way to Honolulu."

"Why do they fly so far? Don't they get hungry first? Or tired?"

"I suppose they might, but I'd guess they eat the things that the ship's cooks throw overboard. The extra food we don't eat."

"How can there be any extra food when Daly is on board?" Anson puts in. Everyone nearby laughs. Daly found his sea legs this morning, and nearly cleared an entire table of food at breakfast.

When I see Anson wants to go into the tent, I decide not to, so I get my broom again to finish sweeping. Cricket interests me, though, and I'm curious to learn if it's like baseball. I decide that, from now on, I'll stop by the cricket tent while I sweep each day. If Anson's there, I'll just keep working. That way, he can't growl at me and tell me to go do my chores. If he isn't there, however, then I'll try to go inside and learn how to play cricket.

I don't work very fast because sweeping is so dull, so I'm still sweeping when the men finish their cricket practice. Once the tent is down, they are about to go to new activities when Spalding asks Ward and Anson to round up all the men and return to this section of the deck in half an hour for an important announcement. While they go find everyone else, and because Anson isn't around to torment me, I stay put. I'm almost sure I know what Spalding will say, especially when I see that the paper he's been studying is a map of the world. He's marked several lines on it, in various colors.

After the captains locate everyone and gather them on the deck, Spalding addresses the group. "Men, we still have many days of travel before us until we reach Australia and have the chance to achieve the main purpose of our expedition. Thus far, you have all acquitted yourselves with the utmost manliness and character. I am sure you will continue to do the same once we reach Australia and play our schedule of games there. I am proud of all of you. The reason I've asked to address you all right now is that because our trip is going so well, I want to extend it."

A buzz sounds among the players as they turn to each other. They all start speaking at once.

Smiling, after a moment Spalding continues, "The contracts you signed back in the United States call for us to play games in Australia and New Zealand and then return to the United States. The contracts do not specify, however, the route by which we must return. Therefore, I now offer you the opportunity to continue traveling around the world after we leave Australia. My agents have arranged for us to play ball in India, Egypt, Italy, France, and the British Isles before returning to New York by an Atlantic crossing .
. ."

At this news, another burst of excited chatter breaks out, each player speaking wildly with the man standing next to him. Few of them, it appears, even had a suspicion that this might happen. All of them light up at the news, however, and even though it is hard to make out what everyone says because they are all talking and gesturing with their arms, or slapping each other on the back, all at once, everyone seems happy. I happen to glance at Captain Anson while the men discuss the news, and he pretends surprise, just like everyone else. He can put on an act when he needs to, it seems. No wonder he's so good at convincing the umpire to take his side.

After a few moments spent scanning the crowd, smiling as broadly as a person can, Spalding claps his hands for attention, then resumes speaking. "I sense no one has objections to this change of plans?"

"No, no objections at all," several men respond.

Fogarty simply replies by howling, "Awoooooooo!"

The group has a laugh. Then Fogarty shouts out, "Three cheers! To the All-Americas!"

"To the All-Americas," everyone responds.

"To the Chicagos!"

"To the Chicagos!"

"To Mr. Spalding!"

"To Mr. Spalding!"

"Awoooooooo," howl the Wolves, all at once this time.

Laughing along with the rest, Spalding ends his announcement by saying, "I wanted to let you men know of this change of plans sooner, preferably before we left San Francisco, but only on the morning we left the harbor did I receive word from my European contacts that such a plan was feasible. Knowing it may delay our return to the United States until nearly April and the start of next year's championship contest, I needed some time to plan the best possible course. Should any of you care to see the route I've planned in full, it will be my pleasure to show you on the map. For the rest of you, we still have a couple days before we get to the Sandwich Islands and Honolulu, so please, enjoy your time as you see fit."

He's lying to the players, and I know it. I don't like this, even though I'd already learned about Spalding's plans. I should probably tell Johnny Ward about this, but I wanted to ask someone else about his brotherhood first. I'm not sure whom to ask, however. I can't ask Palmer because he's in on the scheme. I'll have to figure out some way to ask the other reporter, Newton MacMillan, without making it seem like I know anything already. I'll just work on how to ask the question the right way.

For the moment, however, having nothing better to do, I'm one of those who stays put to see where we are going. I've never seen a map of the world laid out like this before, and like so many of the experiences I've had on this trip, it grabs my attention because it's new. Even though I can't pronounce the names of most of the places, I can follow along while Spalding traces a route with his index finger.

He gives the crowd of players a chance to decide what to do. A handful of them, including Ward, Hanlon, Tener, and Anson, stay behind to learn the entire plan, and so do both Palmer and MacMillan. I find just enough space to follow Spalding's finger by looking between Tener and Ward.

"After completing our schedule in Australia and sailing from Adelaide, we head to this island, called Ceylon. We stop at the city of Colombo. From there, we cross to India to play in Madras and Calcutta. Then, we travel by rail to Lucknow, Benares, Agra, and Delhi, and finish our time in India by crossing to Bombay, which, as you see here, is on the west side of the colony. After that, we steam across to Aden, at the mouth of the Red Sea. We travel up the Red Sea to Egypt, playing in Cairo and Alexandria. Then, the final leg of our journey takes us to all the glorious cities and capitals of Europe. First, we visit Naples, Rome, and Venice in Italy. Then our grand tour continues: Vienna, Berlin, Paris, Madrid, and, finally, London. After London, we steam west to our homes in the United

States. The schedule will be tight, but I think we can manage it all before April."

After Spalding stops speaking, everyone heads off on their own, so they can think about this new plan. Seeing that no one is around Newton MacMillan, I decide this is my chance.

"Mr. MacMillan, can I ask you a question?"

"I suppose so, Clarence. Is it about one of the new places we are going?"

"Not exactly. I've never been to any of them, so they'll all be surprises to me. I wanted to ask you about something I overheard some of the boys talking about a couple days ago."

"Oh? And what is that?"

"Well, I heard them talking about something called a brotherhood, and that Mr. Ward is the president of one. I've never heard of a brotherhood before. I'm curious about what it is."

"Well, now, that is a question, indeed. What do you say we sit down for a moment while I try to explain things."

After we've found some convenient deck chairs, he continues. "If you just want to know what a brotherhood does, well, the answer is simple. It is a group of people who band together to achieve a mutual goal. They pledge to support each other with time, money, and other resources. The members believe they can get more accomplished working together than individually because they have more resources to work with that way."

"Are all the players on our trip in Mr. Ward's Brotherhood?"

"No. Only a few of the Chicago players are. Anson is dead set against it, however. Most of the All-America team's players are members."

"What is the goal of Mr. Ward's Brotherhood?"

"That depends on whom you ask, Clarence. If you asked Johnny Ward, he'd probably say something like this: The players in the National League formed their Brotherhood because the owners of the teams in the National League treat them unfairly. Specifically,

Ward feels that the wording of the player contracts is unfair toward the players, especially something known as the reserve clause."

"I don't know what a reserve clause is," I reply, not quite telling the truth. Ward told me what it was already, but I'm curious if MacMillan will describe it in the same way. "Is it a good thing or a bad thing?"

"Again, that depends whom you ask. It works something like this. If a player signs a contract to play with a team in the National League, he is, essentially, bound to that team for the remainder of his career, or until the team decides it doesn't want him anymore. The reserve clause in the contract allows the team to reserve the player to play on their team again next year, and the player has no choice in the matter."

"That sounds harsh for the players."

"They feel that way, certainly. The owners reply it is necessary because without it, players could switch teams freely for each season by selling their services to the highest bidder."

"Shouldn't the players get to play for who wants them the most?"

"Again, the players think so. The owners like Mr. Spalding do not."

"And how do you feel about it, Mr. MacMillan?"

"I do not fall strictly on either side of the dispute. On the one hand, I agree it is rather restrictive on the ballplayers because without any choice of where to play, often their teams treat them poorly and try to cheat them. The teams can get away with it in most cases because the players can't go anywhere else even when they feel upset.

"On the other hand, however, teams and players get some benefits when teams field the same group of men each year. The fans like it because they become familiar with their favorite players. You know how they love Anson, Tommy Burns, Ned Williamson, and John Clarkson in Chicago. The present system also makes things more predictable for the management of each team because the managers know what men they'll have from one season to the next.

"Still, when you get down to it, I'd like to see some changes made. Not allowing the players any choice of where they want to play after signing their first contract smacks a bit of the slavery your people experienced before our Civil War, in my eyes. I'd like to see a compromise worked out, to be honest with you. Perhaps an agreement where players sign a contract for several years at first, but then are free to change teams afterward. I'll admit that I've not had a chance to thoroughly sort through my thoughts on the matter, Clarence. If you want to know any more than that, I suggest you speak with Ward or Hanlon about things."

"That might be a good idea. Thank you, Mr. MacMillan."

I don't need to talk to Ward because I already have, but I also decide that if Ward is on one side of a question, and Anson is on the other, I know where I should stand. I thank MacMillan again for sharing, then wander back to my chores.

Another thing almost all the ballplayers do while we travel toward the Sandwich Islands is make bets. On everything. Besides the Calcutta Pool that Spalding mentioned, they bet on the weather. They bet on what direction the wind will blow tomorrow, what kind of soup the cooks will serve at dinner, who will be the last to get up from eating, or which one of a group of passengers will sit down first while taking the air on deck. Fogarty even offers five-to-one odds that the ship will not sink before reaching Honolulu. Anson almost takes the bet, until he realizes that Fogarty is joking.

The top deck of the *Alameda* has an entire room meant for nothing else besides playing cards. The players go there often, especially in the evenings, and poker is their game of choice. This, of course, gives them many more chances to bet. Most of the players play at least occasionally. I can't play, even though I know how, because I have no extra money to bet, and no one will loan me any. Although he is one of the smartest and most intelligent men in the party, Ward never plays. Neither does Al Spalding. On the evening of the sixth day out from San Francisco, however, I join Ward and Spalding in the ship's library. I can't read any of the books, but I'm not there to read. Spalding sent me to find Johnny Ward because Spalding needed to speak to Ward and Anson about what to do when the ship reaches Honolulu.

"John, Adrian, I am sorry to distract you from your repose, but we have an issue that could become serious, and I need your help to make sure that it doesn't. As you know, we left San Francisco one day later than our original plan called for. Our initial plans had us docking in Honolulu this morning and playing a game of ball for the people there this afternoon. Because of our delay, however, we will arrive on Sunday rather than Saturday. This would not be a problem, except for one unusual circumstance. Although the Sandwich Islands have a king, the influence there of Christian missionaries is very pervasive. They are Congregationalists, most of them, and I have a strong feeling they will object to our playing a game of baseball on the Sabbath. I do not know what the king's attitude toward the matter will be."

"Well, if there's a king, why doesn't the king just do what he wants and let us play?" Anson asks.

"The politics of the islands are rather more complex than they seem on the surface. My agent in Honolulu, Harry Simpson, informs me that the king, whose name is King Kalakaua, does not always prevail in matters of policy due to missionary interference."

"What would you like us to do, then?" Ward asks.

"First, remember that our goal is spreading the popularity of baseball, not involving ourselves in affairs of local politics. There must be no lobbying by the players, of either the king or the missionaries, under any circumstances. Likewise, you two must help me make sure that the men do not complain if the missionaries do not allow us to play. The men will be restless after a week at sea, and with another long sea voyage ahead of them, their moods might turn a bit sour. Make sure they keep their views on the matter to themselves and cause no problems with the politics of the islands. Are we clear?"

"Sure, Mr. Spalding," both men agree.

Then Anson adds, "Do they even have grounds for baseball in Honolulu? Or is even having a ball field too indecent for the decorum of the missionaries?"

"Harry Simpson informs me the grounds are of high quality and that the local population is anxious to see us play. Whatever the odds of that are, we must be sure we show our hosts our appreciation when the time comes."

"We'll do what we can, of course," Anson says, and then all of us take our leave of Spalding.

I leave really hoping we do play. Then I can keep my promise to Mr. Miller and show him my marching routine.

Chapter 13

November 25, 1888
Honolulu, Sandwich Islands

"That's quite a big rock, isn't it, Mr. Burns?"

"Certainly, Clarence. It's named Diamond Head."

"We're very lucky, aren't we, Mr. Burns?"

"Why is that, Clarence?"

"The weather is so warm and sunny here. I didn't know it could be so warm anywhere in the world in November."

"We've sailed a good distance south from California, Clarence. The farther south you go, the warmer it gets."

I don't understand why that is true, but it makes me happy. Maybe it's like in Denver, where the air was thin, but I couldn't see it.

"I heard Mr. Spalding say that the grounds here are very nice. You and the boys should be able to play your best ball today."

"Yes, we are supposed to play in front of King Kalakaua himself."

"Have you ever met a king before, Mr. Burns?"

"No, Clarence. Have you?"

"No. But I've heard lots of stories about them. My friend Tommy and I talked about them sometimes. He'd been to school a couple times, and they told him stories about kings and queens at school."

"And what happens in the stories?"

"Well, the king has expensive clothes, for sure, and hundreds of servants who do whatever he wants them to, and a big palace. Usually, they get to eat from plates made of gold or silver, and they ride on horses when they aren't eating. And since we're going to a warm place, I'll bet the king has more servants who wave palm leaves around, so he can stay cool when he isn't riding his horse. Oh, and he'll have a beautiful wife. All the kings in the stories have beautiful wives."

Burns gives a hearty laugh. "Well, Clarence, I guess we'll find out if the stories are true before today ends, won't we? Where is your friend Tommy now, may I ask?"

"He died, Mr. Burns. The Chicago police shot him one day."

Burns raises his eyebrows, then bites his lip a moment. "That is a tragedy, Clarence. I'm very sorry to hear about that. But look, it's almost time to dock. There's a crowd of people to meet us, too."

When the *Alameda* comes to a stop and drops anchor in Honolulu Bay, the people gathered to meet us on the dock seem very excited. We are almost ready to debark and march down the gangplank, with Spalding at the head of our group. I am at the rear of our party, but I can still hear what everyone says because most of them are excited to make port and they're shouting to each other.

At the foot of the gangplank, I see a thick crowd of white men who I think must be Americans. "Who is elected?" they call out.

"Harrison," Spalding replies. "Didn't you know? The election was more than two weeks ago."

With this announcement, about half the men in attendance send up a series of cheers. A couple toss their Greeley hats in the air. These hats have a circular crown, like a top hat, but it's dimpled. They also have a broad brim, shaped in a circle, that goes all the way around the hat. Most of the hats are white, but a few are black or gray.

The others on the dock look down and shuffle their feet, snap their fingers, mumble under their breath, or display various other forms of disappointment. I think I see one man crying.

When the last cheer dies down, one man, who wears white duck trousers, white shoes, and a linen shirt, steps forward from the crowd. He is also wearing a white, broad-brimmed Greeley hat.

"Al!" he shouts. "My apologies, Cousin Al, but they do not have telegraph wires here on these remote islands quite yet."

"George Smith!" Spalding shouts back. "I had forgotten the fact. Yes, our man Harrison is the winner, thank the Masters of Wisdom and Compassion. It is good to see you."

"And you, too. As the official head of King Kalakaua's royal welcoming delegation, welcome to the Sandwich Islands. May your stay be a pleasant one."

Smith then gives a wave and says, "May I present to you the Royal Hawaiian Band of King Kalakaua, under the esteemed leadership of the noted Bandmaster Berger."

Peering over the side rail of the ship again, I can see the band assembled to greet us, and after Smith gives it a wave, it begins playing. All the musicians dress like Smith does, in duck trousers and Greeley hats. Their first number is "Yankee Doodle."

Smith gives another wave, and several young men, just a few years older than me, come up the gangplank, bearing garlands of roses and ferns. They also wear duck trousers, but instead of Greeley hats, they sport straw hats instead. They start to drape the garlands around the necks of the ballplayers, but some of the men look uncomfortable at this.

Anson growls, "I don't want no flowers from some kanaka."

Fred Pfeffer also tries to shoo the young men away in his twangy voice, grumbling something about pagan idolatry. Even John Ward tries to decline by extending his arms, palms outward.

I hear John Healy say, "No gifts from a corrupt bourgeois monarchy for me, thank you."

Spalding, however, has one on and has already helped one of the boys drape a garland around his wife's neck. He calls out to the reluctant players, "Men, this is a form of royal greeting. Come now, and give it a try."

"These garlands are called *leis*, and they are a sign of the king's welcome and favor," George Smith, who I now notice wears one himself, chimes in. "It is how the islanders greet favored visitors. It would be most impolite to decline."

Some of the players grumble a little more, but eventually, they give in and wear the leis. The band starts playing "The Star-Spangled Banner." I keep waiting for my lei, but I don't get one. They just forgot one for me, I guess. I suppose it would look silly over my bandleader uniform, anyway.

After that little episode, we walk down the gangplank of the *Alameda* and the players take carriages to our hotel, named the Royal Hawaiian Hotel. The Royal Hawaiian Band plays "The Girl I Left Behind Me" while we climb into the carriages. I happen to look at John Ward while the song plays, and he looks down, or stares off at nothing. I suppose he misses his new wife very much.

The players travel by carriage to the hotel, but I get to march out in front of them. I am quite hot, between the warm weather and my new marching uniform, which is nicer than ever. I now have a scarlet jacket, white khaki pants, black boots, and a gold-braided cap that the players bought for me in San Francisco, so I'd look more like a proper bandmaster. The band follows behind me, playing a tune that I've heard many times in Chicago, "Marching Through Georgia." Even I know that this song is about General Sherman's famous march from Atlanta to Savannah during the Civil War. I smile when I think about how Pfeffer must feel when he hears the tune.

After we get to the hotel, I change into my other set of clothes, the set I got in Hastings. I'm still very warm because they are also too thick for the weather here in the Sandwich Islands, but they are all I have, so they'll have to do.

After I've changed, I wander over to our group just in time to hear George Smith say to the players grouped around him, "You have about an hour to get yourselves settled in. His Majesty will receive your party at 11 a.m., and, I'm pleased to announce, King Kalakaua also invites you to a feast, which we call a luau, at 6:00 this evening. It is a high honor to receive such treatment. The king is very anxious to meet American baseball players and wants to extend to you every courtesy while you are here. We'll march to the royal palace as soon as everyone is here and ready."

That means I must change clothes once again, and put my sweaty marching uniform back on. I wish I could do without the scarlet jacket and its fancy white trim, but my job is mascoting and leading parades, so I put it back on. However, because I don't have any baggage, it doesn't take me very long to store my things in my room and return to the hotel lobby. I find Newton MacMillan sitting in a comfortable chair with padded armrests, writing something in his notepad.

"Clarence, you're looking sharp and ready to do your duty, I'd say."

"Thank you, Mr. MacMillan. May I ask you something, sir?"

"Go ahead, my boy."

"When those young men came onto our ship and put the leis around the necks of all the men, I heard Anson call them kanakas. What does that mean? I thought these were the Sandwich Islands, not the Kanaka Islands."

"The word, I believe, refers to people who are native to these islands. It may be a general term for any islander of the South Pacific, in fact, although I wouldn't place total confidence in the last part of my statement. At the risk of confusing you further, you may also hear people refer to the Sandwich Islands as the Hawaiian Islands. That is where our hotel's name comes from."

"Why have all those names for them and not just one?"

145

"Well, Clarence, if I'm not mistaken, the word kanaka has somewhat derogatory connotations."

"Derogatory?"

"That means you call someone a kanaka to make them seem less important than you are, or worse than you. If Anson said it like you report, that was probably his intent."

"I think I understand that."

"It's like how people in Chicago refer to colored people like yourself. As you know, sometimes they use polite terms like colored, but sometimes people use less polite ones when they are angry or they're being mean."

We talk for another minute or two about why someone would call other people kanakas, but now other players begin arriving in the lobby, and our group heads to the dining room of the hotel.

The cooks serve a dish I've never had before. It is a pinkish mush covered with cream and sugar.

"This, my friends, is called *poi*," George Smith tells us. "You eat it by taking your index finger, scooping out a mouthful with it, and putting it in your mouth, and then repeating the process until the poi is gone. The dish is native to these islands, and a very popular one."

With that, he takes a scoop with his finger and starts eating. I find it tasty, but just having regular meals on this trip, everything seems good to me. Once everyone finishes his helping of poi, Spalding gives the order to form up and march to the palace, so we head out the front door of the hotel.

Once everyone is there, Spalding repeats the plan for the day. "We are to meet King Kalakaua in a formal reception first, then, hopefully, play a game of baseball, and then return to our hotel and change from our baseball uniforms and attend the luau."

While Spalding reminds us of these things, I have time to take in our surroundings a bit more. The Sandwich Islands are mountainous. The city of Honolulu seems quite small compared to Chicago or San Francisco, but it is no village. Several streets lead down to the harbor and several rows of houses line each cross street. The streets slope gently upward, away from the water, and beyond the houses, I see the foothills of the mountains. Today I feel a light, salty breeze and lots of warm sunshine.

Tener stands next to me. Somehow, he's acquired a Greeley hat of his own, which makes him seem even taller than he normally is. When Spalding finishes his instructions, I ask, "How many people live in the city?"

"Something like 20,000," he replies.

"What are those trees with the gray trunks and the branches with the leaves clustered at the top? What about those other ones, the ones with the round, brown globes hanging from them? I don't think we have any trees like that in Chicago, do we?"

"No, we don't, that's for sure. Certain trees grow better in some areas than others because of temperature, amount of rainfall, and so forth. These ones require warm temperatures to grow well, much warmer than we have in Chicago this time of the year. The ones with the gray trunks and wide green leaves at the top are palm trees. The ones with the brown fruit are coconut trees, and those others over there with the yellow fruit are banana trees."

Before Tener can tell me any more about the trees, though, it's time to begin. I glance around. A great many people turn out to see the parade. The king's Royal Hawaiian Band is present once again, and they start into the tune "Yankee Doodle" for the second time while we start marching up the street. From the corner of my eye, I see William Miller, my wrestler friend, watching with the other parade goers. He smiles at me. I tip my cap, smile back, and start up the street toward the King's palace.

Luckily, the palace isn't very far because in the warm weather it doesn't take me long to get hot again while I'm wearing my uniform, marching, and tossing my baton. The Royal Hawaiian Band is just finishing its second song of the march, "Hail Columbia," when we arrive. A crowd of onlookers, some white, some Hawaiian, and even a few who look Chinese, lines our route the entire way.

The king's palace is not anything like I expected. I thought it would have tall walls with towers and one hundred rooms, at least five or six stories, along with white horses and fancy fountains made of gold. They usually looked like that in the stories Tommy told me.

Instead, from the outside it just looks like a very large house, the size of houses you see in the nice neighborhoods of Chicago. Palm trees line the walkway to the front doors, but I can't find any fountains or men on horses with swords and armor. When we enter the grounds and start down the walkway, we pass underneath an arch featuring a fancy coat of arms, which does have armor and crossed swords, and some Hawaiian words: "*Ua mau ke ea o ka aina i ka pono.*" I'll have to ask someone what that means.

I'm disappointed to find that the palace has no stone walls or towers for protection, either. It does have three stories, with the main stairs leading to a double door on the second floor, a railed balcony and porch in the front, and many windows. The people who built it used light gray-colored stones on the outside. I like how it looks. It's just smaller than I imagined.

While I study the king's palace, the men organize themselves into pairs for their introduction to the king. While they do so, I overhear George Smith speaking with Harry Palmer.

Palmer says to Smith, "I rather like these Hawaiians. As a group, they seem to possess regular features and bright, intelligent faces. Just look at all the pretty women, too. From the looks of things, these people consider our arrival an event of no small importance."

"You can scarcely imagine the anticipation yesterday," Smith replies. "Everyone radiated excitement at the chance to see baseball played by professionals here in the Sandwich Islands. Your failure to arrive on schedule, however, was a sad disappointment to many a resident of the city. Yesterday morning, all Honolulu was awake early to welcome you and watched for the signal announcing your arrival. The Royal Hawaiian Band assembled at the place arranged on the docks, and the government tug had steamed up ready to convey a party of our citizens as far as Diamond Head to welcome you. Business was generally suspended, and everybody was on the street in holiday attire, even more so than today. All were so impatient to meet you that it wasn't until 3 o'clock that we gave you up and decided that you would not reach here on Saturday as planned. The local people and the king are going to do the best they can for you, but whatever we do, we shall never cease to regret that you did not arrive yesterday."

"It is a pity, but we were delayed in San Francisco waiting for the mail from England to arrive, or at least so I hear. Spalding needed to hear from his European contacts whether it was possible to tour there before we set out. Your reception is first-class, all the same. Here is the question of the hour: Will we be able to play a game of ball today or not?"

"I fear not. But we will talk it over after the reception and see what develops."

Smith stops there because the party needs him to lead the delegation into the king's audience chamber. Unfortunately, it's Anson's duty to make sure everyone is where he is supposed to be, and when he gets to me he growls, "Stand down, Clarence. You aren't part of the group that gets to meet this king fellow."

"I'm not?"

"Hmpf. Not at all. This is for the Chicago and All-America baseball teams and their players. You are a member of neither, boy. You'll have to wait outside until we are done."

I know that complaining is useless, so I slump down on the white marble palace steps while everyone goes inside. I wonder how long I'll have to wait and how long it takes for this many people to meet a king. While everyone but me files in past the royal guards, I gaze down at the streets stretching below, back down to the harbor, just staring off into the distance.

Everyone has been inside for a couple minutes when I hear a "Psst!"

I turn and see one of the royal guards waving me over. "How come you don't get to join the party?" he asks me. Although he's clearly a native of the islands, he speaks perfect English.

"I don't know. I guess because I'm not a member of the ball teams. I'm just the mascot," I say in a quiet, dull voice, looking down at the ground.

"Well," the man says with a mischievous grin on his face, "maybe you can't go inside, but if you want, I'll let you stand here in the doorway and watch what happens. Anyone who can lead a parade like you deserves to at least see our king, even if you don't get to shake his hand."

My eyes look up at the guard, and I smile back and walk over beside him. "Are you part of the king's army?"

"I suppose you might say that. Even though our army only has about 60 people. We aren't that much of an army. We mostly do ceremonial things like stand guard while important guests visit. Look at my gun."

He holds it out to me, so I can see it better. It's a rifle with a shiny black barrel and polished silver-gray metal.

"It doesn't even have bullets in it. Mostly I just keep my uniform nice, so I look good whenever someone important visits."

"Can I ask you a question?"

"Sure."

"When we passed under the arch on our way to the palace, there were some words in your language carved into the stone. What do they say?"

"In English, our words *ua mau ke ea o ka aina i ka pono* mean 'The life of the land is perpetuated in righteousness.'"

I look inside the king's palace and see that it has an entrance hallway with a double staircase leading to the upper floor. The stairs are wood, although I'm not sure what kind, and shine brightly because they have so much polish. One stair is on the right, the other on the left, and they meet on a balcony overlooking the doorway I'm standing in.

To my far left is a waiting room where the players have left their hats, walking canes, and so forth. Both the entrance room and this waiting room have white plaster walls, but the waiting room also has many pieces of wooden furniture, also polished and shining brightly. An unarmed man wearing white trousers and a purple shirt stands watch at the doorway, white-gloved hands folded in front of him.

The entrance hall lacks fancy decorations but does have many paintings along both walls. The friendly guard sees me looking at them and says, "Those are the king's ancestors."

At the opposite end of the entrance hall, underneath the balcony, are a second set of double doors that give way to the throne room. They are open, so I can see a little bit of what happens inside.

The throne room is much bigger than the entrance hall, although without being able to go inside, I can't see how much bigger. All the men from both teams are in there, however, so it must be large. I can even get a glimpse of King Kalakaua at times. He appears to be in his late forties or early fifties. To my surprise, he doesn't wear a crown or have a sword, or a scepter, or any other item to show his royalty. Rather than a robe or a plush cape with fur trim, he wears a black Prince Albert coat, along with light-colored pants and leather shoes.

"Do all the guests have to bow to the king?" I ask the guard.

"No, it doesn't work that way anymore. I hear a lot of people ask that before they go in to meet King Kalakaua, but usually he just shakes their hand and skips the bowing."

"Does the king like guests?"

"Yes, most of the time. He enjoys meeting new people and sharing our hospitality with them."

"I thought he would look different. He dresses a lot like people do in Chicago, where I'm from."

"The king tries to stay apace with the latest gentlemen's fashions," the guard says with an amused smile. "He considers it important to demonstrate that the Sandwich Islands are modern and in tune with the progressive spirit of the age."

I guess whoever told those stories to Tommy about kings has never been to the Sandwich Islands because they got a bunch of things wrong when it comes to kings.

Now the players start leaving the throne room, which means it's time for the band and me to perform once again. "Thank you for the chance to watch," I say to the kind palace guard.

He smiles back. "Happy travels to you and your friends. Oh, and by the way, I really hope you get to play a game of ball today."

After I lead our march back to our hotel, that is what everyone wants to know. Will the ball game take place? When we arrive, I see a gathering of very well-dressed men, each of whom seemingly drove to the hotel in his own carriage, who ask to see Spalding. They, unlike the people who met us at the dock, have on expensive tailored suits, most of them black, and wear top hats. Several sport walking canes as they hop down from their carriage. One of the men steps forward from the others. He is wearing a business suit with a tie. I edge closer to listen, close enough to see the diamond gleaming in his tiepin and the gold shining from his cufflinks.

"Mr. Spalding," he begins, "I am John Cummins, owner of the Cummins sugar plantation on Oahu. Because this island is home to many fans of the great American National Game of baseball, several of the great planters of the island, me included, have circulated this petition on your behalf. We've collected over 1,000 signatures in the past twelve hours, requesting you to play a game of baseball this afternoon. I will let you examine it if you wish, but as it clearly reads, we will be happy to defray any expenses you incur while playing ball today."

Cummins hands over this petition, and the other wealthy planters assembled outside the hotel lobby nod their approval. Spalding looks the men and their petition over for a moment. Then he gives a short, and probably well-rehearsed, speech in answer.

"Gentlemen and citizens of Honolulu: I thank you for this demonstration of your interest in our party and in the National Game of the Americans, and I assure you that if it is possible for me to comply with your request, I will do so. Every member of the Chicago and All-America teams has expressed a desire to give you a game, and I am equally anxious to have them do so. When we left Chicago, however, we did so with a determination to act in accordance with the laws and wishes of the communities we visited, as far as Sunday games were concerned. At St. Paul, Denver, and San Francisco in our country, we played Sunday games because it was an established custom in those cities, and if your people wish it here and your city authorities give their consent, I see no reason why the game should not be played. I will let you know definitively within fifteen minutes."

After that little speech, Spalding, Smith, Cummins, and a few other well-dressed, important-looking people get into a pair of carriages and depart, I guess to find out if the laws will allow a game. Like I often do when I'm confused about what's happening, I go looking for Harry Palmer and Newton MacMillan, our writers for the tour. I spot Palmer first this time.

"Mr. Palmer, why won't the city authorities let us play today?"

"I am a tad murky on some of the details myself, Clarence, but I believe it has to do with the missionary element here in the islands. I'm afraid the Congregationalists who brought Christianity to the islands are rather serious about observing the Sabbath."

"That's what Mr. Spalding said to Mr. Ward and Mr. Anson yesterday evening."

"Yes, I'm sure he's well aware of the situation. I'm afraid he meant the little speech you just heard to mollify the petitioners. I doubt he thinks there will be a game."

"Why don't the missionaries want us to play? Don't they like baseball?

"It has to do with certain Christian traditions, including the idea that Sunday should be a day of rest. Some Christians take that instruction more seriously than others do. It appears that those who made the laws for the islands take the instruction to observe the Sabbath rather seriously. One member of our welcoming committee told me that the authorities can arrest and fine people just for driving their carriage on Sunday."

"Why doesn't the king change the law, if he is the king?"

"That is a tricky question, Clarence, but it appears the system of government here does not allow for that to happen."

I'm reminded once again of just how little a person can learn about kings from stories. None of the things in the tales I've heard are true, it seems, if the King of the Sandwich Islands can't even have a game of baseball when he wants one.

"As to why the laws reflect the wishes of the missionaries rather than the king, some people have reached a higher stage of civilization, of development, if you will, and so the world needs them to guide its lesser peoples toward progress and civilization. The missionaries are in a more evolved state of society than the people of the islands, or at least that is what they believe."

"It sounds like an excuse to tell other people what to do, if you ask me. Why is what the missionaries believe better than what the king, or the people of the islands, believe?"

"The missionaries believe their faith in the Bible puts them in a higher state of civilization than the native religion of these islands, and it is their duty to share their ways with the people here, and that includes resting on Sunday."

"They get to do what they want because they think they are better than the people here, then. Do you believe that?"

"I think such things might have been needed at one time here, yes. Today, however, such rules seem unnecessarily oppressive. These blue laws are obnoxious to people of cosmopolitan tastes, and if Honolulu and these islands ever want to become the resort location that nature destined them to be, they will have to outgrow such restrictive practices."

"What is a blue law, Mr. Palmer?"

"Blue laws are laws meant to regulate the morality of the public."

"That means they are another way to force other people to act like you would, right?"

"That is correct. Like I said, there might have been a reason for them once, but now, I look around, and it appears that these islands now enjoy a state of civilization and advanced progress of which many people around the world could feel proud. They are not on the level we've attained in the United States, certainly, but they appear well on their way. They may reach our stage of development some day. I am sorry, Clarence, but now I must take my leave and compose my notes of what just happened before Mr. Spalding returns."

A short time later, Spalding does return. He steps down from his carriage and prepares to address the group. Excitement rustles through the crowd.

"Surely, he was able to arrange a game," I hear someone say.

"No doubt about it," another offers.

"They won't go against the wishes of so many people, will they? They must let them play," a third person puts in.

Spalding commences speaking. "After deliberations with the city magistrates, I have determined we cannot play ball today. They inform me that the law strictly forbids Sunday amusements, and that a fine or time in prison will be the result if we try to play." He then reads the law about Sunday amusements to the crowd.

After Spalding finishes, the mood of the crowd turns ugly. One man standing behind me shouts out, "Hang the law! We want a game of ball." Others grumble similar things.

Another man shouts, "We've been waiting for this for two months! The grounds are ready, and everyone wants to see baseball."

A third says, "It's time we put a stop to such silly laws!"

Spalding holds up his arms for quiet. "My friends, I know your passion for our great American game. No one wants to play a game more than the players you see before you. However, as you know, we must steam for Australia tomorrow. We are simply not in a place to issue a challenge to the laws here today. It has always been my intent to observe local customs and laws while on our trip, and however obnoxious we find the law against Sunday baseball, we cannot afford the delay such a challenge would entail."

The people remain angry, but little by little, they accept the fact there will be no baseball today. While the crowd disperses, and the people take their carriages back to wherever they came from, many of the players start to grumble. They seem just as disappointed as the people of Honolulu are.

"I am sorry, boys," Spalding tells them, "but what I told the crowd is the truth. We cannot have any delay here, as much as you men want to play ball. I know it is a weak consolation, but we now have a few hours to explore the city before the luau this evening. You might not have seen it when we arrived in the harbor this morning, but the United States warship *Alert* is also in port. The captain sent me word that any of you are welcome to board the ship and have a look around, should you desire it."

Some of the boys greet this news with enthusiasm. George Wood, an outfielder on the All-America team, volunteers to lead a party to visit the ship. Wood is unusual among our group because he was born in Canada, even though he has lived in the United States most of his life. Some of the players call him a dandy because, like young Billy Earle, he always dresses up very stylishly. Despite that, he always acts politely, holding doors and chairs for people, women especially, and I don't think I've seen him lose his temper once in the four weeks since I joined the tour.

He says, "I've never seen a modern warship. We don't have too many of those in Canada where I'm from."

"Clarence, why don't you come with us?" Anson asks the group. "We'll put you in one of the cannons and see how far you fly!"

Almost everyone laughs. I try to slink away and hope everyone will forget about me.

Before Anson's jokes at my expense go any further, Spalding interrupts him. "One thing you should know, George, Adrian, and anyone else who wants to visit the *Alert*. The captain also said that two of his officers are from Paterson, New Jersey. All of you, I'm sure, remember that Paterson is Mike Kelly's hometown. They probably think that Kelly is with us because I put his name on some of our promotional materials before he changed his mind about coming, so be prepared for their disappointment when they find out that he isn't here."

"We'll handle it, Mr. Spalding," Wood declares. "We all miss not having Kel along, too, but we'll make them understand he was the one who let us down."

With that, Wood and a handful of other players board a carriage and head back to the harbor. Since I don't fancy finding out what the inside of a cannon looks like, I choose not to go even before anyone asks me, although I have no need to worry because no one asks me.

Another group, made up of those who feel they've spent enough time on boats recently, consider their options of what to do. Mr. Cummins, the plantation owner, offers a tour of his sugar plantation to the group. Again, I decline to go because Pfeffer is in this group, and I'm scared he'll ask me to do another plantation dance once we get there.

That leaves me without much to do, so I sit on the hotel balcony and watch the waves at sea. No one comes by to talk to me, and I don't want to talk to anyone else, just in case someone suggests doing something else to me. At least I can get out of my bandleader uniform and cool down a bit. The view of the water is beautiful, too, I suppose, but I've been looking at the ocean for a week now, and it's starting to look familiar. So, I just dangle my legs between the rails of the balcony, stick my head between them, and stare off into the distance.

Chapter 14

November 25, 1888
Honolulu, Sandwich Islands

"Clarence, my boy, what do you think of the Queen's Grounds?" John Tener says to me while he passes a dish of rice.

"Is that the name of this park?"

"Yes, it's the official residence of the Queen of the Sandwich Islands. I do not know why the king and queen have separate palaces, but these lawns are broad, spacious, and well-kept. Any ball team would be proud to play on such a field. Look over there, do you know what those are?"

"You mean the banana and coconut trees?"

"Well done, Clarence. You remembered."

I note lots of other kinds of trees, plants, and shrubs here, too, whose names I don't know, but I don't think now is the time to ask about them. Instead, I point to the torches blazing around the edge of the park.

"Do you know what kind of lights those are, Mr. Tener?"

"Not for certain, Clarence, although I know they burn oil. I've seen people refill them from time to time. Impressive to keep all of them lit for almost two hours now."

In the center of the grounds are two large tents, each measuring about 100 feet long. King Kalakaua has spent most of the evening in one, along with many other Hawaiians who must be his attendants or officials. No sign of the kindly guard from earlier today, however. The king shakes hands and chats pleasantly with those who wish to greet him and does so for the first hour-and-a-half of the luau.

At 7:30, the king moved to the other tent for dinner, and we've all joined him to eat. I'm happy that Tener is sitting next to me at dinner, so I can ask him things. He speaks to me again.

"Clarence, what a gathering! Look at all this food, my boy. Would you like a bit of roast pork?"

"Yes. Is that turkey you have on your plate?"

"It is. And here, have a bit of this coconut."

"I thought that coconuts were brown."

"They are on the outside, but the insides are white. Try a bit of pineapple, while you're at it. You won't find this in too many places in Chicago."

I try both, and decide I much prefer the pineapple. "I don't recognize that fruit," I say, pointing to one with an orange color and small, black seeds in the middle.

"It's called papaya. Would you like some, or perhaps a bit more poi, instead?"

I nod, and soon another plate of poi sits in front of me.

"There's only one thing that could be better here, Clarence."

"What's that?"

"Sitting on the ground like this, well, my long legs are cramping a bit. I'm not used to eating this way."

I'd barely noticed in my excitement over the food. It doesn't bother me, anyway, because back in Chicago I often sit on the pavement and eat. Compared to that, the rush mats we're sitting on aren't bad at all.

Instead of complaining, I ask, "Who are all the young ladies in white dresses walking around?"

"I believe they wave their large fans to keep the guests comfortable. It's part of creating a hospitable atmosphere for the guests, Clarence, just like the guitar music and singing we hear coming from somewhere in the park."

I never thought I'd see the day when I'd be eating food with someone fanning me. I'm not sure what to say about it, and before I can think of anything to say back to Tener, the king rises and begins speaking. Like the soldier I spoke with at the palace, he speaks perfect English.

"Honored guests, in the true tradition of the hospitality of my islands, I wish to provide you with all the festive entertainment I can. To compensate for certain laws that denied you the opportunity to play a game of baseball this afternoon, I arranged this luau in your honor."

The players and other guests cheer and wish the king health and long life.

"In addition to the luau," he continues, "we have another tradition on our islands that I wish to share with you this evening. Another of our ancestral customs is for the women of the islands to perform the hula, one of our dances, for guests of honor."

Another round of cheers follows this announcement. I half expect the Howling Wolves to break forth in a wail of wolf howls, but thankfully, even though they've had plentiful amounts of liquor by now, they appear more interested in finding out how the hula dance works than in hurting our ears.

King Kalakaua raises his arms for quiet once again. "Unfortunately, the laws of our island do not allow for the public performance of the hula, for the Congregationalist missionaries who made the laws consider the dance too indecent for the public."

The men boo as one. Not at the king, of course, but at his latest announcement that, once again, laws about behavior are about to deny them fun and entertainment. I just watch to see what happens next. The king is smiling, so I think he has something tricky up his sleeve.

In addition, I don't know why it comes to me just at this moment, but I also realize that, although I've seen most of the players this evening, Johnny Ward is not around. I wonder where he has gone. I usually keep track of where he is, just in case I might need protection, but looking up and down the rows of people, I don't see him.

Meanwhile, the king says, "I find this disagreeable, just as you do. However, the laws merely prohibit public performances of the dance. Therefore, I've arranged for private exhibitions at various places throughout the park. Any of you who want to see the hula performed in its traditional style are welcome to follow these young women to one of the spots and watch this most graceful dance for yourselves."

A chorus of cheers greets this announcement, followed by applause and many toasts to the good health of King Kalakaua. The young women move off, escorted by members of the king's royal household. No one asks me if I'd like to go and see a dance, so I stand and wait to see what happens.

I expected Jim Fogarty to be first in line to watch the hula, but strangely, he walks back toward the queen's palace. Probably because the queen's palace is where they serve the alcohol, and he just wants to drink a bit more before watching the dance, but just out of curiosity, and having nothing better to do, I follow. I also notice that since the king finished speaking, the flaming torches in some areas of the park have gone out, and no one refills them.

Fogarty walks to the bar, like I expected, but instead of getting a drink, walks by. Now I'm curious what he's doing. When he gets to the end of the hallway, he turns a corner to his right and disappears from my sight. After a couple moments, I turn and walk back outside, stopping to take in the view from the porch while I think about how to kill time until the end of the party. Even though the day was nice and warm, the evening is perfect. I can still smell a hint of salt in the gentle breeze.

After I've stood there a minute or two, I just happen to glance back inside the palace doors in time to see one of the women serving the drinks walk away from the bar and go down the hallway in the same direction as Fogarty.

I look to the other end of the porch, and notice another doorway there. It's wide open, so I walk to that door. The porch is empty except for me because most people are now at the hula dance, so I squat down and peer around the corner, feeling safe no one will notice what I'm doing. From here, I can see the length of the hallway where Fogarty went. My timing is just right. The moment I poke my head past the door frame and look down the hallway, the woman slips into one of the rooms while a man's arm closes the door behind her. It looks like Fogarty's arm, as best I can tell from this distance.

I know I shouldn't be spying around like this, but with everyone dispersed and watching the dances, I hope the danger isn't that great. I creep toward the door I saw close. Even though I walk carefully and my steps are quiet, they do make a tiny sound when I step on the thick blue carpet. I look over my shoulder. Still no one around. I get to the door. Still no sounds in the hallway. I press my ear to the door and listen. It's Fogarty's voice, all right, although I can't quite make out what he's saying. The problem isn't the thickness of the door but the fact that Fogarty's words aren't very clear. However, between his grunting and the moaning of the woman he's with, I have a good idea of what they're doing.

Just then, I hear a click. Someone just unlocked one of the other doors in the hallway! I need to hide!

I look up and down the hallway, but I'm right in the middle, and I'll never make it to either end in time. My only chance is ducking behind one of the planted ferns that line the edges of the hallway, so that's what I do. Luckily, it's a very large fern, and I'm small, but still, it's only a plant. It's the best chance I have, however, so I duck down just as the door opens. A head peeks out. It's Johnny Ward!

"Thank you," I hear him say. "It was wonderful."

"You are amazing," a woman's sultry voice purrs. "You're sure you can't stay another day? I'd love to show you a few more tricks." I hear a kiss.

"I'm afraid not," Ward says. "I'm also afraid I must get back to the party before someone notices my absence."

"Aww, are you sure?" Another kiss. "I'll make it worth it for you."

Peeking through the fronds of the fern, I see Ward scan the hallway. Lucky for me, he's looking for people walking around, so his gaze is at face level, not toward the floor where I hide. He hasn't noticed me yet.

"No," he says with a very friendly smile. "But thanks again. I'll go first. You follow after a few minutes."

With that, Johnny Ward, the recently married captain of the All-America team, steps out into the hallway, adjusts his tie, and walks toward the open doorway leading back to the party.

After taking a few steps, he stops. "Clarence, what are you doing there?" he turns and says to me, frowning deeply.

I need to think of a clever excuse. Quickly. "Mr. Ward," I manage to stammer, "I have something important to tell you. I didn't know where you were, but someone told me they saw you over here last."

"What might be so important that you had to tell me now?" he asks, still frowning, hands on his hips.

"I have important information about your brotherhood," I say, playing the only card I have.

His frown gets deeper and his lips tighten together. "Go on, then, but first, let's walk outside."

Once we find a place outside the palace I tell him, as well as I can remember, everything I heard Spalding, Anson, and Palmer talking about that evening in the Baldwin Hotel in San Francisco. I repeat what I heard about the Brush Plan really being Spalding's creation, about how Spalding chose Ward and Hanlon to come on

163

this trip partly so that they wouldn't be able to do anything about it, and how Palmer and Anson are both in on the plan. By the time I've finished, his mouth hangs open.

"You're sure about this?" he finally says to me when I'm done.

"You can keelhaul me or throw me overboard if I'm lying to you, Mr. Ward."

"I'm tempted to do that anyway, just for you snooping around, but, if you promise to never tell another soul about where you found me tonight, I'll offer you a deal instead."

"What is the deal?"

"I want you to, as best you can, try to find out more from Spalding, or Anson, or Palmer about their plans. I don't want you to shadow them around every day or listen outside of their ship cabin at night," he looks me straight in the eye and nods slowly while he says this, "because eventually they'll catch you, and the game will be up. However, if you happen to be around them and overhear anything, I want to know about it. I'll reward you with a nice, shiny, silver 50-cent souvenir for every good piece of information you bring me."

"I want to help, but it sounds risky, Mr. Ward. What if they do catch me?"

"Perhaps it's risky, but you're clever, Clarence. If worst comes to worst, and they suspect you, pretend to be a dumb kid who just blundered by. I know you're smarter than that, but Anson will go for it. Besides, is there any person in the world who hates you more than Anson does?"

"No, I think he's about the worst."

"Wouldn't you like to get back at him, then?"

"It does sound rather tempting. Okay, I agree to help."

"Excellent," Ward says. "Now, we'd better return to the party by separate routes. I need to find Hanlon. Tell no one else about this," Ward finishes, holding his index finger right between my eyes. "No one. Understood?"

"Yes, Captain Ward."

While Ward disappears into the night, I see him slip his wedding ring out of his pocket and put it back on his left hand. I wait a moment and then walk back to the gathering. I don't want anyone to notice me. I decide it's a good time to go back to the main tent because Spalding warned everyone before the luau that we must return to our steamer by 11 o'clock because we set sail tonight rather than in the morning.

I've made it only halfway back to the main tent, however, when someone does notice me. It isn't Anson or Pfeffer, thankfully, but Jimmy Ryan, which is almost as bad because he's become almost as hostile toward me as they are. I've never learned what caused him to have a change of heart and not like me, except that he spends lots of time with Anson and Pfeffer.

"Clarence, where have you been? We've been looking all around for you. King Kalakaua wants to meet you."

Although Ryan pronounces his words clearly, something seems a little different about him. When he turns around and walks back toward the tent, he wobbles a bit, so I suspect too much liquor. Still, his words take me by surprise. I had no idea the king even knew who I was.

"The king wants to meet me?"

"He does," Ryan says over his shoulder. "We've told him all about you, and he wants to meet an African. Although I can't fathom why."

"But I'm not an African. I was born in Kentucky."

"Same thing. Come along now."

Ryan enters the king's tent, and I follow. King Kalakaua and his royal household have resumed their seats. Ominously, Anson and Pfeffer are there, too, along with Palmer and Burns. Tommy Burns appears to have partied too hard, however, because he is leaning over the back of his chair, staring down, with a dumb look on his face. All these things make me nervous, so nervous that when the king speaks to me, I forget how to address him properly.

"You must be young Clarence Duval," King Kalakaua says to me.

"Yes sir, Mr. King."

Anson pounces on my mistake. "Address him as Your Highness, you dumb coon."

"I'm sorry," I stammer. "Please forgive me, Your Highness."

"Not to worry," the king, who luckily continues smiling rather than getting upset, says. "I've been called worse things than that. Have you enjoyed yourself this evening?"

"I have, very much so, sir. I don't usually get food this good back home. I very much enjoyed eating pineapple."

The king smiles at me again. "I imagine. It is one of my favorites, as well. What did you think of the hula dance?"

I didn't see the dance, so I must make something up on the spot. "The ladies are wonderfully skilled dancers, Your Highness."

"I understand you know some dances yourself, Clarence. I would like to see one."

"It's a fair way back to our hotel to get my marching baton. I don't know if I could toss it into the air and do my routine inside of your tent."

"No, I do not mean that kind of dance. Your friends, Mr. Anson and Mr. Pfeffer, tell me you are skilled in the plantation dances of the American Negro. I request that you do a plantation dance for me. I have never seen one."

Now I know what happened. Anson and Pfeffer must have tricked the king into thinking I like to do dances. Before I can even begin to protest, the two of them start clapping their hands, and Palmer, Burns, and Ryan join in.

"Give us a dance like the Negros dance in Alabama!" Pfeffer shouts out.

I squeeze my hands into fists and look down at the ground, hoping everyone won't see my face turning red. I want to run away. I can't, however, because the king doesn't know Anson and Pfeffer tricked him, and he has been a kindly host to us.

What do I do? I can't run away, but I hate dancing. I look up, not caring if anyone sees how angry I am. The king just looks at me, not aware Anson and Pfeffer tricked him, waiting.

"Dance, you coon! The king said to." Pfeffer gives me a little shove in the back.

I make up a silly dance, just like I had to do on the train platform back in Salt Lake City. I go on for three or four minutes, prancing around while singing nonsense about picking cotton all day. Finally, everyone stops clapping, and I stop. I'm almost ready to cry, but I can't do that in front of the king.

"Well done," King Kalakaua says. "Well done, indeed. I have always wanted to know how the Negro dances in America. I would ask to see another, but I fear it is time to send you on your way. Accept this present, Clarence, as a token of my thanks." The king shakes my hand and puts a coin in it.

To what's left of the group, he says, "I will always remember your visit to my kingdom fondly, but I fear the time has come when our ways must part. Your ship departs shortly."

I look at the coin the king handed me. It's a ten-dollar gold coin! I've never held such a valuable thing in my life. He says a few other words to the people present, but with all that just happened to me, I don't really hear them.

When I walk outside the tent, I can see most of our party gathering on the lawn, but I barely notice that. I am so ashamed, I don't even notice which players I ride with in the carriage. I just keep my head down or look out the open side window and blink back the tears. Or close my eyes and wait for the trip to end.

I'm not only ashamed and angry. I'm also confused. I always knew that Pfeffer and Anson hated me, and Ryan was getting that way, too, but until now, Palmer and Burns had both treated me decently. Now, I don't even know if I can trust them or anything they've told me so far on the trip. I know they were drinking and were at least halfway drunk, Burns more than halfway, but I don't care. How can I travel around the world if I don't have any friends at all?

I don't bother keeping track of time, but at some point, we are back at the hotel. Each of the players grabs his travel bags from the lobby, I pick up my knapsack, and we are back in the carriages, traveling down to the harbor to embark on the *Alameda* once again. After we get underway, I find a place on the steamer deck where I think no one can see me, and I cry. I put my head in my hands and sob until my eyes sting. After several minutes of that, I'm still upset. I take my gift from the king, the beautiful ten-dollar gold coin, and I throw it as far into the ocean as I can. It plops into the black water, and it's gone forever.

Chapter 15

December 1, 1888
South Pacific Ocean

I've stayed in my cabin almost the whole time since Honolulu, except to wash dishes and sweep the decks. I don't have the heart to talk to anyone because I don't know which people I can talk to anymore. It's lonely, but being lonely beats doing plantation dances. I also come out to get meals, most of the time, but it isn't until the first day of December that I venture out on deck by my own choice.

While hiding, I try to think of who I might still talk to. It's a short list. Maybe Newton MacMillan, the newspaper writer. I think he's okay. At least, he's never done me wrong so far. John Ward makes the list, especially since we made our bargain, but he spends his time talking to Ned Hanlon, who I know doesn't like me, so I don't see him very often. They are probably talking over things that are important to their Brotherhood. John Tener is probably the closest thing to a dependable friend I still have. I sit near him at meals whenever there's an open seat nearby. Several other ballplayers on the trip haven't ever been mean to me, but they mostly ignore me and don't care what I do. Ned Williamson, Ed Crane, Jim Manning, Tom Brown, George Wood, and Billy Earle are in that group. Spalding has important things to do and doesn't pay attention to me. The only times I've seen him the past few days, he's either eating a meal or looking at his map. Other than that, I haven't seen him since that horrible night in the Sandwich Islands.

The other thing I do, besides my chores, is that a couple of times, I've snuck up to the ship's library early in the morning when most people are still asleep and borrowed a couple of the books that look easy to read. I have them in my cabin, and sometimes I try to practice, but I've only spent a few months in school, so I don't get very far. Perhaps I need to find someone to teach me more about reading.

Although I'm still scared, eventually, I decide I should leave my cabin. It does get stuffy staying in one room. To escape the boredom, on December 1, I go up to the main deck and wander around. The weather is warm but pleasant, with a light sea breeze.

First, I head to the stern. The brown canvas cricket tent is back up, and I hear some of the men practicing. When I get closer, I can hear Anson's voice inside the tent, however, so I turn around.

I go the other direction, toward the bow because I hear some music playing. It seems that some passengers brought musical instruments and created a volunteer band. I'm just getting near them when they finish a catchy number. Sadly, the first voice I hear is Pfeffer's drawl.

"That's the way, gentlemen, that's the way! It warms my heart to have a few other true Southerners with us. Let's have another classic tune from the old days. I wish someone would find the nigger, so we can make him dance for us!"

Again, I retreat. I'd better try crossing to the other side of the ship. I do so, only to bump into Jim Fogarty and Tom Daly on my way.

"Clarence!" Fogarty proclaims. "You're just who we were looking for. We need your help, boy. Come with us."

I have no idea if this is a good thing or not. Fogarty and Daly do appear sober, which, while unusual, is promising. It's hard to tell if they like me or not; being two of the youngest members of our group, they spend so much time clowning around and drinking, I don't know if they take things seriously enough to hate anyone. It appears that whatever credit I earned in their eyes that night at the train depot in Utah Territory is gone. They insist I go with them, however, so I take my chances.

The two men hustle me over to a gathering on the port side of the ship. Various deck chairs are off on one side. In them sit some of the ballplayers; I recognize them as the Howling Wolves. Ned Williamson is there, with his wife, although she doesn't really look at me or seem to notice I'm there. Mark Baldwin and Bob Pettit sit next to them. Tom Daly walks over and joins them. The only Howling Wolf missing is Marty Sullivan, the Chicago outfielder who caught me when I leapt aboard the train that night.

Sitting on deck chairs across from the Howling Wolves are several other people who are not part of our group. A couple of them are sailors on the ship. They wear bright white clothes with blue trim, and they're smiling when I arrive. My sense of danger lessens a bit.

I see two chairs set apart from the rest. Fogarty walks over and occupies one. He bangs together two blocks of wood he obtained from somewhere and calls out, "Ladies and gentlemen of the jury, this court is now called to order. Our sergeant-at-arms, Clarence Duval, is now present and ready to do his duty."

Here, Fogarty winks at me, and now I know that one of Fogarty's games is afoot. He continues by saying, "Mr. Duval, will you please escort the defendant, Marty Sullivan, to the witness stand." He points to Sullivan.

I finally notice that Sullivan stands off to one side, his hands tied in someone's shirt and his head down. Fogarty motions to the empty chair, so I take Sullivan by the arm and lead him there.

"Mr. Sullivan," Fogarty begins, "you are charged with bringing a curse upon the good ship *Alameda* by being seated and minding your own business when an albatross fell into your lap. The sentence for this crime is solitary confinement until we cross the Equator this evening, thus lifting the curse. How do you plead?"

"Your Honor, please allow me to speak in my defense. It is true that, approximately one hour ago, I sat taking in the view from the deck when an injured albatross fell into my lap. You see, said bird struck the smokestack of our vessel, injuring itself in the process, and plummeted deckward in consequence. Through no fault of my own, I merely happened to be sitting directly below the bird when it fell. This proves a lack of premeditation on my part to curse our vessel. As further proof, I have already paid due penance for my actions; may it please the court to note that said albatross, upon falling into my lap, proceeded to peck me on the arm, leaving a bruise before I could discard it from my lap and onto the deck. Therefore, your honor, I plead not guilty to the charge of cursing the *Alameda*, owing to lack of intent to curse the ship and to the inconvenience already suffered in massaging the pain from my arm."

"The jury will note your testimony, Mr. Sullivan. I understand that a member of the crew would like to testify in this case? Sergeant Duval," Fogarty says, facing me, "please escort the witness from the stand. Next, bring Mr. Robinson to testify on behalf of the cursed crew of the *Alameda*."

I do as Fogarty requests and lead one of the sailors to the witness chair. He looks like he's been a sailor for several years. His beard reaches his chest, and some of the strands of hair have gone to gray. I see several tattoos on his left arm, and Robinson's face has the leathery, weathered look of someone who's been at sea for years. Still, he's smiling and has a hop in his step.

Fogarty continues. "Sailor Robinson, as a man with years of experience, you would like to provide expert testimony regarding this case?"

"Indeed, Your Honor," Robinson says, now speaking very earnestly while looking Fogarty straight in the eye. "On behalf of the crew of the *Alameda*, I wish to testify as to the seriousness of this event. For nearly a century, all sailors have known what bad luck it is to kill an albatross while at sea. Fortunately, in this case, no one killed the bird. It only suffered burns from the hot smokestack and an injured wing from the collision. Still, it is best to take no chances under these circumstances, for none can escape the consequences of this unlucky act. The defendant has, most certainly, cursed the crew because he was the first man to touch the injured bird, and so Mr. Sullivan is the focus of the dark magic afflicting us. Therefore, on behalf of the crew of the *Alameda*, I urge the court to find the defendant guilty and keep him away from the rest of the crew until we can nurse the albatross back to health and it can fly once more."

"Your honor, I request permission to cross-examine the witness," Sullivan declares.

"Permission granted."

"Sailor Robinson, does the steamer *Alameda* employ any cross-eyed men among its crew?"

"No, it does not. That would be bad luck."

"Do you prefer black horses or white ones?"

"White horses, of course."

"Do you expectorate over your right shoulder, or over your left?"

"Over the left shoulder, certainly."

"May it please Your Honor and the jury to note," Sullivan pauses for effect, "that Sailor Robinson's answers to these questions clearly demonstrate that he is a man of excessive superstition. Of course, no difference exists between black and white horses, either physical or metaphysical, nor does the shoulder over which one spits have any practical significance. Therefore, I move that my case be dismissed as nothing but fear and paranoia on the part of a few crew members."

Fogarty nods. Somehow, he still has a straight face. "The jury will consider your testimony and this evidence, Mr. Sullivan. You may step down now, Mr. Robinson. Sergeant Duval, please escort him back to his deck chair."

Once I've done that, Fogarty faces the rest of the Howling Wolves seated in their deck chairs. "Will the jury render a decision?"

The Howling Wolves circle their chairs for discussion. It doesn't take long, however, for them to return their verdict.

Mrs. Williamson stands up and faces Fogarty. "We have made our decision, Your Honor."

"What is the jury's decision, my lady?"

The Wolves let forth their usual howl.

"Guilty as charged! Court adjourned." With that, Fogarty bangs his blocks of wood together with a grin, and then he leads Sullivan away to solitary confinement, wherever that happens to be.

Because no one needs me anymore as a sergeant, I wander off again in search of something to do. My path takes me by the ship's library. Typically, the library is empty of ballplayers, at least whenever I've gone in for a look in the morning, although Ward, Tener, Palmer, and a couple of the other men go in to read now and again. Today, however, to my surprise, many people have gathered there, including some of the ballplayers. I notice both Ward and Tener are present. Because this is about as safe of company as I'll find today, I go in and sit down behind them quietly.

I soon discover why so many people have come to the library at this moment: An Englishman stands in front of the group speaking. At least, his accent sounds English. He is an older man, past sixty for certain, but he stands tall and erect. The man also has an enormous beard that is a mixture of gray and black hair. It reaches the middle of his chest. He paces back and forth while he speaks, hands clasped behind his back, and his voice projects very clearly. I think he just finished a story of some kind because several of the boys start peppering him with questions.

I turn to John Tener to find out what's going on. "Who is this man, Mr. Tener?"

"This, Clarence, is Major General Strange of the British Army."

Then John Ward speaks out. "General, what can you tell us about your service in India? Were you there during the Mutiny of 1857?"

"Ay, I was. Marched across the scorched, burning plains of the North with my column, pacifying villages as we went. I arrived in the colony in October of '57 and went to Benares. There I earned my first of four commendations while quelling the Mutiny when I decided to make an example of some mutineers my men captured by tying them to the mouth of a cannon before opening fire.

"I was part of Campbell's relief of Lucknow in 1857, too, and we recaptured the city in March of '58. The rebellious Nawabs nearly had us whipped once, but with iron discipline provided by my officers, my sepoy troops held on, and we drove them back. A close thing it was, but by God, we British are the finest race of soldiers alive. No offense meant to our American friends, of course."

Several listeners nod. It seems they took no offense. Ed Crane asks another question, and while he does, I tug on Tener's sleeve and ask him something else.

"Mr. Tener, what are Nawabs and sepoys? I don't know what they are."

"The Nawabs, I believe, were the princes in India who tried to rebel against British rule back in 1857. The sepoys are the Indian troops that the British used to help put down the rebellion."

"The British came to America to get Indians to help them fight?"

A laugh. "No, Clarence. The country of India, where these Indians live, is in Asia. We are going to go there and play ball before our trip is over. It is confusing, I know, but they are a different people than our Indians, even though they have the same name."

Then Tener decides to speak up and ask Strange a question of his own.

"General, after all that meritorious service to the British Empire, the military glory, and high adventure, how come you have to travel amongst such relative nobodies as we Americans? Why not a British military vessel, like you deserve?"

"I was hoping you might ask that, my young American friend. For, after all I've done in the name of Her Majesty, Queen Victoria, to spread civilization to the benighted, backward colonial masses and maintain the glory of the Empire, I'm afraid my tale does not end in a happy manner. Although I've spent my life bringing enlightenment, Christian values, and morality to the pagan hordes of India and fought for Her Majesty the Queen for the better part of three decades, my reputation has fallen on hard times. However, as a gentleman and honorable member of the British Army, I will tell you the full story and leave you to judge the merits of the case.

"In 1884, I retired, temporarily as it turned out, from the Queen's service and took up residence in Alberta. The province of Alberta, I'm sure you recall, is one of the provinces of our Dominion of Canada, just across the border from your Montana Territory. There, I planned to raise horses on a ranch for the remainder of my days. Good, strong horses fit for military service, in order that I might make one final contribution to the glory my country.

"My retirement proved brief, however, because the next year the Troubles of 1885 broke out in Canada. Perhaps this merited coverage in your American newspapers, perhaps not, but in that year, the Canadian government had an unfortunate bit of trouble with a group of savages known as the Métis, some of who were from your nation."

"We have many Indian tribes in the United States, which you know well, that sometimes cross the border into your territory," John Ward breaks in. "But I've not heard of the Métis. What can you tell us of them?"

"Very little you need to know, save that they are another of the buffalo-hunting tribes of the Northern prairies. The word Métis is French, as you've probably guessed. In our more civilized language,

176

the word translates as 'mixed' or 'mixed-blood.' Your newspapers
may also refer to these people as Cree Indians, but in truth, they are
a mixture of many peoples, some European, some Indian. Although
they tend to look more Indian than white, many have European,
especially French, names."

"You mean they're mongrel half-breeds." I hadn't even noticed
Anson come in, but sure enough, there he is, standing to my right at
the back of the room.

"Some use that term, yes," Strange continues. "Regardless of
what name you give them, in '85 they began something we British
call the Northwest Rebellion. They claimed to be protecting their
homeland, but as roving buffalo hunters, they have no real homeland
in the eyes of civilized people. Their leader, as it turned out, was an
American citizen, Louis Riel, if you recall the name."

"Where is the villain now? Languishing in prison somewhere, I
hope?" Anson replies.

"Oh, we did much better than that. After defeating the rebels at
the Battle of Batoche, we captured and hung the traitor Riel in
November of 1885."

"You did both our nations a favor, then," Anson answers.

"This all sounds to the good so far, General," Tener interjects.
"But you gave us the impression that somehow your government did
not fully appreciate your services in suppressing the rebellion."

"Yes, I was just getting to that part. My role in winning the Battle
of Batoche was that I raised a volunteer force of Albertan ranchers
and farmers to deal with the insurgents. We took a heavy toll on the
women and children of our enemy in the teepee settlements and log
cabins of the rebels on our way to the battle, where my company
fought bravely and honorably. However, some young and ambitious
junior officers reported that my men and I engaged in unnecessary
violence against the women and children of the mixed-bloods. They
accused my men of looting, raping, and pillaging too frequently
along our route to Batoche. These young officers also claimed I had
recruited vigilantes, rather than volunteer soldiers."

"Those scoundrels!" Anson shouts.

"Yes, indeed. Sad to say, their reports caused enough of a sensation in London that the army's high command decided to deprive me of my commission as an army officer. After all I'd done in the name of Queen and Empire, the War Ministry in London dismissed me for killing some rebellious savages in time of rebellion."

While everyone thinks over the general's story and begins commenting to each other, the thought occurs to me that, perhaps, it was unnecessary to kill women and children, especially if it happened on the way to, rather than during, the battle, but most others in the room angrily curse the villains in the high command of the British Army, so perhaps I don't fully understand the situation.

Strange continues his appeal to his new friends, saying, "I leave you to judge whether my treatment is just. In my effort to validate my conduct and restore the good name of my family, I travel to London alongside you noble Americans. Furthermore, as befits a man whose grandfather fought for the great Wellington against Napoleon at Waterloo, I've begun a book of military history, a memoir that will, I trust, restore me to the good graces of my superiors by giving the true account of my conduct and service to the Empire. I've decided to title it *Gunner Jingo's Jubilee*."

All assembled agree that the title is a good one, and wish the general luck in his quest to restore his honor. I try again to understand what is so honorable about killing unarmed women and children, but perhaps I'm just not old enough to understand such things.

"Excuse me, General," Ward asks at this point. "You said that some of the Métis who took part in this rebellion were from the United States?"

"Yes. Because the Métis have no permanent homes, some of them freely cross our mutual border, which they call the Medicine Line. Back in the days of the buffalo, they did so mostly for the hunt. Now that the buffalo are gone, they claim they are visiting family members, although because they are uncivilized heathens, I often doubt this claim."

The buffalo. I don't know why the buffalo are gone, but somehow, it makes me sad to know that they are no more. I've seen photographs of them, of course. They were huge, shaggy beasts that used to graze on the grasses of the Dakotas. They were so big compared to people they looked like they weighed at least one thousand pounds! Even though all they did was eat grass, whenever I saw them in the pictures, they seemed to have some strength and calmness, some nobility, about them, somehow. Well, maybe those aren't the right words for it. I don't know if an animal can be noble, but I just liked the way they looked in the photographs.

For no good reason, I decide that when I get back to the United States, I'd like to go looking for a buffalo, just to see if any remain out in the West. Maybe I'll even meet a Métis person. If they are homeless, like General Strange reports, then we will have something in common. Perhaps they can help me find a buffalo. While everyone files out of the ship's library, I decide I'd like to try that someday. He said some lived in Montana Territory. That name has a good sound to it. Maybe I'll go there.

Chapter 16

December 2, 1888
South Pacific Ocean

"I think there may have been something true about the curse of the albatross, Mr. Burns," I say as the ship's motion throws me against the wall of the passageway. Ouch! I smash my right shoulder before I can brace myself.

"What are you talking about, Clarence? What curse?"

"Yesterday, an albatross fell on Mr. Sullivan, and the sailor said it cursed the ship."

"That's nonsense."

"Well, it did get really stormy right afterward, didn't it?"

The ship tilts the other way now, and tosses my left side against the wall this time. I remembered to brace myself a bit, though, so it doesn't hurt as much.

"Yes, this is a big storm, but birds don't cause storms to happen, Clarence. If there's any cursing to be done, you should be cursing me."

"Now I'm the one who doesn't follow, Mr. Burns."

"I did you wrong in Honolulu, Clarence. I drank too much and wasn't on my guard when Anson and Pfeffer started talking to the king about having you dance. It was my idea to invite you on our trip, anyway, so I should have watched out for you better."

Slam! Now it's back to my right side hitting the other side of the passageway. I need to keep paying attention to what the ship's doing, so I don't hurt myself.

Burns continues. "Why are you out and about now, Clarence? Oh, that's right, you don't get seasick easily. Your sea legs are very strong."

"I just want to see the big waves, Mr. Burns. I've never been in a storm at sea, and I want to know what they look like."

"Well, let's go and look."

We reach the deck, both holding fast to the railing while we watch. It is difficult to describe what it's like to be at sea when a storm strikes. Words fail to describe the situation and do it justice. It is very scary the first time it happens. The waves get bigger. Much bigger. In calm waters, large ships like ours bob up and down very gently. Even though some people get seasick from this at first, after a day or two, most people are not sick anymore.

Now, however, that gentle rolling is gone. Instead, whenever we reach a wave, the bow of the ship rises, and when we crest the wave and it passes by the ship, you slam down rapidly. In the process, every wave coats the deck of the ship with a new sheet of salt water, and things get slippery if you go on deck. At least I'm relieved of my sweeping duties for now.

"I'm nervous, Mr. Burns. Will the waves throw us overboard if we walk around?" I half-shout to Burns, just so I'm sure he hears me.

"I don't think so, unless you do something stupid like go to the bow of the boat and put yourself at risk," he yells back.

"Will our ship sink?"

"No, that's not likely, either. Maybe in the old days, when ships were wood, but with modern ships that shouldn't happen. Still, I'm glad we have you on board for good luck, Clarence."

Even though Burns tells me things are safe, I'm not sure I believe him all the way. I'm more than a little scared to stay on deck or try to move around the ship.

Then, we both hear a loud crashing sound.

"Did we hit something, Mr. Burns? Is the ship going down?"

He laughs, although I can hardly hear him because another wave throws spray all over us. I can taste the salt water while it runs off my face. "No, Clarence, that is the gong for dinner, remember? Let's go. I think my stomach is okay to eat. How's yours?"

"Fine, I think."

"Follow me, Clarence."

Burns half-pulls, half-drags me up the stairway to the dining room because neither of us can stay steady on our feet. At least the stairway has handrails, so we don't crash into the walls quite so violently.

When we reach the door to the dining room and while Burns pulls it open, I take another look back at the waves. One very big one looms up in front of the ship like a gray wall. Then the nose of the ship starts climbing up the wave until we reach the top, followed by another swift drop into the trough between the waves. I probably shouldn't have looked because now that I've seen how big some of the waves are, I'm even more scared than before.

My curiosity about the waves satisfied, I'm grateful when Burns pulls open the door that leads to the dining room, shoves me inside, and slams it shut behind us.

Another thing that changes on a ship during a big storm is that normal activities, like cooking and eating food, get a lot more difficult.

When we finally get our bearings and look around, we find chaos. It's hard to describe how funny it is to watch the passengers try to eat while the ship tilts back and forth. Most try to time taking bites of food in between the waves that rock the ship. Some, although not all, succeed. Everyone sports a stained napkin on the front of his or her chest, not to mention stains in other locations. The smarter diners, it seems to me, have given up trying to eat anything that requires sauce or garnish, because that tends to end up on their napkins, the tablecloth, or the floor.

Burns and I sit down.

"What should we do, Clarence? How does one eat under these conditions?"

"Look over there, Mr. Burns."

I point at one of the waiters. He has on a dark dinner jacket over a white shirt and wears a black bow tie and white gloves, just like the waiters usually do. The man has a plate of food in hand and is about to hand it to a diner politely when the ship crests a wave and drops down suddenly.

The poor waiter loses his balance, and the food, several slices of roast beef covered in gravy, slop all over the table. Some of the gravy splashes the chest of the diners, one man and one woman, on the other side of the table.

"I beg your pardons, sir and madam! I'm ever so sorry."

As quickly as possible, the waiter grabs a cloth napkin and tries to blot out the stains on the table while the passengers do the same to their clothes.

I expect them to scold the waiter, but, instead, they just laugh.

"Oh, Clarence, watch this!" Burns points to another waiter approaching a different table.

Knowing the ship is about to drop down again, he goes to one knee for balance. It works, but when he rises, the ship starts riding up the next wave, and he loses his balance and falls over backward, buttered pieces of corn spilling all over the floor.

Laughing, one of our ballplayers, the burly pitcher Ed Crane, extends his hand to the unfortunate man and helps him to his feet. The waiter bows, gathers the rolling pieces of corn from the dining room floor, and returns to the kitchen.

We watch the struggling waiters for a while longer. A few make it to their tables and deliver their food, and when they do, everyone nearby claps enthusiastically. I'm impressed at everyone's good mood. Instead of misfortune, they've taken the storm and decided to have fun with it.

"Well, Clarence," Burns tells me, "I think I will pass on any food that won't stay in one place on my plate."

"I think I have an idea, Mr. Burns."

I reach out for the basket of dinner rolls at our table. I take one, and then another. Soon, nearly a dozen of them lie piled on my plate.

"A capital idea, Clarence. Just eat food that can't stain your clothing or slide around. Well done, my boy."

Burns calls for another basket of rolls, and that's our dinner for December 2.

Once the storm passes, the rest of this leg of our voyage passes without many interesting incidents, except one. It happens on December 8, just when we sight land. Even though our main destination is Australia, it seems our next stop is Auckland, New Zealand, and once we know we are only a few hours from port, our players gather on the main deck for some announcements from Spalding. Even the captain of the ship, Captain Morse, is there.

As usual, I look for a safe person to stand next to while Spalding talks. MacMillan is there, and I have not spoken with him for several days, so I choose to stand by his side and hope he won't mind my presence.

Spalding begins by saying, "Gentlemen, as we near port at Auckland and the latest stage of our voyage on the *Alameda* comes to an end, I believe I speak for everyone here when I offer our most hearty thanks to Captain Morse for his skilled and careful handling of the ship these past weeks."

Almost all the players shout something in agreement, while the captain smiles at the acknowledgment.

"Therefore," Spalding continues, "on behalf of the Chicago and All-America teams, it is my pleasure to present to you, Captain Morse, the sum of two hundred dollars as a token of our gratitude and appreciation of our time aboard your vessel."

Captain Morse's face brightens considerably at this unexpected news, which is saying something. Whenever I've seen him on this voyage, which is usually at meals, he's always smiling, talking pleasantly with the passengers, or telling a funny story to someone. One reason I see him frequently at meals is that he never misses one. Although I see no way to decide the winner, some of the players have a bet going, with a prize for the one who correctly guesses the weight of Captain Morse. The most common bet is something near 275 pounds, although some guesses go quite a bit higher than that. The overweight captain starts into a speech to thank Spalding for the gift when Newton MacMillan turns to me.

"I'll say, Clarence, the captain has been a gentleman of the first order on our trip. He is quite the storyteller. Several evenings during the past two weeks, we have had the pleasure of listening to his tales of sailing the Pacific. He claims to have twenty-three years of experience as a captain, and no one questions the claim. The captain also says he was an athlete in his younger days, which some of the men are rather more inclined to dispute. Has he told you any of his stories?"

"I'm afraid not, Mr. MacMillan. No one ever invites me to visit with the captain. I haven't had the chance to because I have to wash dishes and sweep the deck."

"That is a pity. I've not seen you much this past week, Clarence. What have you been up to, besides your duties?"

"I spend the days mostly keeping to myself, sir. I watch the waves, and I think about things back in Chicago. Even though they feed us mighty well on this ship, I worry a bit about what I'll do when the trip is over."

"Well, you still have a few months to think about that, my boy, just as long as we don't miss too many more days between now and then."

"We missed a day, sir? I don't think I understand."

"If you've been spending time in your cabin, perhaps no one told you. Two days ago, it was Thursday, December 6. Yesterday was Saturday, December 8. We missed Friday altogether."

"I still don't follow, Mr. MacMillan."

"Thursday evening, we crossed over an invisible line called the International Date Line, which means that the day on the calendar moves forward one day. Because we crossed near midnight, the calendar moved forward two days instead of one, essentially. So, except for a couple minutes near midnight, we skipped Friday."

I'm still not sure I understand how an entire day of the week just disappears, but I don't get to ask any more questions because the captain finishes his speech and Spalding rises from his seat to address the group once again.

"You are most welcome, Captain Morse, and we shall never forget your kind hospitality to us aboard the *Alameda*. However, I must take this opportunity to inform the men of one new development. These past days, I have pored over maps and schedules and timetables, and, to my dismay, I have concluded that the planned leg of our tour that takes us across India is too ambitious. I do not believe we would be able to accomplish such a journey while still leaving ample time to tour in the great cities of Europe like so many of you desire to do. Therefore, after we sail from Australia to Ceylon, we will proceed due west on our way to Egypt from there.

"I am sorry, men, for I desire to see some of the mysterious Orient and learn its eternal wisdom just as much as you do, but I am afraid the days are too short if we are to return to America by April and the start of the championship schedule. In the meantime, however, we are near to landfall in New Zealand, and I know you are all anxious to put your feet on solid ground once more and resume playing ball. Let us prepare to debark, so we are ready when the moment arrives."

A few of the men mutter something under their breath, or look over their shoulders and frown, but most take it in stride. Knowing nothing about India, I don't know if I am happy or sad about it. I suppose it depends on whether people in India like parades. My favorite feeling is leading the ballplayers onto the field in front of a cheering crowd of people. I'll have a chance to do that again soon, I hope. Maybe it will help me shake the misery and sadness of the past week.

Before going to my cabin to prepare my knapsack, however, I get up my courage and decide to speak to MacMillan again.

"Mr. MacMillan, sir, may I ask you something else?"

"I suppose, Clarence. Despite what Al just said, we still have ample time before making port."

"Since you write for the Chicago newspapers, you know a lot about reading and writing, don't you?"

"I guess I do. I know less than some, but more than most, if I may say so."

"When we put out to sea again and leave Australia, would you help me learn to read better? I promise to try my best to learn. I want to learn how."

"How much schooling have you had, Clarence?"

"Not that much, sir. A year or so, when I was younger, but never all at the same time. My parents tried to make me go for a little while, before they disappeared. I can say the letters, and read some of the easy words, but I can't read books very well. I want to learn to read them better. I think it's important."

"You're right; it is very important. I will think about your request, Clarence. There may be some time for me to teach you a thing or two. First, however, I think we'd best get ready and pack our things. There's no hurry, but no sense in dawdling, either."

After MacMillan finishes speaking, I realize how nervous I am and how fast my heart pumps. I'd never thought too much about reading when I lived in Chicago. You don't need to read to do odd jobs like sweeping floors and washing windows. But, I've had a lot of time to think on this sea voyage, and I've decided that if I'm ever going to do more than odd jobs during my life, I need some of the skills that grownups have. One of those skills is knowing how to read and write.

Chapter 17

December 14, 1888
Sydney, New South Wales, British Empire

"What city is this again, Mr. MacMillan?"
"Sydney, in Australia."
"We're finally in Australia."

"Aye, we are, my boy. You'll have to come out of your cabin again and go ashore with us, Clarence."

"It's true I've been hiding in my room again, for almost the entire two days since Auckland, but I'm not hiding from anyone this time, Mr. MacMillan."

"Was it the weather, then?"

"Yes, sir. Two more days of storms, and the water always splashing the deck, and the booming noise each time we strike another wave, it was all a bit too much for me, I'm afraid."

"Are you still nervous the ship will go down? Tommy Burns said you were."

"Not so much, sir, at least, not anymore. I don't think I'll wash overboard, either, because and no one else has yet."

MacMillan smiles at this, and strokes his mustache. "Things have been rather rocky of late. Even I got a bit weary of the ship lifting up, then down, up, then down, for hours at a time."

"Me too. I thought I had good sea legs, but I think they've deserted me these past days. I haven't felt very well. Miserable, in fact."

"So, you are ready, like the rest of us, to touch *terra firma* once more."

"Does that mean solid ground?"

"Very good, Clarence."

"Yes, Mr. MacMillan. It's high time, I think."

"Well, the storm did let up earlier this morning. How do you feel now?"

"Better, but not quite myself. I don't know if I'm quite ready for a parade yet."

While we speak, our ship enters the harbor in Sydney, and the scene is not what I expected.

"Wow! Look at all those ships, Mr. MacMillan. Are all of them here to greet us? They are all different sizes, too."

"Yes. I see steamers, tugs, even rowboats. And look over there, Clarence, at the Sydney lighthouse."

"I see it! Look at the size of that American flag. Over there, look! The people are waving at us, or waving their handkerchiefs, their fans, or their umbrellas."

Instead of replying to this, MacMillan just smiles and shakes his head back and forth slowly.

"Some of these boats have American flags, too. Are they cheering for us?"

MacMillan still doesn't say anything, but I think they must be, because now all the boys at the ship's rail start cheering and waving back. MacMillan takes out his notebook, and starts scribbling down notes for his next newspaper article, so I wait a bit before asking him why our arrival is so special.

When he stops, I ask him, "Mr. MacMillan, it sure looks like everyone in Sydney is happy to see us."

"So it would seem," he says, still with half a smile.

"How come so many people came to greet us? This is a lot different than Honolulu, or even San Francisco."

"So it would seem."

"They must really love Americans here in Sydney."

"So it would seem."

"Why is Billy Earle crying?"

"I think the response to our arrival and the affection shown by the colonists of Sydney have overwhelmed him. Or, maybe, he's just glad to see land again, so he won't be seasick for a while, but I'll assume the best and tell my readers back in Chicago that it was the glory and pomp of our reception."

"You don't seem to feel the same. Is that because your newspaper just wants you to keep to the facts?"

MacMillan gives a broader smile while he scans the scene. "No, Clarence, rest assured that the readers of the *Chicago Herald* will find a soul-stirring account of our arrival when my letter describing events reaches our press in Chicago. You can bet that they will read all about the beautiful display of love for all things American by the freedom-loving people of Australia. Indeed, I'll tell them it is a diplomatic event without precedent and complete proof of the grand success of our expedition."

"Your tone of voice sounds different than usual. Is there something else going on that I can't see?"

"I have my reasons for displaying some sarcasm, yes. Prime among them is the fact that Leigh Lynch, Mr. Spalding's agent in Sydney, has arranged for this day and promoted the event for the better part of a month. I wouldn't be surprised if Lynch has paid some of these people to sail out and greet us. That certainly fits with Al Spalding's character as a businessman."

"He paid people to come and greet us? Why would Mr. Spalding, or Mr. Lynch, do that?"

191

"It is good business, Clarence. The greater the story our arrival becomes, the more the local newspapers will write about us and promote our ball games here in Australia. That means more people will pay to see the games, and Mr. Spalding will make more money. It is a form of advertising."

"Is that also why you plan to write about things and make them seem so perfect for your newspaper article?"

"It is. The people of Chicago want to read that our trip is a grand success in every way. They want to read how people all over the world love Americans and that those people will adopt baseball enthusiastically once we expose them to it. Because that is what they want to read about, later, when I write about our games here in Australia, I'll tell them about how we instantly convinced many foreigners of the superiority of baseball once they witnessed the game firsthand. That sells newspapers and helps me keep my job. I'll wager my friend Palmer is writing the same thing right now."

"I see."

"I know what you're probably thinking, Clarence. It isn't lying, exactly; it's just portraying things in their most favorable light. All the newspapers do the same thing because they need to sell papers to people and make money if they want to stay in business, and people want to read about success, so they can feel good. Americans want to believe that Americans are the best at everything, so I tell them that we are. That makes them happy, so they read my columns more often in the future.

"Look at all these boats and ships in the harbor. How many do you think we can see? Fifty? Seventy-five? One hundred? I have no idea exactly how many, and I don't plan to count them, but it's a great many ships. When I write my newspaper article, I pick the most favorable number and write that there were one hundred ships in the harbor to greet us. Even if Leigh Lynch paid some of them to be here, others are here on their own, so I can write that we saw an enthusiastic gathering, and I'm still telling the truth. For the most part."

"I think I get it."

"Any exaggerations aside, it is a stirring view, is it not? Besides the lighthouse, the harbor has parks that go all the way to the water's edge, English residences made of stone in the old style, modern frame houses, and so many beautiful trees."

"What was the big building at the mouth of the harbor we just passed? The one across from the lighthouse."

"A fort to guard the approaches to the harbor. Its name is Fort Dennison, I believe. And see, Clarence, the wide avenue ringing the docks, where all the carriages wait? So clean and orderly, compared to the docks of Chicago."

"Yes, sir, it certainly is nice. How much longer until we land? My sea legs are getting a bit more tired, if you catch my meaning."

"You are not the only one, Clarence, trust me. To answer your question, I'd say not long. We will land at Woolloomooloo Dock, the captain tells me. I had to get him to spell it for me; the name is quite a mouthful. It is probably a leftover from when the dark savages were the only ones populating this beautiful land."

I'm not sure how I should respond to this last statement. For a moment, I have a flashback to Denver and the newspaper article about hunting kangaroos with spears among the cannibals. I shuffle my feet and look at the ground for a moment while I think.

"Look at the city now," MacMillan goes on, taking no notice of my hesitation. "Civilization, progress, manufactures, and substantial buildings. The city of Sydney is almost as modern as what we left back in the United States. I do believe they've paved some of the streets, too. Impressive for a colonial city, wouldn't you say?"

After we land, throngs of people continue cheering us along our route to the hotel. I wonder, after what MacMillan told me, if Lynch paid these people to be here as well. I suppose I'll never know, but I don't really mind the warm welcome. I don't have to lead a parade this time; instead, I ride in a carriage with a few of the players. Again, I don't mind because my legs remain a little shaky.

When the carriage stops, I find out that Lynch had to make accommodations for us at two separate hotels. One, called the Grosvenor, is where we are now. It isn't nearly as big as the Baldwin Hotel in San Francisco but looks very modern all the same. I'm standing in a wide courtyard in front where all the carriages pull up. The building has five floors. The first features a shaded walkway that serves as the entrance to the lobby. To the right and left of the walkway broad, green canvas awnings overhang large windows, so the people in the hotel's dining room won't have bright sunshine disturb their meals. The second and third floor rooms have large balconies that face the courtyard and give a fine view of part of the city. These rooms also have large windows shaded by thick curtains. On the top two floors, the windows are smaller and less grand in size, and they don't have porches to take in the air, although I'd imagine the view up there helps compensate for that.

Some of the players, plus Spalding, get down from the carriages here and hand their belongings to the hotel porters. This is not where I get to stay, however, and I note with some concern that none of the Howling Wolves seem like they're staying at the Grosvenor, either.

The other hotel, the one where I stay along with Fogarty and the other Howling Wolves, is much smaller and rundown-looking. I guess we are here to keep us from disturbing the nicer guests with our presence. We must unload quickly, however, and then return to the Grosvenor, to keep to the agenda for today.

After we arrive back at the Grosvenor, I see Spalding standing nearby, dressed in his nicest suit. It's a black tuxedo suit, with bow tie, navy vest underneath the tuxedo jacket, and expensive, tailored black pants. Another man, who I gather is Leigh Lynch, stands next to Spalding and claps his hands to draw attention.

"Hasty now, my friends," Lynch says. "We are expected for the play within the hour. An American who lives here in Australia, Jimmy Williamson, runs the Royal Theater in Sydney, and he has extended an invitation for all the ballplayers to attend tonight's performance. Like its name suggests, the Royal Theater is a high-class affair, so you'll want to wear your best suits."

"How are we going to wear our suits?" Ned Hanlon asks Lynch. "The ship's crew is still unloading some of our luggage down at the docks."

"Oh dear. Oh my," Lynch says. "This is an unwelcome development. I'm afraid the bad weather must have delayed you ever so slightly and upset our schedule. Whatever will we do? No suits to wear, oh my."

"We will have to go as we are, I suppose," says Spalding. "We'll apologize for our appearance, should the need arise. Not attending would be the grosser insult, I would say."

"Yes, I'm afraid there's nothing else for it," Lynch answers. "Well, men, do your best under the circumstances, dismal as they are. I'll head over to the theater now and inform Mr. Williamson of our misfortune."

This time, it's John Ward's turn to tell me that I must stay at the hotel rather than go to the performance. When he walks toward me, he walks slowly, his head is down, and he's looking off to the side.

I decide to say it first.

"I'm not to see the play, am I, Mr. Ward?"

"I'm afraid not, Clarence. The invitation is for the ballplayers and newspaper reporters only. Maybe one of these days you'll get a chance, my young friend. Not tonight, however." He sighs. "I know, it isn't right. Maybe next time."

He says this last sentence with so little energy in his voice, I'm pretty sure he doesn't mean it.

The next morning at breakfast I overhear Jim Fogarty, Tom Daly, and Mark Baldwin discussing the previous evening at the theater. They must have returned very late, for even though their rooms are near mine, I was long asleep before any of them got back.

195

Daly says, "Smashing good performance last evening. I enjoyed it enough I wasn't even thirsty for a beer until the speeches at the end."

"Yes, *Struck Oil* was fine as far as plays go, but a dreadfully boring affair those speeches were," Baldwin answers him. "I'm sure that whatever that legislator, Mr. O'Connor, said was fine in a political sort of way, but who cares? They could have cut that from the program, along with Spalding's reply, and got us back here thirty minutes sooner. That might have left us time for drinking somewhere along the way. Still, I'm sure Pfeffer and Anson enjoyed the encore performance, the one about the dangers of Chinese immigration."

"I guess we should feel honored that Williamson invited us up on the stage, though; that was a nice touch," Fogarty chimes in. "I half expected that when Pfeffer got up there he might overturn some of the Chinatown props, just like he did in that Joss house back in San Francisco, but he held his temper this time. It would have made quite an ending to an eventful day."

Baldwin says, "Yeah, we should have given him a few drinks of good Kentucky whiskey beforehand. That might have been fun, but it was only our first night in town, and we didn't know the good watering holes yet. By tonight, we'll be ready," he finishes with a smile and a high-pitched laugh.

Daly adds, "This life really ain't too bad. Play some ball, sail around on the water, and drink when you can get it. Just imagine if Mike Kelly were here. He'd have found a way to get whiskey last night, I'll bet you. We're all just amateurs, compared to King Kelly."

Next, it is Fogarty's turn, and he says, "Men, I have an important question we must consider here and now. You have seen the notices posted for us that we are to meet the mayor of Sydney before our game today. That means we'll have to sit through another round of speeches. The question, then, is shall this be the day when the Howling Wolves make their first appearance on Australian soil?"

"If you want Old Man Anson to rip your arms off, I'd say go ahead and howl," Baldwin says with another little laugh. "But if you want to keep your arms attached so you can play ball again, this might be a good time to stay mute. Besides, they sometimes have alcohol at these official functions. You wouldn't want to jeopardize that for the rest of us, would you?"

They go on, but I don't learn much else of importance because they spend most of their time trying to decide where to go drinking after the ballgame this afternoon. If the pattern holds, I will not have the honor of meeting the mayor of Sydney, so I'll have more free time on my hands for shooting craps in my hotel room and practicing reading with the children's book MacMillan bought for me today. I decide I'd better read the book first.

I don't get to meet the mayor of Sydney, but a carriage brings me to the place for today's game just in time, so I'm standing there, looking at the Sydney cricket grounds. When Johnny Ward walks over and stands beside me, he whistles when he sees the field where the teams get to play today.

"Clarence, you were the mascot of the White Stockings for most of this past baseball season, right?"

"Yes, Mr. Ward, I was."

"Did you ever go to Recreation Park in Detroit for a game there?"

"No, sir. I mostly just saw the games at West Side Park in Chicago."

"Well, let me tell you something, Clarence. Everyone in the National League knows that Detroit has the best grounds in the league. It's flat, the clay on the base paths is soft, and it doesn't have too many rocks. The infielders usually get a clean hop on ground balls in Detroit. Every visiting team likes to play there. But I'll tell you, lad, Recreation Park is a sandlot compared to the grounds of the Sydney Cricket Association."

"I think it is very nice too, Mr. Ward. Much nicer than in Chicago, I'd say."

"Just look at it, my boy. Perfect green grass, and soft, too. Flat as a billiard table. No rocks. No potholes or ruts in the field to dodge when chasing the ball. And see the white picket fence that encloses everything. Perfectly constructed and newly painted. With rows of seats, what, would you say, twelve or fifteen rows of them?"

"Yes, that looks about right to me."

"Then there's the clubhouse. Nothing in the National League is nearly that spacious."

"Are you talking about the large white building over yonder?"

"Yes, that's the one. I know you didn't get to go inside, but I did. It has comfortable armchairs, pegs to hang your hat and clothes on, and, I'm told, after the game, there'll be refreshments for all the ballplayers."

"It sounds first-rate, Mr. Ward. How come none of the baseball parks in America are like this?"

"I can't answer with certainty, Clarence, but my guess is that, partly, cricket here has held the public's attention for quite some time, and, also, the people who run the cricket clubs in Australia are not so interested in squeezing every single dime out of their team like baseball owners are in America. I know you've never met the Triumvirates in Boston, Clarence, and trust me, you don't want to. They are the worst when it comes to their treatment of their players and their fans. The South End Grounds are in horrible shape most days, and the accommodations for the players are third-rate, at best. A more disagreeable trio of human beings would be hard to find."

"I think I've heard other people say that about the Beaneaters as well, Mr. Ward."

"You can put it down for a fact, Clarence. Well, my boy, now's the time to loosen up for today's contest. Enjoy the view."

Ward and I are not the only ones who notice how fantastic everything looks. While I stack the bats for the Chicago team before the game starts, I overhear Spalding talking to Harry Palmer while Palmer writes down things in his reporter's notebook.

"Harry, this is how a first-class athletic facility should look," Spalding begins. "Just look at the care given to the field of play—the quality construction of the grandstand, the perfection of the lawns, everything. This is what I want in Chicago. Imagine how many well-to-do patrons we could attract if West Side Park looked anything like this."

"That has always been your goal, hasn't it? Cater to the respectable classes first."

"Yes. That is why I've worked so hard to rid the game of the gambling element over the last decade. It is why I use Pinkerton detectives to spy on my players, both in Chicago and on the road. It is why I allowed Jim McCormick to go to Pittsburgh after the '86 campaign, even though he won 31 games for us that season. I never got over how he lost us a game in the World Series with St. Louis that year by drinking thirteen beers the night before he was to pitch. That's why Mike Kelly is in Boston now, instead of with us. I've decided that from now on, I will have sober players, or nothing. Chicago has many wealthy and middle-class citizens who will pay fifty or seventy-five cents to see a game of baseball, but they won't stand for drunkenness on the field or the mediocre play resulting from it."

"I think you've got some work to do then, Al. I doubt you need your detectives, or even me, to tell you that several of the Howling Wolves have done a little more than just howl at times on this trip. Daly, Baldwin, Pettit, Fogarty, and Sullivan have done their share of rushing the growler so far and will be on the lookout for where they can find growlers, or whatever they call pitchers of beer here in Australia, again tonight, most likely."

"Yes, those boys are a concern. They are young and adventurous, no doubt, but to be true professionals, they must show more self-control. I'll see if I can get Anson and Ward to lean on them and get them to straighten up.

"To change the subject back to where we began, what would you guess it cost the Sydney Cricket Association to lay out such perfect grounds and construct the bleachers and grandstand and everything else you see here?"

"I don't know the exchange rate for British pounds to dollars, but perhaps $100,000?" Palmer raises an eyebrow as he says this to inquire if his guess is in the ballpark.

"Higher."

"One hundred twenty-five thousand?"

"Higher. According to Lynch, the outlay for what we see approached $200,000 when taking everything together—the grounds, the grandstand, the playing equipment, and maintenance. That's nearly a quarter of a million dollars. These Australians are truly a manly, sporting people."

"No doubt. Compare this to the so-called grandstand at Oriole Park in Baltimore. Their grandstand is anything but grand—unless it be a grand humbug." Both men laugh at this.

"You are quite right. What a tragedy that Billy Barnie does not make more money in Baltimore. It is a thriving, growing city with plenty of wealth, but the combination of sub-par management, sub-par ballplayers, and a sub-par ballpark dooms them to mediocrity, or worse, nearly every year."

Palmer shakes his head and says, "Well, Al, Bald Eagle Barnie may not know much about running a ball club, but he sure makes the American Association's meetings much livelier."

"Yes, that he does. My spies at their meetings would have considerably less to report if not for his shenanigans. You put him together in a room with Chris Von der Ahe of St. Louis and Charles Byrne of Brooklyn, and the sparks fly every time."

"Soden, Conant, and Billings in Boston, however, seem to have the right idea when it comes to building the proper place to see a game of ball, wouldn't you say, Al?"

"They do, in some respects. Their grandstand is first-class, certainly. Two decks, even. Combine that with the rabid sports fans of Boston, and they are bound to make a pile of money, even if the field itself is so rough that it sometimes looks like it's just seen a cannon bombardment."

The two men talk for a little while longer, but soon the ballgame begins. It is a good one. The All-America team wins in the final inning, with the score standing 5-4 in their favor. The crowd of Australians is immense; I hear Palmer mention a guess of 5,000 or 6,000 spectators once the game begins. Perhaps Spalding was right when he said the Australians are a sporting people.

Chapter 18

Two days after our first game in Sydney, we are back for another. First, however, our players try their hand at the Australian game of cricket.

"It is time to see if all the practicing in George Wright's tent onboard the *Alameda* is going to help, Clarence."

"I think so, Mr. Palmer. Do you know how to play cricket?"

"I've learned the basics by reading about them on board the *Alameda*, but that is all. How about you?"

"No, sir. I've practiced my reading a bit lately, but I'm still just learning."

"Well, Anson seems to think he knows the game. Look at him out there, coaching the players on how to hold the bat, where to stand, and everything."

"Yes, Mr. Palmer. It looks like he's about to bat. But Billy Earle is tossing the ball in there differently today. He keeps his arm straight instead of bending it to throw a pitch. Is that how it's supposed to work in cricket?"

"I believe so, yes. You call the player who delivers the ball the bowler in cricket, and they must use a straight-arm delivery. I hear that in our practice sessions on the *Alameda* that Billy was the best at this, other than George Wright, so he's the bowler today."

I turn to watch the action. Earle bowls the ball to Anson, who hits a lazy and weak fly ball that the opposition catches easily.

Anson lets loose a string of curses such as I've rarely heard. I know he's bet heavily on his skills in cricket, but after the All-America team put him out on his first swing, they are all giving him a hard time and teasing him. He is on his way back to the Chicago bench when his temper explodes.

"Where is Duval?" he shouts. "Where's the little Ethiopian?"

I am sitting on the Chicago bench, of course, just where I always sit during the games. Tom Burns is beside me. I look at him; he simply shrugs his shoulders.

"There you are!" Anson roars. "Come on, you little nigger, follow me." He still has his bat, which in cricket has two flat sides. He uses it to point to a spot in the far corner of the cricket grounds. "Over there."

I fear this might be the end of me.

I head out to the place Anson pointed to, and he follows close behind.

"I'm sorry, Master Anson, I really am," I plead. "I'll try my best to bring you better luck next time you bat, honest."

Anson has about two dozen cricket balls. He drops them on the ground and then walks about fifty or sixty feet away. "Start bowling them to me."

"But Master Anson, I didn't get to go into the cricket tent on the ship. I don't know how to bowl the ball."

"Just throw the ball overhand like a baseball pitcher. You should be just the right speed. That's my problem. These cursed cricket bowlers throw the ball too slowly for me. Now, start bowling."

I try my best, although my best honestly isn't very good. Anson reminds me of that fact frequently. After I've tried bowling him all the balls and apologized for poor pitches on several of them, he says, "That's enough. Now, go pick up all the balls and bring them back to the bench." Then he storms off, occasionally stopping to swing his cricket bat violently through the air as he walks.

It isn't long before I hear him cursing again. When I finally round up all the balls and get back to the bench, I learn why.

"Oh, there's Clarence," Fogarty yells from his spot in the field. "Hey Anson, could you hit Clarence's bowling? Or was he too fast for an old man?"

George Wood then says, "Clarence, next time, take a little off your pace, just to be sure Anson can keep up. Don't go so hard on him."

The big captain boils with rage by now; I can see his face getting redder by the second. I back away from him, even though I'm already at least thirty feet away. The other players aren't letting up, however.

Tom Burns says, "Do you owe Clarence money, too? Or were you too scared to make a bet with the kid?"

Although I'm worried Anson will take his frustrations out on me again, the captain finally gets himself under control, mutters something under his breath, and then marches to the Chicago bench and sits down. I stay where I am and watch the rest of the match from there. I didn't win any bets from Anson, but if I had any money to spare, I'd wager that Anson has a plan for getting even with everyone.

After the cricket match and the ballgame that follows are over, I expect everyone to pack up and return to our hotel like always. Instead, everyone sticks around for second event. Another of the first-class passengers aboard the *Alameda* is a man everyone calls Professor Bartholomew. When the players conclude their game, which the All-America team wins, 7-5, Bartholomew starts unpacking his gear, and soon, he is in the center of a circle of fascinated onlookers.

I also notice that very few of the spectators leave their seats. They must know what's next. Clearly, something big is afoot, although I don't know what. Most of the things the professor unpacks are unfamiliar to me. MacMillan and Ward are chatting and pointing at various pieces of equipment that the professor has brought to the cricket grounds, so perhaps they understand what is happening. I walk over to see if I can pick up anything.

"Ah, there's our little bowler," MacMillan says in greeting. "Pity that Anson made such a weak showing today and decided to take it out on you. I understand he'd made a considerable number of bets on his performance and needed someone upon whom to take out his frustrations. Shame he didn't pick on someone his own size, however."

"I'm afraid I didn't make much of a bowler," I respond. "But no one would let me inside Mr. Wright's cricket tent to practice on the boat."

Both men laugh a bit. "In a few years, perhaps you will be," Ward says.

"Mr. Ward, Mr. MacMillan, can you tell me what is going on here with Professor Bartholomew? I don't recognize any of the things he is setting up."

Ward answers, "The professor is what people call an aeronaut. What he is doing, Clarence, is setting up a balloon. He is going to attempt an ascent in the balloon for the amusement of the crowd today. Do you see his carriage there? He will stand in that, with the balloon above his head, and rise up into the air."

"He is going to fly into the air in something that big? How?"

MacMillan replies, "I believe it works something like this. You heat the air inside the balloon with that apparatus," he points out one piece of equipment, "and because the air is warmer inside the balloon, it is lighter than the air on the outside of the balloon. If you get enough hot air and a big enough balloon, you can float even heavy things like people off the ground. That is why the balloon is so big."

"That's amazing. He's is going to fly through the air in that little carriage?"

"Believe it or not, Clarence," Ward adds, "it is my belief that someday, people will fly through the air. Except they won't fly in balloons; instead they'll fly in machines. It will look something like a flying train."

"I didn't know you had such a vivid imagination, Johnny," MacMillan says with a friendly smile.

"Some of my classmates at Columbia described it to me," Ward counters. "No scientific principle forbids it from working. The trick is to get a motor that is powerful enough, but also light enough, to achieve true flight. Mark my words, Newton; someday it will happen. People will fly. I just hope you and I live long enough to see it, my friend."

"If it works like you say, Johnny, perhaps we can use it to go to Kansas City if the National League owners ever get it into their heads to put another franchise out in the Cowboy City. Remember when we had to make those marathon western railroad trips in '85 and '86? Depending on where you began, it sometimes took a day and a half to reach Kansas City. The best move the League ever made was to drop Kansas City and bring in Indianapolis before the '87 season."

You'll get no argument from me on that score," Ward concurs.

"Look!" I exclaim, "I think the professor is about to take off."

Indeed, Bartholomew had given the crowd a short address while Ward and MacMillan discussed the future of people flying, and now he is ready to go up in his balloon. First, however, he does something entirely unexpected. The professor waves toward our group with his arm, beckoning to us. Then, he calls out, "Clarence, come over here."

I look at Ward and MacMillan for how to respond. Ward gives me a gentle shove in the professor's direction. "Go on, Clarence, go see what he wants."

Still unsure, I trot over to where Professor Bartholomew stands. The balloon behind him is full of air now. The only thing keeping it on the ground are some ropes the professor has tied to pegs in the ground and wrapped around other pegs on the rail of the balloon's carriage.

When I approach, the crowd murmurs in surprise.

Soon, I've reached Professor Bartholomew. His shakes my hand and gives me a warm smile. "Would you like to go up in the balloon with me today, Clarence?"

"Me?" I can't believe it.

"The balloon is strong enough to bear your weight, and it's quite an experience. You'll never get the chance again, will you? Plus, even a scientist like me doesn't mind having a mascot for good luck with him."

I look around. Everyone is watching. I'm not sure what I should do, because I'm scared.

"Well?"

I swallow hard. "Yes, sir!"

"That's my boy! Step right in here, Clarence."

Professor Bartholomew, who is a short, somewhat overweight man and nearly bald, motions me into the carriage with his arm, and then he waves one of his meaty hands to the excited crowd. He closes and secures the door to the balloon's carriage and starts untying the ropes that keep us on the ground. He adjusts a knob on the machinery that gives off the flame to heat the air in the balloon, and the flame grows a little bigger. Finally, he lifts the last rope off its peg, and we start up into the air.

While we rise above the cricket grounds, the crowd cheers, but then the voices on the ground get quieter. Soon they are indistinct, just a dull murmur, and then I can't hear them anymore.

"Well, Clarence, what do you think?"

The view is so amazing that I'm nearly speechless. "I've never done anything like this before. How high do we get to go?"

Then, another thought occurs to me. "And how do we get back down when it's time?" I probably should have thought about that before getting into the balloon.

"The answer to both of your questions is the same, my friend," says the professor. "When you want to go higher, you turn this knob," he points to the one I saw him adjusting when we were on the ground, "and that releases more heat and you drift upward. When you want to get back down, you turn the knob the other way, the flame gets smaller, and you descend. We can stay aloft until we run out of fuel to burn."

He answers my next question, about how long we'll be in the air, even before I can ask it. It seems like he's done this before.

I'm still scared a little, even though the professor just looks around, taking in the view, seemingly relaxed. He even starts humming a tune, but I don't recognize which one. We're drifting high above the cricket grounds, but the winds have blown us a bit to the west, toward the town. I just stare down at the ground in wonder.

At first, I'm scared to touch the hand rail of our carriage, and I just stand in the middle. I'm scared it will tip to one side if I do. But, after Professor Bartholomew does it, I relax and try it myself.

I can see all manner of things about the city of Sydney from this height. I look down at the streets, and I can see the square patterns they make. There are people moving on the streets, but they look like little ants from this height. I point to one crowded and busy part of the city.

"What's that, professor?"

"I believe that is the railway depot. See all the railroad tracks, and how they converge together?"

"I thought the United States was the only place with railroads."

"No, Clarence. Although the United States has many railroads, it was the British who got the idea first, so far as I know."

I never saw any railroads in the Sandwich Islands, so I figured the United States must be the only place that had them. I guess I was wrong about that.

I forget about the railroads quickly, however, because it's so incredible to just see an entire city while you calmly float above it. The green trees, the houses, the smoke rising from the smokestacks of a handful of factories. I stop concentrating on how scared I am and just enjoy the view for a while.

It takes me a little while to notice because I'm so busy looking at the city of Sydney, but after floating along for fifteen or twenty minutes, the wind has really picked up. I hear Professor Bartholomew start to fidget and make nervous sounds. "Hmm, no, this won't do at all. Blasted wind, why has it come up now?"

"Is everything okay?"

"I think we'd better drop down a bit, Clarence. This wind is stronger than I expected."

The professor turns the knob on his machine, and I feel our balloon start dropping bit by bit, but it's too late. With a frightening whoosh sound, a big gust of wind hits us, and I see what worries the professor. The strong wind has a big effect on the flame that keeps us in the air. The flame doesn't go out, like I fear it will, but something else happens that is just as bad. The flame touches the rigging of our balloon and sets it on fire! In seconds, the flames leap upward toward the balloon's top.

"Professor, what do we do? Our balloon is on fire!" I shout hysterically.

Luckily, the professor keeps his cool. Maybe this has happened to him before?

"I'm grabbing our parachute. We'll have to jump for it, but this will save us." While he says this, Bartholomew puts on what looks like a backpack. "Quick now, Clarence, we haven't much time."

With that, he spins me around by the shoulders and grabs me from behind in a bear hug. His arms reach under my shoulders and clasp around my chest. He yells to me, "Grab that strap with your right hand, Clarence, and . . ."

Just then, one of the lines holding our carriage to the top of the balloon snaps, and we lurch to the side of the carriage. Not expecting this so soon, Professor Bartholomew loses his balance and we tumble over the side!

Now we're falling through the air, but he's still holding on to me. I scream as the noise of rushing air fills my ears. Through my panic, slowly I realize the professor is shouting something to me. The noise in my ears is so loud, and the panic in my brain is so intense, I can barely hear him, even though he's yelling and he's right behind me.

"Pull! Pull!" he's shouting to me again and again.

I look down and realize I still have the cord in my right hand. I give it a hard yank. A silk parachute opens above us, and suddenly we slow down with a sharp jerk. It's a good thing, too. We're not very far above the ground. Another few seconds, and we might have struck the roof of one of the houses in town.

I take what feels like my first breath in ten minutes and then exhale. My heart is thumping so loudly, I can hear it pounding in my ears.

"Well done, Clarence, well done!" Professor Bartholomew says to me, not yelling quite so loudly anymore. "It looks like we'll survive this little incident after all."

"Little incident?" I reply. "What does it take for you to call it a big incident?"

While I say this, I can see some of the crowd, including some of the ballplayers, running in our direction.

"It's a figure of speech, Clarence, just a figure of speech. Maybe in bad taste, given our circumstances just a moment ago. Okay, now, we're almost down. I need to maneuver us, so we don't crash into a house or a tree."

I'm starting to breathe easier finally, but then I hear an unusual sound. It's getting louder. "Professor, what's that noi . . ."

Before I can finish the last word, the carriage from the balloon hurtles past us as it plummets to the ground, and it clips our parachute on the way, shredding the fabric. The carriage misses hitting us by only a couple feet, and before I can think of anything else, Professor Bartholomew drops me in surprise, and I'm falling again.

I look down and realize my only chance is to grab a tree branch, so I don't crash into the ground.

I grab at one, and get it!

"Ouch!"

I scream from the wrenching force on my arms and shoulders. The force of stopping so suddenly makes it feel like the branch has torn my arms away from my body. I hear a violent thud behind me, which must be the professor hitting something solid.

Then I hear a sharp crack!

The branch I grabbed snaps, and I drop.

I can't grab anything to break the fall this time. I only have time to guess the distance to the ground, fifteen or twenty feet, before I crash into a grassy lawn, landing on my side, and black out.

Who knows how long I lie there, but it's probably only a few minutes because when I come to, I look up and see people everywhere. My blurry, unsteady gaze finds John Ward's face first.

"Clarence, you're awake! Are you okay, my boy?"

I just lie there a moment, while the other onlookers ask similar questions with their strange accents. Finally, not feeling any crippling pain anywhere, just an enormous bruise on my side, I try to flex and stretch my arms and legs a bit.

"I suppose so, Mr. Ward. At least, I don't feel like I've broken anything. My hip and ribs feel a good deal bruised, however." I wince when I rise to one knee.

"That was sharp thinking to break your fall with that tree branch, lad, and then some good luck to land in a nice, soft patch of grass. It's a minor miracle you and Professor Bartholomew are both in one piece."

"The professor is okay, then? I heard a loud thud just as I grabbed the tree branch. I feared it was him hitting the ground and being killed."

"No Clarence, I'm still alive, and only a little the worse for wear," I hear the professor say from behind me. "What you heard was my body hitting someone's roof. I think I've probably broken my left arm, but I managed to grab the edge of the roof with my right hand and hang on until these people arrived to catch me. I should have known better, I suppose, than to try an ascent today. I was so excited by the grand occasion, the size of the crowd, and the spirit of the moment, however, that I decided to risk it despite the danger of the wind. Serves me right, I suppose, that my hubris and lack of judgment ended in grand failure. Well, I'll have to pick up the pieces and try again another day."

Several of the ballplayers give him a hearty slap on the back and volunteer to help him gather the wreckage of his carriage. As for me, I vow that I'll never go up in one of those things ever again!

In the carriage ride back to our hotel, I close my eyes for a while. I have a deep bruise on my left side, for sure, and my shoulders still hurt a good deal. Because I already saw the view of this part of Sydney on the way to the cricket grounds, I just close my eyes and put my head back.

Maybe they think I'm sleeping or don't care if I hear them, but Ward and MacMillan are also in my carriage, and they start talking about what happened.

"Did you set the whole thing up with Clarence, Johnny?" MacMillan asks.

"Sure did."

"The professor was okay with it?"

"Yes. I asked him if I could fly with him yesterday when I learned of his plans. He said no because the weight might be too great. It's a pity he's too fat."

"So, you asked if he'd take Clarence instead of you."

"Not at first. I got that little inspiration after watching the way Anson bullied the young chap today during our cricket match. It seemed a fair recompense for the lad at the time, even though it turned out more dramatic than I thought it would."

"Agreed. The idea was right decent of you. No one could predict the wind would set the balloon on fire. Does anyone else know that you're behind this?"

"No, and I think it would be best if things stayed that way, don't you?"

"I suppose so, yes. No one will hear a peep from me. How much did it cost you to arrange, if I may?"

"Nothing. The professor is a tolerant man, it seems, who has taken a liking to young Clarence, but he's rather intimidated by Anson, so he keeps it to himself."

I stir a bit to pretend I'm waking up but wince again when I shift a little. My ribs and hip remain very sore. The bruises are in just the spots where it's hard to move without feeling it. Ward and MacMillan change the subject and talk about the ball game the rest of the way back to our hotels.

After all the excitement at the cricket grounds, I'm flat worn out and very sore, so for once I don't mind that I'm not invited to the grand dinner that evening planned by Sydney's welcoming committee. The hotel's fare is fine with me. It serves chicken as the main dish, along with steamed potatoes, and it's tasty enough, plus I'm not sure how far I can walk after my fall, anyway.

To my great surprise, I see that John Healy, the lanky pitcher for the All-America team whom I painted faces with in Utah Territory, also stays behind. With no one else to talk to, I decide to ask him why he isn't with everyone else. Carrying my dinner plate, I limp over to his table where he eats alone.

"Mr. Healy?"

He looks up from staring at his plate and his eyes slowly focus on me, as if he'd been thinking of something from long ago.

"Clarence, my lad, pull up a seat next to old John. I could use a bit of company this evening. How're your ribs?"

I can see from the empty tankard in front of him that he's had some of the hotel's ale before I got downstairs. Talking to him might have been a bad choice, after all. However, he isn't slurring his words yet, so maybe this is the first drink. Either way, I think I'm stuck talking to him for a while.

I say, "I'm a bit on the sore side, but I'll be okay before long, I think, Mr. Healy. How come you didn't go to dinner with everyone else? Usually, I'm the only one who doesn't get to go."

"Oh, the opportunity to go was offered, and I went to the banquet hall to have a look at it, but for my own reasons, I declined to stay."

Without knowing why, I ask the question, "Will you tell me why? I promise not to tell. Most of the players barely talk to me, so I don't have too many chances to tell anyone, really."

"I suppose so," Healy says, his brogue a little more pronounced than usual tonight. "But only if you swear an oath never to tell anyone. Deal?"

"Deal."

"You swear it?"

"Yes."

Then Healy lowers his voice and says quietly, "Well, okay, then. Do you know where Ireland is, Clarence?"

"No, sir, is it somewhere in the United States?"

"No. Although many Irish people live in the United States, the island of Ireland is far away, across the Atlantic Ocean. I'm from there."

"I thought you said you were from Illinois, just like me."

"Well, yes, Illinois is where I was born, but my parents came to our country from Ireland almost twenty-five years ago. That is why, in a way, I still consider Ireland my home. Does that make sense?"

"I suppose so, yes. Is Egypt the place in Ireland your family comes from? I've always wondered why people call you 'The Egyptian.'"

Healy gives a hearty laugh at this question but then returns to his quiet voice. It's clear he doesn't want the other guests to hear what he says. "No, my boy, Egypt is not in Ireland. You see, when I first started playing ball, everyone knew that my hometown is Cairo, Illinois. Cairo is near where the Ohio and Mississippi rivers combine, right down at the southern tip of the state. Cairo also happens to be the name of a great city in the land of Egypt, on the banks of the Nile River. Egypt is a place on the continent of Africa. That is how I got my nickname. My hometown in Illinois just happens to have the same name as a famous city in Egypt, so people started calling me 'The Egyptian.'"

"Don't you like being called 'The Egyptian'? Is that why you didn't stay at dinner tonight, because you got tired of everyone calling you that?"

"No, Clarence, and this is where you must keep your vow of secrecy. When Spalding decided to extend our trip around the world, it became my goal on this trip to free Ireland from the oppression of the British."

"Ireland is not its own country?"

"No, it isn't. It has been a colony of the accursed British monarchy for centuries. A country becomes a colony when another country takes it over with its military forces. Along with political control, the British apostates brought their vile Protestantism with them. The Irish people are Roman Catholic in religion and, like me, proud of it. My goal is to help the Irish get their independence back and free my people."

"How are you going to do that? Will playing baseball help the Irish get their freedom?"

"Playing baseball? It will not be enough by itself, no. My hope is, however, now that we're traveling to the British Isles, I'll probably get to meet some people highly placed in the British government. Perhaps I can learn some information that will be helpful to Ireland's cause. I have no more definite plans than that at this moment."

"I think I see. What does that have to do with skipping dinner tonight?"

"Australia is another land colonized by the British imposters. Some of the people at this dinner tonight are representatives of the British monarchy. It makes my blood boil just to think about them and the oppression they stand for, let alone shaking their hands and pretending cordiality toward them. If I hear the anthem 'God Save the Queen' one more time, God as my witness, I just might do someone in. If my mission is to succeed, I need to keep a low profile, and I have difficulty doing that among all these officials, diplomats, and other imperial lackeys."

I don't tell Healy this, but pretending to be nice is something I understand very well, and I am very good at it. It is a talent you learn quickly when you are colored and need to deal with white people. He continues speaking quietly, his Irish brogue growing a little stronger.

"You should have seen the banquet hall, Clarence! Over one hundred feet long, sixty wide, and with a dome eighty feet high. There were marble carvings, some of them gilded, beautiful oil paintings, and a chandelier with hundreds of little globes that reflect light in thousands of brilliant flashes. It also had British flags everywhere, vase after vase of roses, a grand piano, and a dozen other luxury items that I couldn't afford to buy in fifty years."

"It sounds very nice. How come that makes you angry?"

"Where does all the wealth to buy such things come from? It comes from the sweat of the brows of the Irish! These English landlords, they took over Ireland, and now they charge the Irish rent to farm their own land. Then they take the wealth of Ireland and use it to afford pianos, and roses, and statues, and build banquet halls with eighty-foot domes! That is why Ireland must be free!"

What Healy just said to me sounds like how things work in Chicago. I've walked past the mansions of wealthy businessmen during the day and slept in the bunkhouses, basements, barns, and cellars of the people who work for them at night. Some of them talk just like Healy does right now.

I consider bringing this up, but, instead, I say, "So you are trying to help the Irish be free and not get pushed around by the British anymore?" This also sounds an awful lot like the Métis that General Strange told us about on the ship recently, the ones who fought to

216

keep their homes in Canada. I don't like the thought of some people pushing other people around.

"Yes, that about says it, Clarence."

"I want to help you on your mission, Mr. Healy."

"That's my boy. I knew I could count on you."

"What should I do?"

"Right now, I want you to do nothing. Just keep quiet about our little conversation we just had. I do not know if events on our trip will allow me to do any more than simply gather information. Until I know more, I want you to keep quiet and say nothing about anything. Say nothing to Ward, Spalding, or Anson, or anyone else. Got it?"

"Yes, Mr. Healy."

"Remember, you made a vow not to say anything."

"I remember, Mr. Healy."

"Now we can finish our dinner. These Brits and Australians may be in league with the Devil himself, but at least they are decent cooks and brew some passable ale. Give credit where credit is due, I suppose," Healy finishes with a wry smile.

Chapter 19

December 23, 1888
Melbourne, Victoria, British Empire

"How does this look, Mr. Burns?" I ask while I straighten my new hat.

"You're looking very American, Clarence. It's a shame no one thought of getting these straw hats before now. Just don't take your ribbon off. A person just doesn't look as good without it. Don't you agree?"

"Yes, Mr. Burns. The bands of red, white, and blue ribbons do look rather dandy."

"So they do. At this rate, I might be mistaken for 'The Count of Macaroni.'"

"The Count of Macaroni?"

"That's what we ballplayers call Tony Mullane."

"Who is Tony Mullane? I've never heard of him."

"That's because he's not a National League player. He is a pitcher with Cincinnati in the American Association. He always dresses up sharp and fancy and stylish, so some people just call him 'The Count of Macaroni.' Mullane is also a good pitcher, so when he's in the pitcher's box, people refer to him as 'The Apollo of the Box.'"

"Who was Apollo, again?" I ask. I recognize that name because it was in another of the books I've been reading with MacMillan, but I can't remember for sure who he was.

"Apollo was a Greek god."

Oh yes, that's right. We read about Zeus, Hera, Hades, and a bunch of other gods in a book that MacMillan found. I'm learning quickly, but I still have a long way to go in my reading lessons.

"I see you decided to put your hat pin in your suit, Mr. Burns."

"Yes, I thought the American flag would look nice in my lapel. How about you?"

"I don't have a suit, so mine will have to stay on my hat, I suppose."

"Yeah, I suppose so. Still, it was very proper and patriotic for that cigarette salesman to give them to us. It wasn't enough to entice me into buying any cigarettes because I find them most disagreeable, but a few of the boys bought some."

"I agree about cigarettes. I don't like them at all, which is fine with me because I never have the money to buy them even if I want to."

We arrived in Melbourne three days ago after taking a train from Sydney. I overheard Palmer say that the train was a special one the Australians got up just for us. From listening to Palmer talk, he sure seems impressed with the hospitality of the Australians. I heard him read another of his letters to *The Sporting Life* to some of the ballplayers, just to make sure he hadn't forgotten any important names or details, and he almost glowed as he read. I think it's strange that he can be so happy with everything while the exact same things make Healy so angry. I know I gave my word to help Healy free Ireland, and I plan to keep it if I can, but if Palmer and Healy can feel so differently about the same thing, perhaps that means I don't understand some of the finer points about traveling to foreign lands quite yet.

It's Sunday morning, and I've nearly finished breakfast when Spalding walks into the dining room and asks everyone to listen for a moment.

"Good morning, men. I see everyone looking fit and ready to play more baseball. I want to commend you on your work here in Australia thus far. Nearly 12,000 people came to the cricket grounds to watch us play yesterday, and you put on a show that did our country, our flag, and our National Game proud. I can barely recall a crowd that large back in the United States. You are making possible the future of baseball in Australia with your work here."

Several players clap, and I see Fogarty prepare his wolf howl, but Spalding sees it, too, and holds up a hand for quiet.

"No howling this morning, John. It's Sunday, after all."

Everyone laughs at this, including Fogarty.

"Besides, like you demonstrated with your speech last night, you can make people howl with laughter without any lupine sound effects."

"I thought about using some last night, but my favorite Australian animal is the kangaroo, and I don't know how kangaroos howl," Fogarty replies, to another round of laughs. He goes on, "Although with the number of rabbits we've seen since dropping anchor, when we reach London I plan to petition Parliament to make the rabbit the national animal of Australia. I don't know how there got to be so many, but the colony positively swarms with them."

"You might hold off on petitioning Parliament," Ward tells Fogarty. "Instead, you should put your brain to work. I've heard that Australia has something called the Inter-Colonial Rabbit Commission and that this commission offers a prize of £25,000 to anyone who can demonstrate an effective way to get rid of them."

"Twenty-five thousand pounds of what?" Fogarty replies.

"The pound is what the British call their currency," Ward tells him. "It's like their dollar bill."

"So, how many dollars is that?"

"I don't know for sure, but enough to buy all the beer you can drink between here and London."

"Speaking of London," Spalding says, "that is part of what I wanted to speak to everyone about this morning. While you have been playing baseball and exploring the town, I've been working with the Lynch brothers to finalize the details for the next stage of our adventure from Australia to Ceylon and then Egypt. It is now official that India will not be part of our itinerary, but the rest of the voyage is now certain."

All the men applaud the good news and try to give Spalding the traditional three cheers, but again he holds up his hand for quiet.

"Remember, Sunday morning."

After a moment he continues, "However, when we proceed around the globe, I want you men to remember certain things. Up to this point, although outside the United States, we have been among people with a similar language, similar habits, similar love of sport, and similar traditions to our own. Similar enough, in fact, that some of you have been able to make a thorough examination of all aspects of colonial life these past weeks."

He says this with a sideways glance towards Fogarty, Daly, Pettit, and the other Howling Wolves, who have indeed kept very late nights here in Australia. My room at the hotel is next to the one shared by Daly and Baldwin, and while I'm not lucky enough to own a pocket watch, the clock in my room is often well past midnight when they've woken me up coming in from their evenings on the town. Sometimes they have female guests with them, sometimes not.

"Once we leave Australia, however, all that will change." Spalding's smile is gone now, replaced by a sterner, serious look. "We are about to travel to strange countries, among strange people, who have strange and exotic traditions and ways of life. In short, we are about to leave Christian civilization behind and exchange it for the mysteries and superstitious ways of the Orient. Think of our visit to Chinatown back in San Francisco, and then imagine entire cities like Chinatown. That is where we will be very soon.

"Now, the British have a presence in both Ceylon and Egypt, it is true. Although none in our party speak Singhalese, not even Fogarty," laughs accompany this barb at the All-America outfielder's sense of humor, "there will be some officials present we can communicate with. However, these officials cannot be everywhere, nor is it among their duties to watch over American tourists. We cannot depend on them at every turn. Therefore, it is up to each of you to take care of yourselves when we reach Colombo and to stay out of trouble. I expect all of you," another sideways glance in the direction of the Howling Wolves, "to avoid taking too great an interest in native customs, especially those of the native women. Am I understood?"

"Awoooo," Fogarty says quietly, to more laughs.

"Good," Spalding says, smiling once again along with everyone else. "I do not know if my diplomatic skills would be up to the task of extricating you from the dungeon of some Oriental potentate. Remember our voyage on the *Alameda* and General Strange's stories about visiting Fort William and the Black Hole of Calcutta."

"Didn't he say that the Black Hole took place all the way back in 1756, though?" Ward chimes in.

"He did, but it shows the character and barbaric tendencies of the rulers in the places we are about to go. Besides, given the less-civilized lands of the Orient and their more primitive approach to things like hygiene, it would be most unfortunate were any of you to contract that certain disease which disables men from playing ball or taking part in normal activities for weeks at a time. No amount of diplomatic finesse could help you then."

"Yeah, Johnny, even your lawyer skills couldn't get you off the hook for that," Fogarty says to Ward. "Take it easy on the charm when the Sultan of Egypt offers you his harem, all right?"

"Just remember to howl loud enough that we all can hear you when the sultan locks you away for trying to steal one of his women," Ward shoots back with a smile. "Otherwise, we'll never know to get you out before we sail for Italy, and you'll languish there while they cut off your fingers and toes one by one as punishment for your crimes."

"All right, men," Spalding breaks in, "I doubt we'll be visiting any harems, anyway. Remember this, however. We still have receptions to attend back in the States upon our return, and we are still Americans representing our country, our flag, and our game of baseball, no matter where our travels take us. I expect all of you to remember that and acquit yourselves honorably. Enjoy yourselves, certainly, and see all the exotic sites you can lay eyes on, but always remember that we represent America and must uphold her good name."

"Ay," several of the players say in unison.

"I know I can count on you men to do the upright and manly thing. When we do return to New York, the American press will provide us extensive coverage, you can be sure, and I'd like to extol the virtuous, courageous, and exemplary behavior of each one of you."

The next day features a ball game, followed by yet another reception, this one at St. George's Theater in Melbourne. With the temperature pushing ninety degrees for the game, it's easy to forget that it's December 24, Christmas Eve. Nearly 6,000 people take a break from their Christmas shopping and window-looking to come to our game, which is yet another win for the All-America team, 16-13.

At some point since our arrival in Melbourne, Professor Bartholomew found replacement gear for his damaged balloon, and today, he pulls off an ascent and descent without any fires. It's a grand sight to see a person soaring through the air like he does, and the crowd cheers his bravery and courage. I'm still too scared to try it again, however, even if someone ever asked me to go. I repeat my vow not to try flying for a second time.

You can imagine my surprise when, while the men get ready for their evening at the theater, John Ward comes over to me and says, "Clarence, get your bandmaster uniform on, and bring your baton. You're in the show tonight!"

"I am?"

"Yes. They tell me that tonight's performance is a farcical play about American baseball. We've inspired the Australians to dramatic imitation already, it seems. The theater manager wants you to do your marching act, just like in the parade today. Now hurry off and get ready!"

"What is farcical?"

"It means the play is supposed to be funny. Off you go now!"

I finally get to join the boys for a performance! My pulse speeds up, and I have trouble with the brass buttons on my uniform jacket. I button one into the wrong hole before I realize it, and then I need to undo them all and button up again. At least I remember to trade my straw hat for my bandmaster hat. I almost run back down the stairs to rejoin the boys. I get to see the inside of a real theater and be in a real play!

We take coaches to St. George's Theater, with all the players in their evening dress suits. They all look alike, and very warm, in their black suit jackets, black pants, white collared shirts, and black bow ties. Compared to them, I look a little funny in my bandmaster uniform, but when we arrive, no one says anything to me about it.

The theater isn't quite as big and fancy-looking on the outside as some of the other places we've visited, but I don't have time to look at it too closely. As soon as we arrive, Ward hustles me backstage to see the theater manager, so he can explain what part I have in the show tonight. The manager is a large and heavy man who wears stylish glasses. Maybe not as large as Captain Morse, our captain on the *Alameda*, but large all the same.

He greets me, shakes my hand, no, pumps my arm, and says, "Clarence? Clarence Duval? It is a pleasure, my lad. You were superb this afternoon in the parade, and I just knew you'd be perfect for our show tonight. This is a special honor, yes, it is. Your baton act captivated my stage manager today, and we believe you're perfect for this part."

"I'm happy to be in a real play, sir. When is my part, and what should I do when it's time?"

"You'll go out on stage when the show is almost over, right after the conclusion of the third act. When it is time for your appearance, our stage manager, Mr. Grey, will motion to you. There he is, right over there. See him? Simply march to the middle of the stage and toss your baton around until the music stops. Because you're on stage, you'll have to march in place while you do your act, of course. Can you manage that?"

"Yes, sir, I can do that. I usually practice that way."

"Splendid, Clarence, splendid. Welcome to the stage, my boy! Oh, yes, I have one last bit of instruction for you. Until it's your turn to go on stage, just try to stay out of the way of the actors and stage hands, all right?"

"Yes, sir! I've been in lots of plays back home. I know just what to do."

I don't remember very much about the play. I'm so excited for my part to arrive that it all goes by in a blur. The audience laughs often, however, so I suppose it must be a funny play, just like Ward said it would be. Finally, the third act begins. Butterflies flutter all around in my stomach, so I keep telling myself to calm down. I want to make the boys proud of me and represent my flag, just like Spalding said we should.

After the third act has been going on for a while, I hear Mr. Grey whisper, "Clarence! Come over here, lad!" He beckons me to a spot next to him, just offstage behind the curtain. "Are you ready, my boy?" he whispers.

"Yes sir, I think so," I whisper back.

"When the next song begins, that's your cue," he says to me. "Remember, march to the middle of the stage and do your act.

You'll have a clear path. Good luck, Clarence." He shakes my hand, pats my shoulder a few times, and smiles warmly.

The actors on stage say a few more words, and then they finish, and the music begins. It is a marching song, and even though I'm not familiar with it, that doesn't matter. Nothing can shake my concentration now. I strut to the center of the stage with my chest puffed out and my arms swinging high. Up goes my first baton toss. Uh-oh, I'm feeling so much energy, I almost hit the ceiling! I'd better ease off a little bit. My second toss is lower, and now I'm feeling better. Next, it's time for my routine of spins. I even catch the baton behind my back. Every one of my moves is just right. When the music ends, I catch my baton for the last time, snatching it from the air and waving my arms with style. Perfect!

The crowd erupts in applause. For the first time in my life, I know the cheers are just for me!

The overweight theater manager comes out, grabs my left arm, and raises it into the air. He says, "From the United States, Clarence Duval, ladies and gentleman!"

The audience begins chanting something. I turn to look at the theater manager. "They want an encore, Clarence. Are you ready?"

"I get an encore?"

"Yes! The people loved your performance so much, they want to see another!"

"Yes, I can do another." My smile goes from ear to ear.

The theater manager steps forward and eventually the cheers die down a bit. "Ladies and gentlemen, Clarence has agreed to do an encore performance. Now, some of his American companions tell me that Mr. Duval, besides his excellence in marching, is also a highly skilled performer of the primitive art of the plantation dances of the American Negro. For his encore, he will perform a plantation dance for our pleasure!"

The lump in my throat is so big, I can't breathe for several seconds. I simply stand with my mouth open. This was the greatest moment of my short, unhappy, homeless, orphaned life. Now, the greatest night of my life is in ruins because I'm supposed to do a stupid dance before an audience of rich Australians and Americans, just so they can see a colored person look foolish. Led by the theater manager, the audience starts a rhythmic clapping while I stand there debating what I should do.

"Come on now, Clarence, start your dance," the theater manager says to me. He looks at me very seriously, and lifts his eyebrows in expectation that I'll dance.

I don't know if he was in on the plan from the beginning or just taken in by a trick to embarrass me, but I want to swing my baton and strike his fat face. I look out at the crowd, eyes darting back and forth, looking for a sign of what to do from someone. Most of the players are clapping, too. My glance just happens to land on John Tener, and I notice that he has his head in his hands. He is not clapping. Once more, I think about what Spalding said, about representing our flag and our country, but this time I ask myself why I would want to. What would be worse? Humiliating myself so I can stay with our company or just running off and getting away from everyone for good?

The theater manager looks at me again with his jaw set and eyebrows clenched together, and I know I can't delay my decision any longer. I swallow hard. I dance. When I'm finished, the crowd tosses silver coins onto the stage while I slowly walk away, my eyes fixed on the wooden floorboards of St. George's Theater.

When I pass through the curtains and go offstage, several cast members say something to me, but I don't hear them.

I'm back in my room at the hotel. I've spent most of the last hour crying into my pillow. There's a gentle knock at my door. I don't answer.

A short time passes, then I hear another knock. "Clarence, can I speak with you? I know you're there." It's John Tener's voice.

I want to tell him to go away because I'm still furious with the world, but given that Tener is about the only friend I have left, I decide to let him in.

"You've had a tough day, Clarence. Want to take a drink?" He holds out a bottle.

"No, Mr. Tener, I've had enough of white people offering me things."

"I can't blame you, Clarence." He sighs, then takes a quick drink. "Still, it's good stuff, if I do say so myself."

He tips back his head for a second swig and then bends down a bit while stepping through the doorway. Tener closes the door behind him.

"Don't worry, I'm not drunk; this is my first bottle. You sure you don't want any?" Tener says as he tilts the open mouth of the bottle toward me.

I shake my head.

Tener continues, "What happened to you tonight didn't sit well with me. I can't prove it, not enough to satisfy a lawyer like Johnny Ward, anyway, but I have the feeling that Anson set you up. He's the only one, besides Spalding, Lynch, and Ward, with enough pull to speak with the theater manager and suggest such a thing." He takes another drink.

"I don't know. That may be so," I say to him in a flat, quiet voice. In fact, I know it's so, just like in Honolulu, but even as upset as I am, I know colored people don't get to lay blame on important white people like Anson. That's a lesson I never forget.

"I should never have come on this trip," I continue. "Now, I wish I'd never signed that stupid contract with Mr. Spalding."

"Don't blame you for that, either, my boy. Still, you get three square meals a day and warm weather rather than snow. It could be a great deal worse for you, but yes, it could also be a great deal better."

"Mr. Tener, when you get elected, will you make a law so that people can't treat other people so mean?"

"I'm afraid that the law doesn't work quite like that, Clarence. It's hard to enforce prior restraint on what people do."

"I wish that it did."

"Sometimes I do, too. Here, this is for you." Tener takes a small beige sack with drawstrings out of one of his pockets. It clinks and jingles when he hands it to me.

"What is it?"

"It's all the money people tossed on stage after your performance tonight. They didn't know about Anson's trick. They meant it as a compliment to you."

"I don't want it." I try to hand the sack back to Tener.

"I know you don't want it right now, but please take it. It contains several dollars' worth of coins. You'll need the money at some point."

"I don't want any money from white people."

"Please take it. I know you don't have any money. You'll probably need another set of clothes before our trip ends. Save it for that. Really, Clarence, the people who contributed money didn't mean to embarrass you."

"I suppose," I say very quietly while I put the little sack into my pocket.

"Can I tell you a secret?" Tener says with a wink.

"What secret?"

"I also put some of Anson's meal money into the sack. If he asks why he's short at some point, I'll just tell him he must have lost it on one of his bets."

It doesn't make me feel much better, but it's something, I guess.

"Well, Clarence, I suppose I should go now. We travel to Adelaide tomorrow, so a good rest wouldn't hurt either of us. You sure you don't want a drink before I go?"

"No, sir, I think I'll take your advice and try to sleep now."

"Oh yes, one last thing. I almost forgot. Here, Clarence, have this. Merry Christmas." Tener reaches inside his suit jacket, into his vest pocket, and takes out a small box tied with bright red ribbon and with a red bow on top, and hands it to me. Then he closes the door and leaves.

It occurs to me that it is Christmas Eve, and Tener is the only one to wish me Merry Christmas all day. I look at the box tied shut with its shiny red ribbon. It's the first Christmas present I've ever received from anyone.

I don't know what to do. Am I supposed to open it now, or do I wait until the morning? The box looks so nice with the shiny ribbon and bow; I don't want to open it too soon. I decide to go to sleep and open it in the morning. Then I change my mind. I don't think I can sleep until I open it. Slowly, I slide off the ribbon and then pack it away, so I can save it. I take the lid off the box very carefully and look inside. It's a small photograph in a metal frame. The photograph shows the cricket grounds in Melbourne, looking toward the seats from a spot in the field. At the bottom, it reads, "Melbourne Cricket Ground, built 1853."

I think for a moment, and then I decide that the best way to keep the photograph safe is to return it to its box and pack the box away, along with my bandleader uniform and baton. I hope the box will protect it while we travel around.

With so many things to think about today, it seems like it takes forever, but eventually I fall asleep. Just like I did after the night in Honolulu, I have vivid nightmares. This time, I'm inside an old shanty house with sagging walls and a creaking floor that looks like it might collapse at any time. It isn't my old home in Kentucky, though; I'm sure of that. An old man sits next to me who I think I'm supposed to know, but I can't quite recognize him. He's drinking coffee from a tin cup, and he hands me a cup of my own. It's too hot, so I set it down on the old wooden table in the kitchen of the weathered, gray sharecropper shack. Then, I hear voices outside, angry voices, and they're coming closer.

The man peeks out the window, which has no glass, turns to me, looking very scared, and says, "Run, Clarence. Go out the back door and don't stop until you reach the woods. Go! Now!"

Melbourne

I run, just as he said to do. I leap from the porch just as I hear the porch door slam behind me. Then, I hear a shotgun blast. I turn to look back to see what's happening, but suddenly, everything fades. I'm awake, and it's Christmas morning, 1888.

Chapter 20

December 29, 1888
Ballarat, Victoria, British Empire

"Are we all here?" Spalding calls out to the group. It is 6:00 in the morning, and I see Ward and Anson counting the players on their teams.

"One short," Anson announces. "No Daly."

Tom Daly. It appears that out of all the players who listened to Spalding's message about representing ourselves well, he's the one struggling most to take the message to heart. The evening after Spalding talked to us about responsibility in the days ahead, even Baldwin and Fogarty came in early and got a good night's sleep. There has been no change in Tom Daly, however. His actions have caused some muttering among the players, and being late right now isn't helping his cause.

"Find him!" Spalding shouts to anyone who can hear him. "Search the sleeping compartments."

A few minutes later Ward appears with a ragged-looking Daly staggering behind him. I've slept in some rotten bunkhouses and seen men with bad hangovers, and Daly is in poor condition this morning. It takes him four tries just to swing his leg up and climb into the carriage waiting for him.

Hills lie beyond the outskirts of Ballarat, and the sun is just rising over them when Daly's friends help him slump into his seat. It's quite a sunrise; all the clouds have that red-pink color, darker near the horizon and brighter higher in the sky, that makes me wonder if I'll ever see something that exact color again.

It isn't long before we arrive at our hotel in Ballarat, named Craig's Hotel. Just like everywhere else we go, a welcoming committee greets us. This one even has a brass band. Inside the hotel the committee prepared sandwiches and coffee, plus brandy and soda for those looking for stronger drinks than coffee to begin their day. Daly heads straight for the brandy, but Ned Williamson and Marty Sullivan head him off and lead him to a seat on the other side of the reception room. They take turns, one man bringing him sandwiches while the other watches Daly and makes sure he stays seated.

Meanwhile, I overhear Baldwin half-whisper to Fogarty, "See, I told you. They nearly always serve alcohol at these official receptions. We've just got to get Tom to ease off for a while, or else Spalding might send him back to San Francisco on the *Alameda* to boil out while we finish our tour."

"Looks like Marty and Ned have him under control for now," Fogarty replies. "But you're right. He needs to learn the art of pacing himself a little better, doesn't he?"

"Do you know the plan for today, Jim?"

"I think it involves some kind of botanical garden tour first. We haven't seen enough flowers and statues on this trip yet, apparently."

Baldwin's face turns downcast, and he twitches his cheeks back and forth. "More gardens? I'm sure they have nice gardens here and all, but how many pretty flowers can you look at before they all just look like pretty flowers? We're ballplayers, not florists."

"We're going to have to look at a few more, it would seem. After that, however, I hear we have something unusual on our itinerary. Something we haven't done or seen so far."

"You mean we're going to visit a brothel finally?"

Fogarty smiles. "Well, I guess that tavern we went to back in Sydney doesn't qualify. Not quite a true brothel, even if the women waiting outside probably worked in one."

"So where are we going, then?"

"From what I hear, Ballarat is a mining center. The people here excel at gold mining, to be precise. I hear we are going to descend into a mineshaft and see what it's like. Well, maybe 'see what it's like' isn't quite the right way to put it. I imagine things are pretty dark down there."

"Really? We'd better keep an extra eye out for Daly, then, and keep him out of trouble in the gardens, or else Spalding might just decide to leave him down there and let him try to climb his way out."

Then Fogarty leans in close to Baldwin and whispers something to him I can't hear. I'm not sure what to make of going into a gold mine, but as long as no one tries to get me to dance for the miners, I suppose it's worth a look.

After seeing the botanical garden, I agree with Fogarty and Baldwin when it comes to gardens. They have lots of pretty trees, flowers, shrubs, and statues, but you can only look at them for so long before they all look about the same. I suppose that someone who really loved flowers and specialized in knowing about plants would really like spending two hours walking around a botanical garden, but for a homeless kid from Chicago, it's a long two hours.

After that, I'm sure the ballgame is our next stop, or maybe the mine, but I'm wrong. Instead, our carriages park outside a large, long, two-story brick building. As we prepare to enter, I see a sign with the name of the building, but I don't know all the words. Tom Burns happens to be walking beside me once again.

"Mr. Burns, what is the name of this place?"

He pauses for a moment, as if he is unsure of whether he should answer. He clicks his tongue. Finally, he says, "We're visiting the Ballarat Orphan Asylum." He gives me a sympathetic pat on the shoulder and walks on.

Orphan. I know that word because it's what I am. I just stand there for a moment, staring at the sign.

"Clarence? Clarence, what's the matter?"

Suddenly, I realize someone's speaking to me. My mind wandered off while I thought about my time in an orphanage. I turn around to find the voice. It's John Ward.

"I'm sorry, Mr. Ward. I was just thinking about when I had to stay at an orphanage once."

"What was it like, Clarence?"

"Well, like I said, I was in an orphanage once, but I ran away. I wish I had a fancy story or dramatic escape that would make me seem brave or heroic, but I was only there for about a week before I ran off. The people there hit me when I didn't do what they said fast enough. The food was lousy, and my bed had fleas."

"There were fleas in your bed?"

"Yes. Or some other bug, maybe, but I think it was fleas. I can get beds with fleas on the streets of Chicago any day, so that wasn't worth staying at the orphanage. I decided it wasn't the place for me, so I left."

"Didn't anyone notice that you were gone?"

"Oh, the people there came after me and tried to find me, for sure, but I knew the alleys and backstreets of Chicago a lot better than they did."

"What did you do next?"

"That's when I ran into Tommy for the first time."

"Who's Tommy?"

"He was my best friend in Chicago. The evening when I got away, it was cold, mighty cold. When it was nearly dark, I snuck into the loft of a small barn at the back of someone's lot. They had a few pigs they kept in that little barn, and I hoped their noise would hide the sound of me bedding down for the night. Well, Tommy had the same idea, and he was there first. When I got up in the loft, I saw him and thought about leaving, but he said it was okay for me to stay."

"Why did you choose the loft of a barn?"

"Well, the roof keeps in a little heat, and you can use the straw to pad your clothes and keep in more warmth that way."

"Wow, I never thought of someone having to do that. What next, Clarence?"

"We talked for a while. I told him about coming up from Kentucky on the railroads. He told me about how he ran away from his home in Indiana. His mother had just died, and his father got sad about it and drank all the time, so Tommy figured it wasn't worth staying around and having his father beat him, and he went to Chicago. After that, we decided to take up with each other and be friends."

"What happened to Tommy? You said he was your best friend. Why do you talk about him in the past tense? Did you have a falling out with Tommy?"

"No. Tommy is dead. The Chicago police shot him one day."

Ward's eyebrows arc in surprise, and he takes a step back. "That is quite a story, Clarence. Now I'm happier than ever you got to come with us. You deserve a break after all of that."

By now, everyone else has gone inside the orphanage. We're the last ones standing on the steps outside. In a low voice, Ward asks me, "Have you learned anything else yet about Spalding and his plans?"

"No, sir, nothing so far. I can't listen very well on the train. It's too loud, for one thing, and I don't have places to hide."

"Just keep your ears peeled, Clarence. When we put out to sea again, you should get more chances. We'd better go inside for now, though. Everyone else already has."

I wonder if orphanages in Australia are just as bad as the one I stayed in, so I go inside to satisfy my curiosity, but we don't get to tour the building. Instead, we go to the orphanage's dining hall for another round of sandwiches and wine. None of the orphans are there, probably because this food is too fancy for them. These Australians sure are friendly to guests, even if they aren't that creative in their choices of food and drink. Still, I can't really complain. I've never eaten as well as I have the last few weeks.

We end our tour by walking to the back of the building and going outside, where the orphanage has a yard for the children to play and a big pool for bathing. By the time I get there, some of the players have started amusing themselves by throwing small coins into the water while the boys dive in after them.

I'm worried that someone is going to ask me to do a plantation dance, so I wander over and stand behind Spalding, hoping he might offer a little protection. He's talking to someone in a dark suit and top hat.

"How many carriages would it take to bring these young boys to see our game today?" Spalding asks the man.

"You want to bring these orphans to see a game of baseball? Why?"

"I have many reasons. It will be good advertising for our party and our country if we show generosity during our tour. The people of Australia, this city included, have been gracious hosts to us. I'd like to return your hospitality. In addition, baseball is an excellent sport for boys to learn. I never underestimate the role of manly sport and recreation in improving the morals and health of a people."

"You speak truly. These boys need all the good examples of manly living that one can provide them. Still, we have almost 200 boys in our orphanage. You mean to bring them all to the game?"

"Is it possible to arrange enough carriages to bring them all?"

"I'll see to it personally. We can always engage a carriage to make more than one trip to our cricket grounds."

"Very good. I'd like to see that all these lads get the chance to witness a game of American baseball. My business manager, Leigh Lynch, will see to the matter of financing their outing."

As a result, we have lots of company for the afternoon ballgame. The orphans, all 200 of them, see the All-America team win another game from Anson's men, 11-7.

It seems a strange order of events, but after the ball game ends, we travel to the edge of the city of Ballarat to visit one of the mining operations there. It's early evening, so there's still plenty of light. We're at the mine now and getting ready to go down into the mineshaft. We need to dress up like miners, however, for safety, and so our group spends several minutes putting on the proper clothes.

The company that owns the mine, the Barton Gold Mine, supplies everyone in our party with the full gear that miners wear, which includes overalls, canvas jackets, slouch hats, heavy boots, and headlamps. Because I'm only twelve, and I'm small, I'm a little surprised that they seem to have plenty of clothes in my size.

When the man supplying our gear brings mine over, I ask him, "Did you have any trouble finding clothes for me, sir?"

"Not at all."

"I thought you might have a hard time finding them because I'm young."

"Young? My boy, we have plenty of lads younger and smaller than you are in our mines. They work right alongside their fathers. As soon as they're strong enough to move rocks around, we send them on down, and they start working."

"You have little children like me for miners?"

"That's right. You don't have to spend as much time digging the mine shafts that way because the ceilings don't need to be as high."

Another employee of the Barton Company stands nearby. He also has mining gear on, so it appears he will be the one who leads our tour. Presently, he says, "All right, men, we have two mining carriages coming up now. Once the men get out and pass their inspection, we'll have some of you board the first one going back down. The rest will take the second with me. Just remember, when we get to the bottom of the shaft, don't wander off. Some of the tunnels go a long way and connect with other tunnels, and if you get lost, well, it may be days before anyone finds you. We'll just look around for a while and then come back up. Stay out of the way of the real miners, too."

Harry Palmer is standing near the speaker and asks him, "Inspection? What are you inspecting them for, might I ask?"

"This is a gold mine. We can't have any of the miners walking away with anything they've just mined now, can we? If we didn't have inspections, someone could find the next Welcome Nugget, and we might never even know it."

"If you'll forgive the ignorance of an American tourist for a moment, what is the Welcome Nugget?" Palmer replies.

"The Welcome Nugget? Only the second largest gold nugget ever found. Some men working for the Red Hill Mining Company pulled it out of the ground at Bakery Hill back in '58. It weighed just over 152 pounds."

This raises the eyebrows of everyone who can hear the mining foreman. Someone found a gold nugget that weighed 152 pounds! I don't weigh nearly that much!

"If that is only the second largest," Palmer inquires, "what is the largest discovery, if I may ask? My newspaper readers back in the United States will want to hear this story, I'm sure."

"That would be the Welcome Stranger. A pair of prospectors named John Deason and Richard Oates found it at a place here in Victoria named Moliagul in 1869. It weighed over 241 pounds."

"Almost as much as Anson," Fogarty says to laughs all around. It's a good thing Anson is waiting to get in the other carriage and doesn't hear him.

Billy Earle waits to go down in our group. He says aloud, to no one in particular, "All these machines, they're so big. I never knew it took so much equipment to mine gold."

John Ward hears him. "What did you expect to see, Billy, men with mules and pans wading into a river? That era of mining history ended more than a decade ago. In the modern age, you need capital, skilled miners, and business acumen to prosper in any business, mining included."

Ward wasn't really scolding him or making fun of him, but I think Earle feels that way a bit because he just looks at the ground with a sheepish look on his face and doesn't ask any more questions.

Meanwhile, Palmer and the foreman banter back and forth a bit more about the incredible size of Australia's gold nuggets while we wait for the inspection to end, and then, it's our turn to board the mining carriages and head down. I end up in the first. Not all the players decide to go. That means some regular miners ride with us in our carriage.

The mining carriages, if that's what you call them, are iron, with large, heavy iron bars for their frame, which is rectangular. The iron rails on the sides of the carriage are chest high for grown men, which means they are about as tall as I am. Smaller iron bars connect each part of the frame, so no one falls out. The carriages are open on top, so it feels like being in a cage, but a cage with no roof.

Tener is one of the men who decides to stay above ground, so I sit next to MacMillan when we begin our drop down the mineshaft. I expect that immediately we'll plunge into total blackness, and I'll need to turn on my headlamp, but that isn't the case. Every so often, lights illuminate our way, so most of the time the light is more a murky gray than an inky black. MacMillan, being the friendly newspaperman that he is, attempts a conversation with one of the miners sitting on the other side of him.

"I say, my friend, how deep underground is the bottom of this shaft?"

"Are you a guest of the company?" the miner responds.

"Yes. We are Americans touring your beautiful land."

"If you're a friend of the company, you're no friend of mine," the young man responds. He shifts so he's looking away from MacMillan.

"Easy, Snelling," another miner sitting nearby says. "It's a harmless question. I don't love the Barton Company any more than you do, but don't blame a tourist for that. He's not the reason your daddy brought you below ground and then died of silicosis."

"It's 1,100 feet to the bottom, by the way," he says to MacMillan.

"Thank you," MacMillan responds. "If I may ask another question, what, exactly, is silicosis? I'm a newspaperman, and I'd like to explain things properly to my readers in the United States."

"It's like the Black Lung disease that coal miners get," the second man responds. "Except that instead of having your lungs fill up with coal dust, they fill up with silica from rock dust. The results are the same, however. You can't breathe very well, and eventually you can't breathe at all, and it kills you. That's why, when you get back to the surface and look around, you'll see almost all young men and boys working here. You'll see no old men. In the mines, forty years old is an old man. Anyone who claims that he's older than forty is either lucky or lying about his age."

The first miner, Snelling, then says, "And for the privilege of choking to death on dust, we get paid just enough so that our own children won't starve. It's not enough, however, to put decent clothes on their backs or to be able to afford to send them to school all year. If they went to school, then they wouldn't have to join their fathers in the mines just to support their family. When you're at your fancy reception after your tour is over, just remember that the money that pays for all the wine and fancy dishes came from the sweat of the children of the miners."

After hearing such discouraging statements, no one says much more until we reach the bottom of the mineshaft.

It's hard to report much about the bottom of the mineshaft, except that the need for all the gear becomes obvious very quickly. The floor is wet, the walls are wet, and the ceilings of the tunnels are wet. I saw some big pumps at the surface of the pit, and I guess they try to get rid of the water, but they are only partly effective. The water drips, constantly, and pools up on the rock floor, and all the miners slosh around when they walk.

We turn on our headlamps, and those help a little. The gray light becomes a little less gray. Still, to me, it seems like everyone is a shadow or a ghost. Maybe it is easier for the miners to know what they're doing in this light when they're used to it, but for me, everything is spooky, like when I'm walking in an alley in Chicago, looking for a place to sleep, and it's a cloudy night, and the moon only shines through here and there.

Another thing surprises me about the mines. The only thing holding up the tunnels are timbers. It seems crazy to me that pieces of wood, large and thick though they are, can hold up so much weight of rock. I wonder how often they collapse. I consider asking one of the miners, but if they are anything like the miner named Snelling, they probably aren't in a mood to speak to me. Plus, the mining company person said not to bother the miners. So, I just stand there and look around.

Oh boy, I shouldn't have thought about a tunnel collapsing. It might bring bad luck, for one thing, but it also brings on a feeling of fear in me. Maybe a word exists for how I feel, but I don't know what it might be. I just know my stomach suddenly feels very ill, and I'm a little dizzy, too. I look around, suddenly feeling very nervous. Then I spot MacMillan walking around slowly. Near MacMillan, one of the ballplayers, Marty Sullivan I think it is, slips in the slimy, slippery tunnel. That doesn't help my confidence. This feels like how I felt when we ended up in the tunnels underneath Chinatown, but worse.

"Mr. MacMillan," I ask, panting, with my right hand on my thigh, "how long until we go back to the surface? I don't feel too good."

"Being deep underground for the first time is a bit of a change, isn't it? I don't think we'll be long, however; just a few minutes more, probably. There's not very much to see down here in this light, anyway. Still, it gives one a feeling for how Dante felt during his descent, does it not?"

I'm feeling even dizzier now, and my throat starts feeling tight, making it harder to breathe. I'm far too scared to bother asking MacMillan who Dante is, or if I'll get to read something Dante wrote in our lessons someday. I return to the carriage and sit down, panting harder. Sweat drips from my forehead onto my canvas jacket. I can see up the gray mining shaft, and that helps a little, knowing I'll find daylight up there somewhere. I'm relieved when the others join me, and we begin rising to the surface.

I'm sitting by Tommy Burns while we go back up. "Quite a sight, wasn't it, Clarence," he says to me.

I respond with a confused mumble.

"Are you okay, Clarence? I can't really tell in this light, but you don't look so good."

I'm trying to find the words, but I can't. My eyes dart around the mineshaft, expecting something bad to happen at any moment. I mumble again.

"Don't worry. We'll be back in the sunlight again soon, Clarence."

We finally get there. I'm sure I was at the bottom of the pit only fifteen minutes or so, but it felt like several hours, at least. Suddenly I realize that sweat soaks through my clothes under the mining gear. My hands shake so badly, it takes several minutes to calm down and get control of myself.

After about fifteen minutes in the daylight, I'm feeling much better and breathing normally once again. Thank goodness for that. Slowly, the panic goes away, and I can walk steadily. The players continue milling around near the top of the mineshaft while we take off our mining gear and return it.

Finally, I can speak to Burns. "I'm sorry, Mr. Burns, that I couldn't answer you before. This weird feeling came over me, and I was very scared. I don't think I'd be a good miner."

"Well, going underground isn't for everyone, Clarence. Maybe even your luck has its limits. I felt fine myself, but I think that Tom Brown over there enjoyed it about as much as you did."

I glance where he points, and see that Brown has also returned his gear but just sits there, staring down between his knees. He just looks dazed, staring blankly at the ground. He rubs his forehead a couple times.

"Your clothes are soaked, Clarence," Burns continues, drawing my attention back to the moment.

"I know. I think it's because I was so nervous. I'm glad it's a warm day; the heat should help a bit to dry me off."

"Was that part of the weird feeling you got?"

"Yes, Mr. Burns, I was very nervous and couldn't wait to get back to the surface. It seemed like, on the way up, the walls kept getting closer."

"You know, Clar . . ." Burns begins, when several explosions rock the pithead, almost in unison.

Wildly, I spin around, trying to figure out what's happening. It appears the first blast hit the building storing the mining equipment. It's on fire already, with a large hole in the side of the structure. Other explosions strike the mining cars on their tracks, scattering rock everywhere. A few stones strike me, but they are small and don't sting too much. Then, I hear another, delayed, detonation, only a short distance from Burns and me.

I watch one of the mining carts fly off its track and skid straight toward me. It's an eerie feeling because even though I can see it's coming right for me, it takes my brain a moment to get my body into motion. Should I duck, or dodge? I hesitate a moment in indecision, trying to figure out what to do. I choose to dodge. Too late. I see the metal side of the cart close on me, even as I start to move. I close my eyes right before the impact.

Slam! A large, powerful object collides with me, knocking me to the side. I land on my back, waiting for the pain of broken ribs. It wasn't the cart that hit me, however. It was Tom Burns. I open my eyes, and I hear the horrible grating noise of the metal mining cart skidding away from us, sparks flying as the corner of the cart scrapes the metal platform at the pithead. It misses falling into the mineshaft, but just barely, as it caroms past.

That isn't the end of the danger. The cart careens toward some of the other ballplayers at the pithead. I hear Burns shout a warning in their direction.

He isn't quick enough this time. Poor Tom Brown. He looks up just in time to see the mining cart bearing down on him. Brown tries to stand up and back away, but stumbles backward over some rock debris. He falls on his back and conks his head. It looks like he's knocked out, but that turns out to be a good thing, because the cart passes over him when it strikes a rock and just misses taking his head off.

Burns and I gasp and then sprint over to the edge of the mineshaft, barely daring to breathe, the fear welling up inside of us. "Not Tommy!" is all that Burns can say as we arrive, gasping, and look down at our fallen teammate.

I drop to one knee in relief when several of the players bend over, lift Brown's head up, and his eyes open. It looks like he's okay, after all.

Finally, Burns turns to me. "Are you okay, Clarence?" he says to me for the second time today. "I kept yelling at you to move, but you were just standing there. Didn't you hear me?"

"I'm afraid not, Mr. Burns. Maybe I was too scared to hear you, but when that cart was flying at me, I just couldn't figure out what to do fast enough. I panicked again. Thank you for saving me. Maybe you have some good luck yourself."

He simply smiles at this.

Meanwhile, the employees of the Barton Gold Mine assemble around us, some of them armed with shotguns and pistols. They can't prevent what happens next, however. We hear one final explosion. The large, crane-like structure that lowers the mining carriages down into the mine starts to crumple and fall toward us. The loud squeal of shrieking metal rends the air as it starts to fall, slowly at first, but then it gains speed. The metal bolts that used to hold the crane together fly off in all directions. Several of the players, and I, are right in its path as it goes down. I see them look up and start to scatter, and I try to run, too.

Just as I turn to run, one of the ballplayers, I don't know who, tries to back away from the danger. As he does so, we collide. Because I'm smaller, I'm knocked backward, toward the edge of the pit. Before I can get my balance back, I stagger at the edge, my arms flailing wildly, and then I topple over the rim of the pit, falling into the mineshaft.

Clarence's story continues in the sequel to My Australian Adventure, *titled* The World Traveler.

If you enjoyed this book, you can find other books in this series, as well as my works of historical research in baseball history, at my website:

robbauerbooks.com

You can also sign up for my Readers Club mailing list to receive notifications about future books and promotions. If you enjoyed reading the book, I would be grateful if you'd leave a short review on whatever website you purchased it from. Favorable reader reviews are very important to authors like me. They help tremendously in attracting new readers and spreading the word about existing books you think others will enjoy. Finally, if you like the book, please consider recommending it to fellow readers of new and original historical fiction.

Thank you!

About the Author

I'm Rob Bauer, author of historical fiction and nonfiction books and owner of Rob Bauer Books. I hold a PhD in American History and was a Distinguished Doctoral Fellow at the University of Arkansas.

My fiction has two purposes—entertaining readers and explaining historical injustice. Although I enjoy adventure and humorous books as much as the next reader, I'd like my books to stand for something a little bigger. All my studies in history put me in a position to do that. Whether I'm writing about how racism damages the individual psyche, the deportation of the Métis people of Montana, the South's prison labor system, or the utter terror of the Belgian Congo, with my books you'll find yourself in powerful historical stories.

I also write nonfiction about baseball history because I've always loved the game, its history, and its lore. I sometimes joke that baseball may be the one thing in life I truly understand. Although I love the statistical side of the game, if you don't, never fear because my histories go light on the statistics and heavy on what baseball was like in the past. They're stories about baseball, but stories with a point.

The history blog on my website offers posts on a variety of interesting historical figures and events. I'd love to have you follow along.

When I'm not working on my next story or writing project, I enjoy spending time at the beach. And, oh yeah, I still read a history book or two. When I'm not watching baseball.

Acknowledgments

I also want to thank the people who helped make this book possible, especially Jim Soular for his help with editing. Ali Holst gets the credit for the cover art and design. Thank you to David Mitchell, Maggie Bergin, Jennifer Johnson, and especially Jennifer Lodine-Chaffey for reading and making suggestions on various chapters. Also, thanks to Mike and Karen Bosso for suggestions on how to publish the book once I finally finished.

41214046R00152